MW00638485

EINSTEIN'S TRUNK

EINSTEIN'S TRUNK

JIM HABERKORN

BONNEVILLE BOOKS
SPRINGVILLE, UTAH

© 2011 Jim Haberkorn

All rights reserved.

No part of this book may be reproduced in any form whatsoever, whether by graphic, visual, electronic, film, microfilm, tape recording, or any other means, without prior written permission of the publisher, except in the case of brief passages embodied in critical reviews and articles.

This is a work of fiction. The characters, names, incidents, places, and dialogue are products of the author's imagination, and are not to be construed as real.

ISBN 13: 978-1-59955-452-5

Published by Bonneville Books, an imprint of Cedar Fort, Inc., 2373 W. 700 S., Springville, UT 84663
Distributed by Cedar Fort, Inc. www.cedarfort.com

LIBRARY OF CONGRESS CATALOGING-IN-PUBLICATION DATA

Haberkorn, Jim, 1951-
Einstein's trunk / Jim Haberkorn.
p. cm.
Summary: The Russians have learned that Einstein has left a trunk full of formulas for making a nuclear bomb that is sixty times more powerful than anything that exists today. His great-granddaughter Yohaba, a brilliant physicist in her own right, and an ex-spy, Rulon Hurt, who was recently fired, are the only ones who can stop them from stealing it.

ISBN 978-1-59955-452-5
1. Einstein, Albert, 1879-1955--Fiction. 2. Nuclear weapons--Fiction. 3. Spies--Fiction. I. Title.

PS3608.A2386E37 2010
813'.6--dc22

2010019595

Cover design by Danie Romrell
Cover design © 2011 by Lyle Mortimer
Edited and typeset by Megan E. Welton

Printed in the United States of America

10 9 8 7 6 5 4 3 2 1

Printed on acid-free paper

THIS BOOK IS DEDICATED TO MY WIFE KIM, WHOSE LOVE INSPIRES me every day, to my daughter Alexandra, and to my son Henry, who passed away in December 2009 and who, like a character in this book, suffered from Asperger's syndrome

1

"IF AT FIRST THE IDEA IS NOT ABSURD, THEN THERE IS NO HOPE FOR IT." —EINSTEIN

LUBYANKA PRISON, OCTOBER 1955—"THIS IS ALL ABSURD. What idiot keeps the secrets of the universe in a trunk?" asked Svetlana Soboleva with impeccable logic right before the bullet entered her head. With the crack of the pistol, she collapsed on the courtyard stones like an empty coat and lay there dying in a spreading pool of wine-dark blood. Her last thought was also her last regret: *But I had so much more to say.*

It had been a bad three days for Svetlana ever since her train arrived in Moscow. She was met at the curb by one of those ubiquitous white bread trucks and five pale, drably suited, dead-eyed handlers. Her next stop had been Lubyanka and a three-by-five foot cell with a hole in the floor and a single hundred watt light bulb that burned incessantly overhead like a lidless eye. She had no sense of time and not even a cockroach for company. Her meager food had been oversalted and her water withheld. In between the interminable interrogations, she sat on the floor in her gray, formless sack of a dress with her arms wrapped around her knees, rocking back and forth and racking her brain for the magic words that would stop the torture—the eternal hope of the damned.

Poor Svetlana. For her entire fifty-one years, she had been a blindly loyal daughter of the Revolution—considered loyal enough to be sent earlier that year on a mission to Princeton, New Jersey. However, in 1955, the ghost of Stalin still ruled Mother Russia, and loyalty did not trump failure.

The only sound she ever heard through her cell door, besides the muffled sobbing from nearby chambers, was of the small clackers the guards carried and continually clicked as they conducted their prisoners through the narrow labyrinth of hallways. Prisoners in Lubyanka were not allowed to see one another or even to speak. The clicking warned when a prisoner was approaching and, according to some unfathomable code, negotiated which oncoming guard needed to take evasive action and which one had priority.

Now Svetlana was dragged from her cell and sent stumbling down a succession of dark corridors toward a meeting, she was told, with Beria's successor, Ivan Serov himself. With a guard behind and one in front, her institutional dress as plain as a shroud, and a clacker going like mad, all the other guards gave way. Despite the rule against talking, she collected her courage as they crossed a courtyard into the blinding sun and blurted out in desperation, "There is no need for this. There is no trunk." As the words trailed off and there was no retaliation, her heart fluttered with hope, and she continued with the opening words of the speech she'd been practicing: "This is all absurd. What idiot keeps the secrets of the universe in a trunk?" And then came the blessed death: a 7.62 mm bullet in the back of her head from a Tokarev semi-automatic pistol.

* * *

Moscow, October 2010—It was Eastern European ugly, this Moscow monument to workers. An old Russian building of squat, square stones layered with equal parts age, smog, and tears. It was a sad building, mostly ignored in the daily rush of a new class of capitalists: four stories and a flat roof with small rectangular windows, built like a mausoleum, or a fortress, or a bomb shelter—take your pick. A crypt for dead files. An archive filled with miracles put on hold, or not yet gotten to . . . or lost.

After a lifetime of working in the Soviet Federal Archives, Anastasiya Rabchenyuk didn't move as fast as she used to. Her sixty-one years of service in the Central Archive of Scientific-Technical Documentation at 109554, Moscow, ul. Mezhdunarodnaia, 10 had bent her back and left her stumbling about with thick, heavy glasses. She spent her days shuffling up and down rows of shelves and talking to the folders in her garden, as she liked to call it. But her iron will and memory were still intact.

This morning, as she teetered atop a twenty-foot ladder, she spied a file that looked out of place. Blue files weren't used in this section until 1986, and this file was much too faded, betraying its origin from an older generation.

She pulled at the file, struggling at it like a difficult weed until she succeeded in prying it from the grip of its tightly packed neighbors. "What are you doing here, my little intruder?" she asked. The folder's texture was different. Very old. "What is your history, I wonder?" She opened it and scanned the contents. No chemical formulas. A KGB stamp on every page, so definitely post-Stalin. An encrypted date. That alone placed it in the mid-to-late fifties. "You don't belong here." She dropped the suspect folder in her wire basket and continued her duties.

At the end of the day, Anastasiya shuffled into Director Kormakov's office and stood stiffly, waiting for him to look up, the faded blue file held firmly against her bosom. Her glasses perched on the tip of her nose. With her practical, thick-soled shoes over bulky woolen socks, and her drab, matronly dress that reached from her neck to just above her ankles, she could have been a stern headmistress poised over an errant pupil. She deeply resented her supervisor, the latest in a long line of incompetent snobs from the nuclear section. Even after the disaster of '86, all things nuclear still received preference.

"Yes, Comrade Rabchenyuk, I mean Ms. Rab . . . " he started to say but stopped himself, exasperated at his slip into the now disavowed greeting. He took a breath and looked up over his glasses and started again. "Yes, Anastasiya. What do you want?"

"I'm here to direct your attention once again to the sloppiness of this operation," she said with rising vehemence. "Stalin himself would roll over in his grave if he could see the slop pit that has become his beloved Federal Archives. It's a disgrace. No one cares. There is no discipline. There are no consequences. What have we come to? We survived the Great War and the Cold War, but will we survive this greater threat?" She bit off each word like it was a hunk of dark Russian bread.

Director Kormakov listened patiently. He knew he couldn't

fire her. On most days he liked her, except when she talked about the years under Stalin as if they were the good old days. His grandfather had disappeared in the 1930s for the unforgivable offense of being the first person at a regional party conference of five thousand to stop clapping after someone rose to yell, "Long live Stalin."

Kormakov glanced over at the picture of Putin that hung on his wall. "What?" he asked. "Isn't our new czar tough enough for you?"

"You mean Putin?" she asked, squinting at the picture. "He is a puppy compared to Stalin. You have no idea what it was like during those times. Stalin's spirit permeated every folder in the archive, every step we took, every conversation we had. We didn't dare breathe. No, nothing. This never would have happened. He would have known. He would have—"

Kormakov cut her off. "What wouldn't have happened, Anastasiya? Does this have something to do with that file you are protecting?"

"Yes, and this file could have changed the outcome of the Cold War—" here she unfolded her arms and dropped the file on Kormakov's desk "—if only it had been properly archived in the first place." She turned and scuttled quickly out of his office without closing the door.

Vasily Kormakov watched her leave and sighed. *Such an odd bird,* he thought. *Still thinking in terms of the Cold War.* When it came to an end, she had been depressed for five years. The war had been her reason for living. And she wasn't the only one. *They never stop to remember what it was really like.*

He ran his finger over the edges of the file. "What could possibly be so important?' he said out loud, wanting to go home. His woman was waiting. The other woman too.

He sat for a moment and then rose in his chair enough to peer through the doorway and check if anyone could see him. Satisfied he was unobserved, he reached into the bottom left drawer of his desk for a bottle of Putinka and a dirty glass. Mild and smooth, or so said the advertisement. He laughed to himself, wishing he had a bottle of Macallan instead. If they had won the Cold War, maybe he would be in Scotland now drinking Macallan Gran Reserva,

1979—no, 1980—and maybe he would be there with his other woman. *Now that would be worth winning a war for.*

He poured a not-so-mild-or-smooth shot of Putinka and flipped open the cardboard folder. He immediately noted the KGB stamp and the seal of the Council of Ministers. Then a page addressed to the KGB Collegium. He sat up straighter and angled the folder into the light.

"What have you dredged up here, Anastasiya?" he said under his breath, suddenly very interested. Then that famous name leaped off the page like a slap in the face. He gripped the report with both hands and read on. After a few minutes, he got up to close and bolt his office door and then returned to his desk and poured himself another drink. He loosened his tie, undid his top button, and settled down for a long read.

It was a formal report from a field agent on assignment in Princeton, New Jersey—a woman. Pages and pages, plus notes written in blue ink in the margins. Something about terrible secrets locked in a trunk. Vasily gave a low whistle. Yes, Anastasiya was right. Men would have been sent to their deaths for this. But then came long sections of nonsense—on billiards of all things. "Did you know," the old scientist had asked, "that a slow massé shot curves sooner, even though a harder shot spins faster?" Further on, the report descended into the agent's painfully detailed explanation for failure.

The trunk was never found. He reflected on that. The agent had every right to be fearful. Vasily looked at the date: October 1955. Only two years after Stalin's death, and many of the 476 Gulag camps in Mother Russia were still operating. He thought of his own grandfather sent to Kolyma in 1936. Perhaps he was still alive at the time of this report. He dismissed the thought and continued reading.

Thirty minutes later he was finished. Vasily closed the folder and pondered the agent's last desperate excuse, written in the margin: "This is all absurd. What genius keeps the secrets of the universe in a trunk?" He considered that for a moment and shrugged. *The same genius who can't match his socks, I suppose.*

It was not impossible that the agent had been imprisoned or even shot for her lack of faith and follow-through, he decided.

Those were chaotic years after Stalin's death. It was a time—how did the Americans put it?—to keep a low profile. Yes. Given the times, it was not inconceivable that the report had been deliberately misfiled and forgotten. There was a small chance of finding the trunk and a big chance of being sent to the Gulag. It was simple arithmetic. Vasily let out a long, deep sigh and refilled his glass for the fifth time.

Now he had his own problem. The report had been misfiled over fifty years ago. Even so, someone had to be blamed. But surely they could not blame him after all these years. He sipped his drink. *Under Stalin's regime, someone would have been shot for misfiling this.* He laughed to himself. *And shot for reporting it. And probably shot for finding it too. What would Anastasiya think of her precious Stalin then?* For a few seconds, Vasily couldn't stop laughing, and then he laughed even louder when he realized he was well on his way to a proper, midweek bender.

He pulled himself together and stared at the phone while swaying slightly in his chair. Yes, in the new Russia, he most likely will be promoted for finding this. He emptied his glass in a single, courageous gulp and then dialed a rarely used number.

Five different times he communicated his message to five different tight-lipped listeners, and five different times he was put on hold. Each time, someone came back after a minute and moved him further up the food chain until he finally heard a voice he recognized from news reports. His blood froze, and he was instantly sober.

He pictured the old, hawk-like face with thin lips and those dark, sunken eyes peering intensely from behind wire-framed glasses. There were no introductions; he was simply told to begin. Seven minutes and thirty blood-pressure points later, and after much rapid speaking and frantic page turning in response to terse questions, the voice on the other end hung up.

Vasily sat there for a minute and realized his heart was racing, and his shirt was soaked with sweat. He had been given two assignments. The voice personally knew Ms. Rabchenyuk and told Vasily to pass on his regards to Anastasiya. He actually knew her name—her first name. Vasily was also told to wait there with the file until someone arrived to take it.

Normally, being told to remain after hours, especially when a certain young woman was waiting in a bar at the Swiss Hotel on Kosmodamianskaya, would have been a source of intense irritation. This time that emotion never registered nor did the disappointment at having not been promoted. He sat there with his trembling hand still on the phone while his thoughts thrashed with the implications of the voice's last words: "There was a time when delivering such news would have been your last, Comrade. Be grateful."

2

"THE ONLY REASON FOR TIME IS SO THAT EVERYTHING DOESN'T HAPPEN AT ONCE." —EINSTEIN

THE APARTMENT BLOCK WAS ON ZURICH'S NORTHWEST SIDE near the top of the Hönggerberg. From the penthouse apartment of the five-story building was a fine view of the Zurich valley to the south and the Swiss Alps to the east. Inside, a man sat at a table eating breakfast: a five-egg bacon and mushroom omelet smothered in La Gruyere cheese; four fried bananas; a protein drink—vanilla; an entire box of *knäckebrot*; and a large bowl of fruit mixed with nuts, yogurt, and cottage cheese. He ate slowly while he enjoyed the view. When he was finished, he pushed himself away from the table, stretched, and reminded himself that the first day on a diet is always the toughest.

After breakfast, Rulon Hurt washed the dishes and made up his mind to head straight for the luggage store to plant the bugs. He left Freya—his close combat weapon of choice—at home but took the Colt and threw on the bullet-proof vest and stomach foam. He wasn't planning on anything exciting happening, but when on assignment, he always felt naked without the vest. As for the foam, well, it was now an essential part of his Clark Kent disguise. He almost couldn't get into character without it.

He wore the small foam pad—a slightly modified Sweet Dreamzzz memory foam pillow from a company called Know-foam—under his body armor to tone down his natural earth mover look. It molded nicely, held its shape, and tended to stay in place. A trick he learned from Magnus, his boss, it made him look fatter than he was, which had the advantage of making people underestimate him—a good thing in his business. Sometimes he also wore a pair of non-prescription glasses when he had a job to do. The disguise was all about being underestimated. No one was afraid of the Pillsbury doughboy with glasses.

Once outside his apartment block, he greeted a few mothers, patted a few little heads, and then walked down the steep, paved path to the bus stop, breathing heavily in the brisk morning air. His collar was turned up, his hands buried deep in the pockets of his long gray coat. A storm had blown itself out during the night, and the clouds were breaking up, revealing patches of blue sky.

He rode the #46 bus for twenty-five minutes down to the main train station and then walked the half-mile down Zurich's premier shopping boulevard to the target.

As always, the Bahnhofstrasse was a pleasant walk, bustling with people circulating between sumptuous stores, the whole boulevard alive with the energy of commerce and the rumble of trams. He passed a nice-looking black-haired girl and immediately thought of Isabella. Beautiful, intelligent Isabella. He kept on walking and passed the Gucci shop a block later. There in the window was Isabella's handbag. A few steps further on, his curiosity got the better of him, and he went back to the shop to check out the price. As expected, it exceeded the gross national product of a small African nation, confirming his impression from their first and only date that Isabella was out of his league. But they had a second date tonight, and she hadn't called it off yet. Maybe there was hope.

Rulon continued east along the Bahnhofstrasse toward the lake, and the crowds thinned. Just before Paradeplatz, he found the street he was looking for, and he immediately put thoughts of Isabella on hold.

Augustinergasse started at the Bahnhofstrasse and then ran off at right angles on a winding, slightly uphill track that ended at a small *platz* barely a hundred meters away. Like many of the older, narrow cobblestone streets in Zurich, it was closed to traffic and had a "Santa's Village" feel to it. On both sides of the street were quaint, multi-storied homes that had been remodeled into upstairs apartments or offices and downstairs shops filled with toys of the adult variety—jewelry, clothes, handbags, and furniture.

The store that interested Rulon was halfway down the street on the right hand side—called the Luggage House. It had an off-white, freshly painted face with brown trim and apartments on the top two floors decked with flowerpots. The bottom floor was the commercial enterprise—the *criminal* enterprise—overseen by a large, ornate street lamp affixed to the building's façade.

Rulon walked nonchalantly past the store to where the street ended at a circle dominated by a stone fountain. The fountain sat in the middle like the hub of a bicycle wheel with a half-dozen little streets and alleys shooting off like spokes. He stopped and turned to look back down Augustinergasse and did a thorough surveillance. Nothing seemed out of place or inconsistent. To his left, a wide alley looked like it led behind the store, and he casually walked over to investigate and found all was normal. On his way back up the alley, he tested what he judged to be the target's back door. It was unlocked. Good to know. Nothing else caught his interest. He walked back to the Bahnhofstrasse and waited by a tram stop, letting a few trams go by while he continued to watch the store and think about the mission.

On the surface, it was simple. There was a store the Company wanted him to investigate. Accountants back home had been watching the place for months. Some lowlife in the States was laundering money through a luggage store that had a full inventory but almost never sold anything and instead declared big losses every year. It was fraud, but in the scheme of things, it was pretty pedestrian. Tax evasion for sure. It could be terrorist related, but it more likely had something to do with drugs. Small potatoes. It must have been a slow month back at headquarters.

Rulon's assignment was to dial up the pressure on the goons running the store and make them do something stupid, like contact their source in the States on his personal cell phone. It was really the source the Company was after.

The perps were three men and a young woman. From the file photos, the meanest looking of the lot was Ivan Markovic, the owner. Nice rap sheet. A regular Ivan the Terrible. The other two were solid, well-built, and swarthy. All three had five o'clock shadows that could sand the paint off a battleship, and all looked like they could handle themselves in a scrap.

The woman was in her mid-twenties and attractive with

straight, red-streaked auburn hair falling past her shoulders; an oval face—perhaps a dash of Oriental thrown into the recipe; big eyes; a spider web tattoo on her neck. She was tall and wore a painful-looking nose ring—a big turn-off. But she looked intelligent. Her file listed her as a physics major at the ETH—Zurich's big technical university. What was her role in all of this? Her name— Yohaba Meleksen—seemed a strange combination, just like her appearance.

Rulon watched the store for a good fifteen minutes. Still no activity. He looked at his watch. *Time to make something happen.*

He pushed himself off a street lamp and crossed the Bahnhofstrasse with the pretence of a window-shopping amble on the opposite side of the street from the target. He stopped in front of a jewelry store and maintained his surveillance via the reflection in the plate glass. In the thirty minutes he'd been doing recon so far, no one had come in or out of the Luggage House. He decided to take a chance and go inside. He needed a new computer bag anyway.

As he walked in, a chime sounded. The girl in the photograph, Yohaba, was standing behind the counter, dealing with some paperwork. With his peripheral vision, he sensed her looking up and dismissing him, but he deliberately avoided eye contact. He glanced around, touching a few suitcases, feeling the leather and acting interested. The store carried a large inventory of American name brands—Liz Claiborne, Samsonite, American Tourister—and a few lesser-known companies. *Maybe if they knew I was a US government contractor, they'd give me a discount,* he thought wryly. The luggage was neatly laid out on the showroom floor and on a double row of shelves that covered two of the shop's walls. Behind the counter was a single shelf with half a dozen pieces of older-looking luggage that he surmised were waiting to be repaired or picked up.

The place had the smell of leather and something else, something old; perhaps it was the building itself. As he roamed closer to the front desk, he could see the girl was working on a page full of numbers.

"*Grüezi,*" he said in the traditional Swiss greeting. Then, with a touch of what he thought was harmless humor, he asked, "Are you the accountant here, or can you help me?"

"I'm doing my homework," said the girl without lifting her head. "Feel free to look around." When he didn't move, she glanced up and huffed, "Do you mind? I'm busy."

He stood there taken aback. *You little brat,* he thought. *Lucky for you this isn't Idaho.* Upon closer inspection, he decided her face looked more Russian than Oriental. As she straightened up to her five feet eight inches, he noticed she was on the thin side. *Yep, three months of moving pipe and Grandma's cooking would fatten her up like a prime heifer—probably improve her personality too.* Her hair was long, and the red streaks would have said goth or punk, even without the nose ring and neck tattoo.

She wore faded blue jeans and an unbuttoned brown vest over a black, long-sleeved Offspring concert T-shirt. On her work surface were three empty Styrofoam cups. The smell of cigarette smoke hung heavy in the air around her, though he didn't see any ash trays. They probably made her smoke outside, but the smell still clung to her clothes and hair. He grimaced. Smokers had no idea. It occurred to him that the back door was probably left unlocked because she constantly went outside to smoke.

He said mildly, "Sorry, but I'm afraid I need your help."

She looked at him, eyes narrowed, and the faint sound of a tongue click reached Rulon's highly tuned ears. She slammed down her pen. It occurred to him there could be another reason why this store wasn't making money.

"If you're in a bad mood, then why don't you come back later?" she replied in a tone that suggested she was the aggrieved party.

"Uh . . . I beg your pardon?" Rulon said, irked at the sheer gall of the woman. "I'm just looking for a computer bag, if you don't mind."

"Well, you're in the wrong place," she snapped. "Do you *see* any computer bags?"

Rulon fixed her with a steely glare and thought, not for the first time in his life, that the Swiss national character had both a good side and a bad side. Apparently, he now faced the bad side. "What's your problem, lady?" he demanded. There was a fine line between being overlooked and being blatantly disrespected, and right now he wasn't in the mood for either. Before she could answer, he added,

"How many customers do you scare away every day?"

That semi-rhetorical question seemed to stump her. She stood there with a bewildered look on her face, but then came the hurt, and her eyes welled up with tears. Immediately Rulon's conscience kicked in. He hated losing his temper.

"Depends on how many customers come in," she finally managed to blurt out from within a darkening cloud of raw emotion. She stacked up her papers and slammed them back down on the counter. Then the floodgates opened in a torrent of angry, frustrated tears. Despite his pang of conscience, Rulon found himself wishing for a fire hose. She suddenly ran off though a curtain into the back room. He stood there, perplexed.

Thirty seconds later, he pushed the curtain aside and saw her sitting in a wicker chair, fumbling through a handbag that looked like a treasure chest with tassels for what he assumed was a cigarette. The bag didn't seem to fit her style, but handbags were a big thing in Zurich.

The room had the feel of a farmhouse attic. There was barely enough room to move through narrow lanes among stacks of boxes, some of which were draped with bed sheets. In the girl's immediate vicinity were two file cabinets, an old, roll-top desk, and some rickety metal shelves holding a collection of shoe boxes overflowing with papers. Behind her was the back door that led to the alley. On the desk next to her bag were a couple of textbooks.

He sat down on one of the boxes and let out a sigh. The box started to collapse but held. "Hey," he said. "Did you ever move irrigation pipes at 4:00 a.m.?"

"What are you talking about?" she asked. "Go away. You're not supposed to be back here."

"On the ranch back home when I was growing up, we had to get up at 4 a.m. every day during the summer and move irrigation pipes to a different part of the field. We got paid sixteen cents per pipe connection. Worked all morning in mud and heat and made twenty dollars. Back-breaking work. You should try it."

"Why?" she asked. "So I can scare the cows?"

"No," he said patiently, "but it would make you appreciate working in a luggage store." That got a small smile out of her. "And because it gives you time to think. It's when I made up my mind to go to college. Like you're doing now. That's something to be proud of." He was trying to make amends for goading her earlier.

"I'm taking physics at the ETH," she said, still focused on finding something inside her handbag. "It's not art or basket weaving. I've got a brain. I'm related to Albert Einstein. He was my great-great-grandfather. "

"You're joking."

"About having a brain?" she asked, mostly ignoring him, still engrossed in her bag. With an irritated sneer and a shake of her head, she pushed the handbag away, frustrated at not finding whatever it was she was looking for. Finally, she looked up.

Rulon gave her his best *gimme-a-break* look. "No, about being related to Einstein. That's something to live up to. Family and ancestors are really important. They leave something with you. Through your genes. More than just looks. You probably have lots of potential in mathematics."

"I do," she said, suddenly perking up. "I hardly have to study, but I still get A's."

"But that doesn't give you the right to mouth off to a customer. You understand that, I hope. Disrespect won't get you anywhere. What would your boss say if he heard you?"

"Same thing he always says." And then lowering her voice as deeply as she could, she said, " 'Hey, baby, how about you and me, huh?' "

Rulon just shook his head. Ever since he was a kid, he'd had a chivalrous streak in him when it came to women that sometimes pushed him into doing some pretty stupid things. He believed it had something to do with his mother dying when he was young. So what he said next didn't come as a surprise, though as soon as he opened his big mouth, the hair on the back of his neck stood up, warning him he was going to regret it.

"Maybe someday I oughta teach your boss a lesson." Sure enough, just as his voice fell silent, he sensed the curtain rustling behind him and heard the slight scrape of a shoe on the wooden floor.

"When the master is ready, the student appears," said the girl, making her eyes go all big and innocent. Looking past him with a big smile she said, "*Grüezi*, boss. Strudel Boy here wants to teach you a lesson."

Rulon turned around, and there stood Ivan Markovic with a package in his hand. He looked much bigger in real life than he did in his picture. Rulon looked him up and down, saw trouble, and surmised Ivan must have taken up weight lifting since the photo was taken. His goatee hid his granite jaw a bit but gave it character. He wore a mint green polyester suit over a half-open white shirt. Two gold chains hung from his neck with gaudy medallions at the end that dangled in his rainforest of black chest hair. He had a massive set of trapezius muscles that rendered his neck all but invisible. *A man with a real head on his shoulders*, noted Rulon. *A regular Bulgarian thick neck.* His suit was taut and looked like it was filled with bowling balls. The whites of his eyes were steroid yellow, and his face was peppered with acne.

"Who are you?" asked Markovic as he set the package on the desk. "And what is this lesson you would like to teach me?" He began cracking his knuckles like he was getting ready to mix it up.

At the sound of his voice, Rulon almost laughed out loud. He sounded just like Arnold Schwarzenegger. Turned out the girl had done a pretty good imitation. But Markovic emanated such a threatening vibe that Rulon knew instinctively to take him seriously.

Rulon cleared his throat and tried to sound bureaucratic. "If what this girl says is true, then I'm going to have to report you to the Zurich Worker's Council for sexual harassment."

This does not have to get out of control, he thought as he spoke. *I will eat a little humble pie, back gracefully out, and then take this guy down later in the course of doing my job, legally, and in cooperation with the Swiss authorities.*

Ivan Markovic took a step forward, and Rulon's threat meter pegged, dumping a fifty-five gallon drum of combat juice into his system. Every hair on his neck stood straight up, and he had that old familiar feeling in his stomach and chest. His brain said he could control the situation, but his body was smarter than his brain. Without consciously thinking about it, he rolled his neck and shoulders to loosen up.

Ivan took another step closer. His hand reached out for the lapel of Rulon's jacket. Rulon slapped it away. Ivan laughed and said to the girl, "Let me take care of Fatso here, and then you and me, huh, baby?"

"That's just what I'm talking about," said Rulon. Ivan feinted with his right hand and reached for Rulon again with his left. Rulon slapped it away again and then took a step back to create a little space. He said, "Look, I don't want any trouble."

"Oh, you won't be any trouble," Ivan replied in a deep, rumbling laugh. He took another playful swipe, toying with Rulon, and Rulon slapped his hand away a third time. This was getting old.

Rulon watched Ivan's hands and feet but was also focused on the center of his chest, trying to spot the telltale signs of his balance shifting as he started a serious attack. Ivan had no idea, but every time Rulon slapped his hand away, it had the effect of kick starting Rulon's internal Harley, and pretty soon the engine was going to catch. Finally, after fending off an attempt to poke his stomach and hearing another one of Ivan's insufferable laughs, former collegiate hammer thrower Rulon Hurt grabbed Ivan's hand instead of slapping it and squeezed so hard that for an instant Ivan's eyes bulged.

As a world-class hammer thrower spins in the circle just before his release, the pull of centrifugal force makes his sixteen-pound ball and chain weigh over 700 pounds, which means you can't throw 250 feet unless you can hold onto a 700-pound weight while spinning like a top—all of which requires the strength of a bull and the agility of a ballerina. Rulon Hurt had once hurled the hammer 258 feet 5 inches. It was during practice at Boise State, right after a girl dumped him. His best throw in competition was about thirty feet less, pretty good for college, but nothing to make him change careers. Still, when Rulon Hurt grabbed a person, it was like being caught in a canal lock.

While Ivan contemplated the fate of his favorite slapping hand with his mouth wide open and on a slow descent to his knees, Rulon grabbed Ivan's other wrist, stuck his foot in Ivan's stomach—hard—and fell backwards, launching Ivan over his body and into the drop cloth he assumed was covering a pile of luggage boxes.

Even before Ivan stopped bouncing, Rulon was on his feet again, ready for action. As he jumped up, he caught a glimpse of the girl disappearing out the back door with her handbag and books. He considered going after her, but by now it had registered that Ivan wasn't moving. Come to think of it, it hadn't sounded right when he landed. Rulon went over to where Ivan was sprawled and saw for the first time that under the sheet was an old piano and a cast iron wood stove.

Ouch.

This first visit wasn't going as well as he'd hoped. He ran to the back door and scanned the alley for the girl. Nothing. Then the sound of groaning redirected his attention back to Ivan. *What now*? He went back to check on Ivan's condition, praying that he wouldn't have to administer CPR. Mercifully, Ivan was breathing. He was knocked out but otherwise okay. Rulon moved him into a recovery position—on his side, mouth down, chin back—to prevent suffocation.

Before leaving, Rulon quickly wiped his prints off the luggage he'd touched. He was in a bit of a hurry because when the girl ran off, he automatically assumed she was going for the police. He made a clean getaway but had enough sense to plant a bug beneath the lip of the showroom counter and another under the edge of the back room's roll-top desk.

3

"If I had my life to live over again, I'd be a plumber." —Einstein

Once out of the store, Rulon beat a quick retreat back to the Bahnhofstrasse. After looking over his shoulder to make sure all was peaceful, he slowed down to settle in with the sidewalk traffic. He headed toward the lake, and by the time he'd reached Paradeplatz, he had made up his mind to hop a tram and swing by the US consulate to check in.

The consulate was on the other side of the lake on Dufourstrasse in a gray, nondescript building with a glass entryway and a terrarium on the ground floor. There were no guards posted at the entrance, and the building was marked by a small, unobtrusive sign. The consulate was in a quiet neighborhood and, conveniently, just down the street from Tres Kilos, one of Rulon's favorite Mexican restaurants. When he arrived at the consulate, he took the elevator to the third floor and walked down the hallway until he reached a door with a small, rectangular bullet-proof window set at eye-level. He saw that Edward wasn't processing anyone, so he walked in.

"*Grüezi*, Edward. How are you?" he said. Edward was seated on the other side of a metal detector, reading a newspaper.

"Ah, *grüezi*, Herr Hurt," said Edward. "I'm fine. I didn't know you were in town." He folded his paper and came over to shake Rulon's hand. Edward was in his late sixties and had manned the consulate's metal detector for over twenty years. Rulon met Edward twelve years ago when Rulon was serving a mission for his church and had needed to sort through some visa issues. Somehow it had come out that they were both gun and movie buffs, which kicked off a long-lasting friendship.

Edward had a full head of wavy white hair and a distinguished looking white mustache that extended far beyond the corners of his mouth. As always, he was impeccably dressed in a dark suit and Leonard tie—his sartorial trademark. "Beat up any bad guys lately?" he asked.

"As a matter of fact, yes," Rulon answered, thoughts of Ivan still weighing heavily on his mind.

"Shouldn't we be converting people, instead, Herr Hurt? Whatever happened to that nice young man I used to know?"

"He's around here somewhere," Rulon replied. He walked through the detector and set off the alarm.

"What is it this time, Herr Hurt?"

Rulon opened his coat and let Edward see the gun.

"You buy American, but you don't think American. Whatever happened to overwhelming firepower?"

"I'm a 'less is more' kind of guy," said Rulon.

"It's not 1911 anymore, Herr Hurt. Americans aren't fighting Moro fanatics in the Philippines or the Apaches back home. I keep telling you to check out the Heckler-Koch UCP. Twenty rounds to your Colt's eight. The times are changing."

"Not enough stopping power."

"Okay, then try the H-K Mark 23."

"Only twelve rounds. Not much more than I've already got."

"How will I ever convince you?" asked Edward.

"You won't. Your credibility is shot. You Swissies are too peace loving."

"We're neutral, not peace loving. There's a difference. And you didn't bring Freya with you today. Did you two have a fight?"

"Never. She always gives me the last word."

"Good. But this fighting with bad guys has got to stop, Herr Hurt. I don't want to have to report you to the Pope."

"Ah . . . wrong religion," said Rulon. As they talked, Rulon smoothed out his jacket, making sure the handgun wasn't too obvious. They chatted for a minute more until a family walked in—a signal for Edward to get back to work. Rulon patted him gently on the arm, and Edward stepped aside to let him pass through the door into the reception area. Rulon walked quickly past the half-dozen waiting people and then through the door marked *Authorized Personnel Only.*

He navigated the consulate's inner sanctum, weaving between several desks and down a hall, seeing a few people he knew and exchanging greetings. It was a friendly and efficient office. Rulon was here to visit Toby, the defense attaché, who, in addition to his other responsibilities, handled security contractors like Rulon. After a few more turns and a long, narrow corridor, Rulon knocked on the last door.

From inside the room, he heard chairs scraping on the floor, and a man said, "Come in."

The "war room," as it was sardonically called, was about twenty feet long and half as wide and featured a painting of Hillary Clinton on one wall. Technically, the US government didn't run any operations in Zurich unless you counted the Friday night after-work drinks at the Jules Verne on Uraniastrasse. Still, as the local staff liked to remind him, if Switzerland ever did become a rogue terrorist state, at least the consulate had a war room.

Toby, his assistant Clare, and Jeff, his second-in-command, were draped around the oval glass table like a bouquet of wilted flowers, a newspaper spread out in front of them. Clare had a pad next to her as befitted the meeting note-taker, and Toby and Jeff had their feet up on chairs as befitted the fountains of all knowledge they fancied themselves to be. Whatever they were discussing, Rulon didn't get the feeling that the fate of nations hung in the balance. With the exception of the Nordic countries, which were in a league of their own, Switzerland was the easiest State Department post you would ever land.

"Well, look who's here," said Toby. "It's Mr. Double-0 himself. Come in, by all means, come in."

With a nod to Jeff and Clare, Rulon said, "I'm just checking in. If you're busy, I can make this short."

"As you can see, we're suffocating with work," said Toby. Then with a friendly wave, he added, "But come on in anyway. There's something we need to discuss. Have a seat."

Rulon saw Clare give Jeff a look and noticed Toby take a deep breath. Clare was forty and liked to wear black. *Always going to a funeral*, thought Rulon. Then a premonition hit him. He floated over to the table and sank into a chair on the other side of Toby.

"I'm being laid off, aren't I?"

As the defense attaché, Toby was responsible for giving him the news. He looked down and started fiddling with his coffee cup. He crossed his legs. "Your contract has not been renewed," he said formally. "We've known about it for a month, but I didn't want to say anything because we thought we had a good chance of getting it reversed."

Rulon didn't know what to say.

Jeff filled in the silence. "But obviously not as good a chance as we thought."

The words didn't quite register. Rulon sat there puzzled. He'd worked for the Company for eight years and had a clean record. He wouldn't say he'd been spectacular, but he was effective. He got along with people and got the job done. What had he done wrong?

He cleared his throat. "Is there a reason?" Clare smiled sadly, and Toby and Jeff looked sincere and concerned. *Well, at least they're trying.*

"Depends on what you consider a reason," said Toby. "It's not personal, if that's what you mean. There are cuts coming down everywhere. If you're looking for something to blame, it's the economy. The War on Terror. The housing mess. The thirteen-trillion-dollar national debt. It's . . . well . . . it's everything. You're not the only one." He leaned forward now, earnestly wanting Rulon to understand.

The three consulate employees offered their concern, trying to make things better. But in the end there was nothing they could say that could help. No matter what the papers said, the economic recession didn't start for a person until he lost his job.

"Well, that's a heck of a thing," said Rulon when everybody ran out of steam and the room got quiet. Would it have been better if Toby told him alone? If they had told him before he went to Stockholm? Sometimes bad news came like a stiletto in the night, sometimes like a mortar shell that took out an entire department. And sometimes it was as unexpected as a long-range sniper sitting in the director's office. There was no right way to do deliver bad tidings, but there were plenty of wrong ways. This way was as good as any. "A heck of a thing," was all Rulon could say.

"As a contractor, you were particularly vulnerable," said Jeff.

"Look, you're good at what you do," said Clare. "You'll land on your feet."

"When's my last day?" asked Rulon.

"Well, here's the good news," said Toby with forced enthusiasm. "You'll only officially be working for another—" he paused to look at his watch "—forty-eight minutes. You're relieved at noon sharp. But you'll be paid for another month. And we all decided you can live in the apartment until we need it, as long as you keep to yourself and don't throw any wild parties. We'll even let you hang onto the BMW until we figure out what we're going to do with it. You can goof off or look for another job or do whatever you want." He hesitated and then added, "We're also kicking in a little extra severance money from the kitty. It's our way of saying thanks for all the things you did for us over the years. Especially Lausanne."

"And Chur," chimed in Clare.

Toby continued. "Yes, and Frankfurt, and all the other nasty little jobs you handled so well."

"I noticed you didn't mention Marseilles," said Rulon. Marseilles was his one big screw-up. The consulate ended up having to parachute in a brigade of lawyers to patch things up.

"Yeah, well, we decided to forget about Marseilles," said Toby. "There were extenuating circumstances there. But here's more good news: we're giving you two weeks' pay for every year. Quick, Jeff, what does that add up to?" Jeff looked up at the ceiling, did a quick calculation, and rattled off a number.

"Does Magnus know?" asked Rulon.

"Yes. We told him last night," said Jeff. "He started blubbering. The guy really likes you."

"What did he say?"

"He wasn't making sense. He said we were worse than the Amazons and told us to tell you he'd call."

A half hour later, Rulon finished signing a stack of forms, and everyone else ran out of things to say. They all sat there looking at one another until Rulon suddenly remembered Ivan.

"What about the luggage store?" he asked.

"Right," said Jeff. "Gotta wrap that up. It's petty stuff anyway. Are there any loose ends?"

"I've got a couple of bugs planted. That's all."

"Well, clean it up. Today, if at all possible. As soon as we've got the bugs back, you'll be officially off the clock."

Jeff spoke up quickly. "You know, when we say 'laid off,' we mean we don't have any work for you here in Switzerland. It doesn't mean the Company can't place you somewhere else. And we haven't given up hope yet. We'll be waiting a month before we cut you the severance check. There's still a chance we can get you back on the payroll."

"Yeah," said Clare, "you were our favorite, even if you did always eat all the fruit in the fruit bowl."

Rulon smiled. "Thanks, but I won't hold my breath. If it's happening here, it's happening everywhere. I'm thinking I might take over my dad's place and go back to ranching for a while. Ride out the economy."

"That's probably not a bad idea," said Toby, nodding his head and conceding the point. "In the meantime, maybe something will come up. Maybe they'll discover another Al Qaeda cell in Köniz. Hey, maybe you can start one." That got a good chuckle out of everyone.

Toby escorted Rulon back through the office. Rulon hardly noticed the pats on the back and well-intentioned good-byes from everyone. He did notice the fruit bowl, however, and managed to grab an apple and a banana on his way out. As he went through security, Edward saw his expression and asked if everything was all right.

"It's a bug's life," said Rulon.

"Woody Allen, 1998," replied Edward. Rulon stopped, totally stunned. Edward had never missed a movie in their little game in all the years he'd known him. Rulon turned to him, his world now toppling on all fronts.

"Edward," he said, "Woody Allen did *Antz* in '98. Not *A Bug's Life*."

"Right you are, Herr Hurt," he said with a soft smile. And

Rulon realized then that Edward knew he'd been laid off and had deliberately missed.

"Thanks," said Rulon, "but you're still batting a thousand."

"You come back and see us, Herr Hurt," he said.

Once back on the street, Rulon let out a big sigh. More than anything else right now, he needed a workout. He hopped a bus back home and ate the apple and banana while staring out the window. Once home, he changed and walked down to the Injoy Gym at Frankentalerplatz for a workout. Whenever he started thinking about Ivan or the layoff, he added ten more pounds to the barbell. When he was finished an hour later, his equilibrium was restored. *It could be worse,* he decided as he toweled off after his shower. *At least I have the ranch.*

Rulon turned his attention back to the Luggage House. There was one last thing to do: get the bugs back. He could do that falling out of bed. But when the hair on the back of his neck stood up, he wondered if his subconscious was trying to tell him something.

4

"You have to learn the rules of the game. And then you have to play better than anyone else."
—Einstein

Later that afternoon, Rulon was back downtown, wearing a pair of gray Brax slacks, a black sports jacket over a long-sleeved black pullover shirt, and black Ecco loafers. As usual he wore his vest and stomach foam and had the Colt, but this time he also brought along Freya as a matter of prudence. He'd already tangled once with this Ivan guy, and his type was always looking for revenge. Rulon wasn't an idiot, his dad was proud to tell people—at least when Rulon wasn't around.

The bugs he'd left behind were two GSM4000u's from a company called JJN. They worked through a SIM card, so all Rulon had to do was call the device from his cell phone if he wanted to listen in. The microphones would last for six days on standby and could transmit continuously for eight hours. After that he'd have had to find a way of getting in and replacing them, not that it mattered anymore.

Rulon stood opposite Globus department store on the Bahnhofstrasse three blocks away from the Luggage House. He dialed the number of the bug in the back room and listened through his ear phones for five minutes while he ate a sandwich. All was quiet. He dialed the showroom bug next and immediately picked up an argument. At first, he couldn't make out the words, just the emotions—mostly fear and anger. He heard a slap, and then a girl screamed. Now he was all ears.

He walked toward the store, picking up his pace as he weaved through the crowd, all the while listening intently. There was a confusion of voices. Maybe half a dozen. He reluctantly threw his half-eaten sandwich into a trash bin and kept walking. He heard a woman's voice that sounded like that Yohaba chick. Now other people were speaking, mostly in high German, but he thought he caught a little Russian too. There was too much going on to make sense of any of it. There was a struggle—something was knocked over—now someone was getting thumped.

When he reached Augustinergasse, all looked normal. Shoppers strolled past the store, oblivious to the scene taking place inside. Rulon casually scanned doorways, roofs, and windows for lookouts and saw nothing. He stopped to look in a shop window and then casually looked behind him to see if anyone was following. Satisfied all was clear, he crossed the street and then walked past the target.

The window blinds were down, and there was a sign on the door that said *Geschlossen*—closed. He continued on to the plaza by the fountain and then made a hard right down the alley behind the store. At that point, he slowed down and performed the same surveillance he had on Augustinergasse, looking in all the likely places for an ambush, asking himself where he would hide if he wanted to keep an eye on things but not be seen. All the while, he listened on the phone to the excitement inside.

In any situation like the one in which Rulon now found himself, there's always the worry that you might be interfering with some government agency that has every right to be there. The Swiss authorities could be paying them a visit. Even the slap and thumps didn't disqualify this as a legitimate government action. But the more Rulon listened, the more convinced he was that these were bad guys, and if it weren't for the girl, he'd let them all shoot themselves.

Fewer people were talking now, and the conversation started to make sense. He heard Ivan's voice, and he sounded scared. Rulon chuckled. Ivan was having a bad day. But there was another voice Rulon didn't recognize that was doing most of the talking.

"Yes, we have been to your apartment. We have nothing to hide," said a heavily accented male voice. Russian. "Here is one hundred francs for the, er, damages. We don't want any trouble, but we did not find what we came for. So now we are here. What could be more logical?"

Just then, a girl let loose just then with a stream of oaths that would have made Robert DeNiro blush. Yes, definitely Yohaba. "What gives you the right to enter my apartment? I'm not saying a word until I see some ID. I don't care what you do to Ivan. You can torture him, see if he cares, but I'm not saying a word. Right, Ivan?"

"Not right, baby," Ivan said. "Tell them what they want to know."

"Ugly here is talking sense," said the Russian. "Tell us about the trunk, and we'll let everyone go. We don't care if you don't have it. If you tell us everything, we all go home, you open the store again, and everyone is happy."

"I told you. I don't know what you're talking about. Yes, I'm related to Einstein, but he died decades before I was born. Are you thick or something?" Another slap, and Yohaba let loose with another verbal howitzer. Men laughing. Rulon made three Russians at least.

"Come. Insolence is not productive. Yes, we know when he died. But the trunk was special, was it not? Surely he talked about it with his family. Did your family have contact with him? Did you know your great-great-grandmother? Maybe he told her something. Do not underestimate us. We believe you know something important. We will not leave here without a lead."

Even over Rulon's cell phone, the Russian's voice sounded menacing. He was willing, in broad daylight in Zurich, to simply lock the door, lower the blinds, and rough people up.

The Russian spoke slowly. "You either give us something to work with, or we think you are holding out. Then we hurt you. You understand now?"

"But there are witnesses," said the girl.

"I do not think there are witnesses." He said something in Russian, and his men laughed. Then, to Ivan, he said in German, "If girl accidentally dies, do you tell police? You can be honest. She understands."

"No. No way. Right, guys?" said Ivan. Two other voices quickly assented. And then Ivan added, "Sorry, baby."

"See?" said the Russian. "Now tell us."

Rulon hated to cut off the call, but he had to check the other bug again. He dialed and listened for a minute, but the back room was still quiet. All the action was in the showroom. He dialed back into the showroom bug. By now he was reasonably certain that the back door wasn't being watched from the outside and that the back room was empty. He moseyed up to the rear entrance and turned the doorknob. Still unlocked.

With his gun drawn, he slipped inside, silently pulling the door shut behind him. Dropping into a crouch, he kept one earplug in to listen to the conversation in the front room and one ear free to monitor his immediate surroundings. He paused for a moment, listening and letting his eyes grow accustomed to the dark. Once adjusted, he scanned the room, always working his gun and line of sight together.

The doorway curtain moved slightly as someone walked by on the other side, their feet breaking up the light that spilled under the gap at the bottom. Silently, Rulon crept forward, light on his feet, like a hammer thrower moving into the circle. He was close enough now to hear voices without the phone. As he passed the rolltop desk, he grabbed the bug that was stuck under the edge. He turned his phone off, holstered his gun, and listened. The girl was trying to reason with them, but they weren't buying it.

"I think you misunderstand," the Russian said. "*We* ask questions. *You* give answers. That is simple thing, yes?" She must have nodded. "Okay, who was Elsa?"

"I don't know," said the girl, a tremor in her voice for the first time. "Einstein's second wife was named Elsa, but she died before I was born. I never met her."

"This is good start. I can see you want to help. Next question. What does it mean that Elsa will be coming back? She is dead. How can she come back?"

"I don't know."

The man grunted. Rulon heard shoes scrape, a man saying "No!" and then the short ugly sound of a fist connecting with someone's face. The Russian continued: "Now, your fingernails, my little girl, are nice and long. I wouldn't even need pliers. I could tear them out with my teeth."

The girl's voice went up an octave. "Stop! Please! Einstein

sometimes spoke in riddles! Tell me what you know, and I'll do everything I can! Just don't hurt anyone else!"

"See that?" said the Russian. "A much better attitude. We're looking for Einstein's trunk. Did your mother or grandmother ever talk about it? Do you have any diaries from that time? Did anyone come take the trunk? One or two men, perhaps? Do you know where the trunk is now? Was there an actual trunk, or was that a code for something? I want to know everything. But first, tell me about 'one ate two.' "

" 'One ate two?' I don't know. Let me think," said Yohaba. After a few moments of silence, she asked, "Was he speaking German when he said it?"

"He was dying. We know almost nothing," the Russian said. "Something about one fish eating two. It was a riddle."

"Then it was English . . . He died in the States . . . One fish eating two, you say? No, you said, *'Einer aß zwei,'* or, 'one ate two.' . . . But if it was in English, it could be taken two ways. He could have said, 'one eight two,' or, *'eins acht zwei,'* and you wouldn't hear the difference. Are you with me so far?" They must have all had puzzled looks on their faces because she went on in an exasperated tone. "The number 'eight' and the word 'ate'—the past tense of 'to eat'—sound the same in English but not in German. Now do you get it, you morons?" Another slap rang out, followed by a torrent of cursing. Rulon looked down and shook his head. Even he saw that coming.

From the back room, Rulon was impressed. The chick kept her cool. She managed to reason through this *eight-ate* business, trying to crack the riddle right after she'd been slapped and threatened. Not bad.

"It could have been a number," she continued, her voice sounding pensive, as though she were thinking out loud. "Maybe the combination to a safe or to a lock on this trunk you've been singing about. Where did you get this information? You must be working for a government . . . you think the trunk has secrets and you want them . . . Trust me, I don't care about the trunk . . . if I knew where it was, I would have sold it a long time ago. But you need to tell me everything you know so I can figure out this riddle. My grandmother said Einstein had a sense of humor and liked riddles. I like riddles too. I think like him . . . .I'm good in math. Just, please, no more hitting. It scares me, and I can't think straight. By the way, what do I get out of it, you know, if I help you?"

"We will pay money. A carrot and a stick. We are civilized people."

"How much?" she asked.

The girl has chutzpah, thought Rulon.

The moment for action was approaching. It was clear that this guy wasn't going to get what he wanted, and things were going to get uglier. Rulon also realized that nobody would be this brazen unless they had immunity. Magnus had warned him a while back that a Russian team was operating in Switzerland. Maybe they worked for the Russian embassy. He would have to factor that in.

Rulon eased a dental mirror from his inside jacket pocket. He quietly lay down on the floor beside the doorway and carefully slipped the mirror between the curtain folds. A slow scan of the room revealed the girl standing by the front desk, looking frail and scared. A short, stocky guy stood behind her, pinning her arms. Ivan stood next to her, his face bruised and swollen. *Did I do that, or did the Russians?* Rulon wondered.

There were two other men in the picture. The guy doing all the talking was bald and probably the leader. The other guy was as big as a gorilla—definitely the muscle. Rulon had heard the voices of only three bad guys, and that was all he could see. He had to assume they were all packing. He rotated the mirror and saw Ivan's two partners tied to chairs. One of them was slumped over, ummoving.

While Rulon lay on his stomach considering all this, he heard the click of a switchblade. He tilted the mirror and saw Baldy twisting a knife near Yohaba's face. Rulon felt something bad moving inside.

He put the mirror away and sat up with his back against the wall.

You can't do these things halfway any more than you can ride a bull without your hand being cinched down tight. So, Rulon did what he always did in these situations. He asked himself, if things went south, would he have any regrets?

It didn't take him long to commit. He was going in there to

help the girl—not a bad way to check out if it came to that. He said a quick prayer. His breathing quickened as he slipped his handgun out again.

Rulon carried a stainless steal .45 caliber Colt automatic with Bo-Mar night sights, but he generally didn't like guns except when hunting. Too lethal. Guns were always perceived as a death threat and were guaranteed to get everyone overreacting. But right now he needed to show the gun just to freeze everyone for an instant.

Rulon also pulled Freya out of her modified shoulder holster and slipped his hand through the strap. Freya was a Wilton demolition model hammer, with a narrow, four-pound, forged steel head and a ten-inch, rubber-coated, spring-steel handle with a leather strap dangling from the end. It had a solid feel and good balance, and it was light enough that he could still control his follow-through if he swung and missed. He was in a tight spot once in a seedy dive in Marseilles and found it in a toolbox under the bar. It had worked really well against a knife—and for clearing a path to a exit. He'd since added the strap.

Sitting there in the back room, he felt a familiar sensation in his stomach and shoulders. Like when he was all set in the bucking chute, his hand cinched tight, and after nodding to the guys on the gate, everything just slowed down. Then it was just him and an insane bull wondering why some idiot was sitting on his back.

Okay.

Rulon slowly stood up and faced the curtain. He could hear the voices. The tones were the same; no indication they knew he was there. His dad liked to say that courage is making a decision to act and then living with the consequences. And Hemingway said courage is grace under pressure. Or was it going berserk under pressure? Rulon could never remember. Two more breaths. He swung Freya back and forth a few times and rolled his shoulders to loosen up. He squared his jaw, hefting Freya in one hand and the Colt in the other.

"Weapons hot," he said under his breath, and then he was through the curtain like a message from Thor.

5

"THE ONLY SOURCE OF KNOWLEDGE IS EXPERIENCE."
—EINSTEIN

"KEEP UP," SAID RULON THROUGH GRITTED TEETH. "DON'T turn around. Walk natural. It's a beautiful day, and we're just another couple on the Bahnhofstrasse."

Yohaba and Rulon walked in the direction of the main train station, trying to melt into the throngs of workday shoppers. Rulon tried to focus on their getaway. He was hurting, but it was sure sweet to be alive. Adrenaline still coursed through his veins, and even with the pain in his chest, he was still ready to rumble. He sensed they were attracting attention, so he made an effort to walk straighter despite the discomfort, but he failed miserably. He'd taken a bullet square in the chest from a silenced pistol, but his vest had saved him. The stomach pillow had helped soften the blow, but it still felt like he'd been kicked by a horse. He grabbed Yohaba's hand, and they hurried on.

"You're hurt," said Yohaba in alarm when she saw him wince.

"I'm okay," he said. "Just keep moving. We're not out of this yet."

Yohaba looked around quickly and scanned the crowd, her eyes going narrow and hard like his did sometimes. "I don't see anything," she said.

Despite what she'd just been through, she was handling herself pretty well. Rulon's opinion of her kept improving. She seemed like a different girl from the pouty, hyper-emotional girl he met a few hours ago. "Neither do I," said Rulon. "But we're not safe. Gotta keep moving."

She pulled up beside him. "I thought you were dead. I thought *I* was dead." Her voice shook. "How can you still be walking?"

He couldn't deal with her questions just then. He was in surveillance mode. It looked like they were in the clear. Nobody was following, or if they were, they were good at staying out of sight. The scene from inside the luggage store filled his mind, but he pushed it out. *Gotta get away*, he reminded himself. *Gotta keep thinking.* He tried to remember his training. In mid-stride he abruptly turned around; everything looked normal.

It was the middle of a Friday afternoon, and Zurich's main shopping boulevard was crowded but not packed wall-to-wall like it could be on Saturdays. There were enough people to help them blend in, but that meant there were also enough people to hide an experienced shadow. Nobody jumped quickly into a doorway or seemed out of place when he turned.

The girl was talking. That was a good sign. *Heck, she's taking this better than the tongue lashing I gave her this morning.* She quieted down for a few seconds and then said very slowly, "I have never seen anything so . . . *violent*. Movies don't prepare you for the real thing." She caught his eye, and Rulon felt heartened by her pluck. But then she started in again with the questions. "Are you a cop or something? Aren't you supposed to yell 'freeze,' or 'put your hands up'? How come you didn't shoot that guy? And if you're a cop, why aren't we calling for backup?"

"I was at the Luggage House to buy a computer bag," he said. "That's all you need to know. And I *was* going to yell something, but they didn't give me a chance." He paused, feeling a sudden pang of conscience. "They *were* all still alive, right?"

"I don't know," she said, stopping to think. "Yeah. I think so."

"Good," he said. "I don't ever want to take a life. I didn't sign up for that."

Yohaba wobbled a bit as she walked, which was understandable, but it occurred to Rulon that there was no way they were blending in. He figured their ages were about right to be walking together, but she looked like the poster child for the punk-rock movement while he looked . . . normal? He was six feet tall, weighed a solid two-ninety, and had the bone structure of a rhinoceros, but compared to Yohaba, he looked normal. Okay, maybe not normal.

They heard an ambulance siren wail in the distance. *That was quick*, thought Rulon. He noticed Yohaba was carrying her handbag. *After surviving a rumble like that, she remembers her handbag.*

Women. He grabbed her arm, and they picked up the pace.

After they'd gone half a block, Yohaba said in a calmer voice, "I haven't thanked you. You saved my life." She took a deep breath. "I've never been so scared. And then you came through the doorway, and it was like the room exploded. And then everyone was on the floor except you and me. There was a shot, wasn't there? You're lucky he missed you."

She kept talking, the words flowing faster as she went on. "I don't think Ivan will rat on you. Hey, I bet to him, you were like Bruce Willis in *Pulp Fiction* when he rescued Ving Rhames. You saved him big time. You should have let me untie them. But I guess Ivan can do it when he wakes up."

Suddenly, she stopped and pulled free of Rulon's hand. "Why didn't you call the police? They need to know what happened. I need to go back." She started to turn, but Rulon held her arm and kept her moving.

Exhaustion hit him suddenly, the adrenaline gone just like that. He spotted the #13 tram and took Yohaba's hand just as she was about to put a cigarette in her mouth. "C'mon," he said. "You can't go back. Just trust me. I'm pretty sure this is bigger than the police."

"Okay," she said so simply it caused him to do a double-take. They pushed their way through the crowd of shoppers in front of Bali's toward the tram. Rulon let her get on first and then paused with his finger on the door button while he took one more look around. Still clear. He hopped on, and the doors swung shut.

They sat together on a two-seat bench, Rulon nearest the aisle. The tram lurched forward. The rumbling of its wheels vibrated up through the hard plastic seat and didn't do his bruised chest any favors. Maybe the bullet *had* penetrated his vest. He felt under his jacket, but there wasn't any blood. He constantly checked the faces around them and on the sidewalk outside. He glanced at Yohaba and worried about her stress level.

"I guess being Einstein's great-great-granddaughter has its drawbacks," he said, angling for a smile and feeling rewarded when he got a small one. That was a good sign.

A man ran alongside the tram and pounded on the door. Rulon stiffened. The tram picked up speed, and the man waved in disgust and melted back into the crowd. *Probably nothing*, Rulon told himself.

He thought about calling the consulate. Until he returned their bugs, he was technically still under contract. He was certain they wouldn't want this mess thrown on their doorstep. A chance to tweak the Russians might entice them, but for now, he put that option aside.

"Really, though, who are you?" Yohaba asked again, drawing him from his thoughts.

"I'm just a nice guy who saw a girl in trouble."

"And to think, I've been avoiding nice guys all my life."

"I'm a different kind of nice guy."

"Yeah, right, you and Kevin Bacon," she said. When he gave her an amazed look, she said, "What? Are you telling me you didn't steal that line from Kevin Bacon in *The River*?"

"No. It's just that there aren't too many people who would have made that connection."

"I'm into movies," she said. "Who do you work for?"

"I'm unemployed." He held out the two bugs he'd retrieved from the store. "I just stopped by to pick these up and saw you were in a jam." He explained what they were.

"Then you put them there this morning. What are you, a spy?"

"Not really . . . not anymore, at least," he said, acutely aware that he'd just been laid off a few hours ago. "I'm looking for a job." To keep things light, he added, "I don't suppose your boss would hire me, would he?"

"I think if he ever saw you again, he'd run screaming in the opposite direction. He's probably got a phobia about fat people now. No offense. By the way, your stomach's moved." Rulon saw she was right and readjusted the pillow. She continued. "We'll just add that to the list of things you'll explain to me later. But for now, can you tell me your name at least?"

"My name is Rulon Hurt."

"Rulon? Really? Sounds like a cowboy name. Are you a cowboy assassin or something?"

"No," he snapped. All this cat and mouse stuff really didn't matter anymore. "Look . . . " he said more patiently. "Oh, forget it. Yeah, I was a spy."

"Wow, a real spy. Do you have a license to kill and maim?"

"Just maim," he said. His brainpower was hovering around an 80-point IQ. He was exhausted, but he didn't feel like sleeping. The post-combat shakes were coming on.

"You're hurt," Yohaba said. "Is it bad? Do I need to get you to a hospital?"

"No, no. No hospital." He grimaced. "Where do you live? Can we go there?"

"I live in Altstetten, near the train station," she said. Altstetten was a neighborhood on the west side of Zurich, south of the river, opposite the Höngg district where Rulon lived, but still along the #13 route.

"Perfect," he said. "If you don't mind, I'm going to close my eyes. Give me a nudge if anything makes you nervous." He closed his eyes, but though his body was tired, his brain wouldn't stop. Still, it felt good to be off his feet. The girl sat quietly beside him, and he wondered what was going through her head. He opened one eye and watched her. She was looking straight ahead, her eyes slightly unfocused—the classic thousand-yard stare. She'd have a good story to tell her school friends on Monday.

Rulon leaned his head against the seat pole and thought about all the things that had gone wrong. What should have been a simple assignment had unraveled like a cheap sweater from the beginning. First, the unexpected fight with the girl's boss. Then getting blindsided by Toby. Then a violent scuffle with the Russians. He just hoped the Russian embassy had a reason to keep things quiet. But wasn't that how things always happened? Some days it just seemed like big cosmic tumblers fell into place while life went to heck in a hand basket, and he couldn't do a thing about it but hang on and ride things out.

Rulon tried putting the pieces together so they made sense—anything to take his mind off the ache in his chest, which, come to think of it, was already settling down.

How do I get myself into messes like this? It had started this morning when Rulon went through the curtain at the luggage store to patch things up with the girl. No, that wasn't quite right. It had started last night in Stockholm over dinner with Magnus.

6

"I NEVER THINK OF THE FUTURE—IT COMES SOON ENOUGH." —EINSTEIN

RULON HAD BEEN IN SWEDEN TO TRAIN THE RESELLERS WHO sold his cover-company's line of laptops and printers. As part of his cover, Rulon worked for a European computer reseller called Portal, which employed people like him in return for preferential treatment on embassy contracts. The training took place in the Portal office in a business park in Solna, just north of Stockholm.

Rulon liked this part of his job—teaching people, making a few jokes, having lunch with the boys. But on this particular occasion, he'd given the same presentation fifteen times in four days. By the time Thursday came around and he was speaking to his last audience, his brain was fried. He spent the last thirty minutes of the class sitting on the edge of the table with his tie undone, telling stories about his bull riding days in Idaho.

After the last meeting, Magnus, his boss, took him out for something to eat. The restaurant was in the old town, and Magnus raved about it as they drove there. From the outside, it had the look of a London Bond Street haberdashery—a grill and glass façade framed with wood and a narrow door with a multi-paned window. The place looked run down, but Rulon was hungry, so he kept his opinion to himself.

Magnus Alstermark was one of those people you couldn't help but like—a Labrador without the slobbering problem, Rulon liked to say. He was taller than Rulon by half a foot but still about forty pounds short of a Viking. He did, however, have the Nordic blonde hair and pale complexion and the red nose of a heavy drinker.

Rulon first met Magnus six years previous during a training course in the mountains near Boone, North Carolina. On the last day, all the students had to walk barefoot across a bed of coals. Rulon and Magnus were next to each other in line. Their eyes locked, and they nodded at the same time. Together, they grabbed the instructor, who'd been irritating them all week. It wasn't one of Rulon's prouder moments, but they were a bunch of tired, fed-up guys in the middle of nowhere. Luckily for the instructor, his shoes didn't burn quite as fast as his clothes, or it would have been a tough five miles back to camp.

It was the start of a beautiful friendship between Magnus and Rulon, just like Humphrey Bogart and Claude Reins in *Casablanca*.

"The stories were good today," said Magnus over a dinner of beef filet and his fifth beer. "They even made sense to us Swedes. But you still never do obscene limericks. How many times have I told you? We will love you if you do obscene limericks."

"It's not my style, you know that," said Rulon. "I'll stick to the cowboy stories. I just want to keep their attention while I go through the boring stuff. You can do the obscene limericks. I'm sure they'd lose something in the translation anyway."

"You're in a rut. And you have no respect for your elders. But that stuff you call boring pays the bills, don't forget. Besides, you do boring very well. You slide-whip us like a pro, and we take it like pros. Plus, you're an American all the way from America. They love you for coming all this way."

"I live in Zurich. It's not so far."

"Yes, but let's keep that quiet, okay? But I think you're liking it here more than usual. Or perhaps it's something else. . . ."

Why not just tell him? Magnus was an old friend, and Rulon wanted to talk about her. "I think I met someone at work."

"What do you mean you *think* you met someone?" asked Magnus. "Were you unconscious when it happened? Does this person happen to be a girl? I've been expecting something like this to happen for six years. If this is true, it's a miracle."

"Yes, you twit, I met a girl," Rulon said, annoyed at the insinuation. "I really like her, and we hit it off. And she's not the first girl I've liked in six years."

"No, just the first girl you've liked enough to tell me about," Magnus said, laughing. "Just take care to not get married too soon.

I like you too much to wish that on you."

"*You're* married," Rulon snapped. "Why would you say such a stupid thing?"

"I say it because while I believe in marriage, I do not believe in monogamy. Monogamy is a pernicious evil invented by the Amazons to torture their male captives." Magnus leaned into Rulon, his breath like smoke from a burning brewery.

Rulon couldn't let him get away with this. "You better not be cheating on Vendela," he said.

Magnus peered at Rulon through bloodshot eyes and announced in a liquid voice loud enough for the entire restaurant to hear, "I would practice monogamy only on one condition." Rulon felt the place collectively hold its breath.

Like an idiot he asked, "What's that?"

"If my wife would renounce the practice of monotony." The restaurant continued its pause for a full second and then came back to life. Rulon could hear again the back noise of muffled conversations, the tinkle of silverware, and the rush of waiters.

"But you," Magnus continued, "you have met someone, you think. You, my friend, need another Sprite. This calls for a celebration." He waved at a waiter. "A bottle of Kung for me—no, make that two—and a Sprite on the rocks for my lovesick friend." Magnus laughed too loudly at his own joke, and the waiter walked away, perplexed. "You know, my friend, you're a bit of a prude, for a spy," said Magnus, suddenly serious.

Out of habit, Rulon looked around, making sure no one was close enough to hear. From his vantage point, he could see the entrance, and he'd observed everyone who walked in, assessing them for threats and feeling wary if they had their hands in their pockets.

Magnus sat next to him on the same bench with the same view born of the same compulsive habit. They both had plenty of experience. Magnus had been around long enough to remember the Cold War, when Stockholm was the setting for some nasty unreported action between East and West. Now he was in management with two kids in college. Rulon was just north of thirty and still playing contact sports, as they liked to call it.

"Technically, I'm not a spy," said Rulon.

"Not again," said Magnus with exaggerated disdain. Leaning closer, the mixed smell of beer, sweat, and peppery filet hit Rulon's face like an exploding airbag. "What difference does it make?" he asked. "Spy, operative, agent, spook. Security specialist. Scalp hunter. It's all the same. You're just being difficult, as usual, *and* you're trying to change the subject. It won't work."

"I'm an investigator. I use my brain. I do my job, and then I turn things over to the authorities. My job is to solve cases, not to hurt people," said Rulon.

"Not unless you have to. And what do you call what happened in Marseilles last year? Please, my friend, save it for the review committee." To Rulon's amazement, Magnus appeared to be sobering up.

"Just tell me about my next job," said Rulon, taking a sip of his Sprite once the latest round of drinks arrived. A little too much ice, he decided, but the Sprite from the dispenser was good thanks to the local water. Rulon fancied himself a Sprite connoisseur.

"Not so fast. First tell me about the girl. I have a right to know." When Rulon gave him a look, Magnus continued. "She could be an agent out to trap you. You can't be too careful—these little Mata Haris are fiendishly convincing. I should know; I fall for them all the time myself. Tell me everything, my virgin scalp hunter."

Rulon asked, "Were you this paranoid when you were my age?"

"No," said Magnus, and then he added gravely, "but I should have been."

There was nobody better in the business, partly because so many people underestimated him. He liked to say that appearing disadvantaged was a real advantage. He also liked to say that Rulon was a natural at it. After a reflective silence on both their parts, Magnus said, "Now, tell me about her. Come."

Rulon just sat there, looking into his drink, thinking about how much to say. Isabella had first shown up on his radar six months ago, when she started working as a product manager for Portal. She was hard to miss for two reasons. First, Rulon was always on the lookout for new employees anyway. For years, the

Russians had been making sporadic efforts to infiltrate the office and identify the OCD operatives who worked there. In the past, though, whenever the Russians sent in a probe, it had always been someone from their part of the world. When Rulon heard she was South African and had verified her authenticity by listening to her accent in the cafeteria check-out line, he breathed a sigh of relief.

The second reason for noticing her was that she was drop-dead gorgeous, with long black hair, a trim, athletic figure, and a wardrobe to match—Gucci accessories, Jimmy Choo shoes, and Armani clothes—not that Rulon was an expert in such things.

"No," Rulon said. "If I tell you anything, you'll do a background check on her."

"Then at least tell me something about your first date. I'll bet you took her to a Mexican restaurant."

"The Desperado serves an excellent fajita plate," said Rulon. "I will not apologize."

"I despair of you. But, come. Tell me something."

Rulon sighed. "Okay. She asked to see my hand and then told me I had the same calluses as her dad, who happens to enjoy shooting pistols."

"Great, you're dating Sherlock Holmes's kid sister. What did you tell her?"

"I told her those were my gardening calluses."

"You are too clever. What else did she say?"

Rulon thought about that for a second. "She gave me a nickname."

"Ah, this is getting interesting. Nicknames can tell you a lot about a relationship."

"That's funny," said Rulon. "She said the same thing. She called me 'Mystery Man.' "

Magnus combed his hand through his blonde hair while he pondered. He next moved to scratching his chin. Then he frowned. "This is a perceptive woman, my friend. Be careful."

"I'm always careful."

"No, you're not," said Magnus emphatically. "You're lucky. There's a difference." For some reason his words struck both of them particularly hard, and they grew silent for a moment.

In a spy's line of work, too much depended on luck, either good or bad. You had no idea when you approached a target if you managed to spot all his defenses or if there was another security layer you happened to overlook, like one more flunky with a handgun who wasn't supposed to be there but who showed up anyway because he left his cell phone behind in the men's room. An operation could blow at any seam, and everyone knew it. The pressure made most agents crazy after a while.

"Tell me, why am I here?" asked Rulon, changing the subject.

Magnus held up a finger as he fished around in his briefcase. He pulled out a file and dropped it on the table. "Here is everything you need. Pictures, background, mission statement, the works. Knock yourself out. This one is pretty routine. Looks like a simple money laundering operation. I'll try and find something a little more exciting for you next time, but right now this is it."

While Magnus drank his beer, Rulon opened the file and read the mission summary and picked through the photos and a few of the biographies.

Magnus may have been Rulon's boss at Portal, but technically Rulon was self-employed—a subcontractor who received assignments though a private security company called Office Crimes Division, a name that conjured up images of accountants investigating white collar crimes—a far cry from what they really did. While OCD was private contracting firm, their agents did have a dotted line connection to the Foggy Bottom boys when on assignment. Technically, when in foreign countries, they fell under their host nation's jurisdiction and got paid out of their budget.

Despite the connection, there was usually no love lost between OCD and the US State Department. It was nothing personal, but the consulate staff saw working with OCD as a lose/lose situation. They didn't get any credit if an assignment went well—the work all came out of OCD headquarters in Virginia—but if something went awry, they were stuck putting all the pieces back together with local authorities, getting the agent out of jail, and settling lawsuits, something that had happened only once with Rulon.

While he traveled quite a bit in Europe on behalf of both Portal and OCD, Rulon spent most of his time in Switzerland, where the Company kept an apartment. The local Zurich language is a German dialect called Schwyzerdütsch that Rulon picked up years ago while in Switzerland as a missionary for his church. The fact that he spoke the language like a native made him a valuable commodity. He may have grown up in Idaho bucking hay bales and riding horses, but that didn't make him narrow or a hick, though it usually worked to his advantage if people thought so.

For fifteen minutes, Rulon and Magnus sat in silence until Rulon looked up.

"A luggage store?" he scoffed. "Come on, Magnus. This is kids' stuff. The night janitor could handle this one."

"Yes," said Magnus, "and I believe you said the same thing before Marseilles."

"No, I didn't. Before Marseilles, I distinctly remember saying, 'I'm sure before this is over, I'll have to fight my way out of a sleazy bar with a sledgehammer'."

Magnus shook his head in exasperation. "Speaking of violent encounters, pay attention. I just heard this morning that the Russians have moved people into Zurich."

"What kind of people?"

"Bad people."

"What for?" asked Rulon.

"To do bad things. I don't know. Word is they're looking for something." When Rulon gave him a look, he added, "What? You think the Thin Man calls me himself and tells me what he's planning? Just be careful, okay?"

"The Cold War is over, Magnus," said Rulon. "You're living in the past."

"Ah, your naivete makes me feel young again, my friend. It's why I worship youth, particularly of the female variety." Magnus drained the last of his beverage. "What time did you say your plane is leaving? I'll take you to the airport on my way back to the office. I'm expecting a purchase order for two hundred laptops. Must keep up appearances." As they both stood up to leave, Magnus was steady as a rock, but his eyes were spinning in opposite directions.

"The P.O. can wait till tomorrow," said Rulon. "I'm driving

you to the airport, and then you're going home in a cab. C'mon, hand them over." Rulon held out his hand for the keys.

Instead of complying, Magnus grabbed Rulon's outstretched hand with both of his and held it close to his face as though he had trouble focusing on it. Somehow, in the space of two hours, the man had gotten drunk, sobered up, and gotten drunk again. "Good heavens, man, look at the size of this shovel," he said. He let go and then draped his arm over Rulon's shoulder. "What was that funny thing you did in college? I've forgotten."

"I was a hammer thrower."

"That's right. To a man with a hammer, every problem is a nail." He laughed uproariously at his own joke. "Tell me, my friend, do you still carry around that hideous weapon of yours?"

"Only when I'm out with you," answered Rulon. "The keys." Rulon gave his hand an insistent shake. Magnus fumbled in his pocket and handed them over.

7

"IF WE KNEW WHAT IT WAS WE WERE DOING, IT WOULD NOT BE CALLED RESEARCH, WOULD IT?" —EINSTEIN

AS RULON SAT ON THE TRAM WITH HIS EYES CLOSED AND YOHABA beside him, he chuckled slightly when he thought of Magnus and his worry that this mission wouldn't be challenging. His thoughts drifted back to the luggage store, and he almost laughed out loud when he recalled the looks on the Russians' faces as he came barrelling through the doorway.

But the rest of the melee wasn't something he wanted to dwell on. The sound of one guy's ankle snapping made him shudder right down to his toes. Still, the hammer was more merciful than a bullet, not that he'd want to be on the receiving end of either. He shook his head to clear the images and opened his eyes just as the tram pulled into Frankental. He looked at his watch. It had been forty-five minutes since he'd busted up the party. He was over the shakes.

At Frankental, they traded the #13 tram for the #89 bus. Seven minutes later, they were walking in Alstetten and three blocks from Yohaba's apartment. Small stores on both sides of the street gave way to the residential area after one block. Yohaba's neighborhood was densely populated with older but well preserved four- and five-story apartment buildings.

As they walked, Rulon felt more alert, and his chest finally loosened up. *Bruised but not broken*, he decided. But now they had other problems. It was risky going back to her apartment, but the bad guys had been to her apartment already, they knew where she worked, and he had to assume they knew where she went to school, so finding the girl wasn't on these guys' top-ten problem list. Plus, she wasn't an agent herself, so she wouldn't be treated like a hard target. So all in all, Rulon felt it unlikely they'd left someone posted there before the fight. And afterward, well, they'd have to figure only an idiot would go back. Seemed like a reasonable risk.

Still, Rulon was nervous when they reached her block. Everything looked normal from a distance—it always does—but he made Yohaba wait by the corner while he walked past her building. No one stood in a doorway smoking a cigarette. No one sat in a parked car. He strolled to the end of the block, turned around, and came back.

"How's it look?" Yohaba asked.

"It looks okay, but stay sharp. If anything happens, stay behind me and do what I say. If I say 'run,' then you run. Got it?"

"Sure, boss," she answered. To Rulon's surprise, she added a bit flirtatiously, "Are you going to hit me with your hammer if I don't?"

"Yes," he said, too tired to play the game.

"This is exciting," she said. "Can I ask you another question?"

"No."

"What do we do if it's the Swiss police waiting for us?"

"Nothing. We let them talk to us or arrest us. Whatever. You've done nothing wrong. You're Swiss, right? I'll probably be deported, but you'll be okay. No big deal."

Yohaba's five-story building was old but still clean and in good repair. They stepped into the entryway, and Yohaba checked the mailbox. "Do you like salmon?" she asked, waving a grocery flyer. "I can buy some salmon, and, how do you say it—'wrestle up some food.' "

"The expression is 'rustle up some grub.' " Suddenly the thought of a nice, juicy salmon steak sounded tempting. "Does that offer include a big salad with a ripe avocado and a liter of Sprite?"

"That could be arranged. But only because you saved my life. I don't want you to think I'm easy."

For the first time, Rulon noticed a red welt on the side of her face. The girl had taken a few hits. He gave her full marks for spunk.

She unlocked the front door, and they took the elevator to the fourth floor. Rulon got out first, looked around, and found nothing out of the ordinary. At her door, Yohaba reached out with her key, but Rulon stopped her and signaled for quiet. The apartment had a Swiss-standard-issue three-bolt security door. He put his finger over the peephole so no one could see out, then took her key and quietly turned the lock. He opened the door just far enough to see that the living room had been ransacked.

The bald Russian was a man of his word. It looked like more than a hundred francs worth of damage, though. Rulon pushed the door open the rest of the way, still on his guard. He took one step into the room, and the door came flying violently back into him. Rulon realized instantly that they had been ambushed. Yohaba screamed.

The door hit Rulon's shoulder hard, but as quick as a cat, he lowered his center of gravity and plowed back into it. There is no give in Swiss apartment doors. They are metal and heavy, and even Freya couldn't get through one of them easily. The door, with Rulon behind it, smashed a grunt out of his unseen opponent as it threw him back against the wall. Rulon released the door for an instant and smashed into it again, eliciting such a satisfying crunching sound that he repeated the move, over and over.

By the fifth crunch, Rulon got into a rhythm. He smiled, imagining the guy behind the door thinking, *Man, she's strong for a girl.* His adversary tried countering with a gloved hand holding a Gyurza automatic, and Rulon immediately concluded he was dealing with another Russian. But before the Russian could angle around the door for a shot, Rulon wrenched the pistol from his grip, breaking a couple of fingers in the process. The Russian howled like . . . well, he howled like he'd just broken a couple of fingers. Not pausing for an instant, Rulon dropped the weapon and dove behind the door, slamming it shut, with Yohaba on the outside.

"Wait there," he yelled through the door.

With Yohaba safe, Rulon gave the man a sound beating until he was sure the guy would have cried out *No mas!*—had he been conscious. When he was finished, Rulon whirled around quickly with his hand under his jacket on Freya's handle, ready for another attacker. Breathing hard, he stood there in a half crouch, listening.

After a few moments, he relaxed slightly and did a quick search of the apartment with his gun drawn. When he came back to What's-his-name, who still lay slumped on the floor amid pieces of a broken coat rack, Rulon noticed that Yohaba was awfully quiet. What's-his-name was blocking the door, so Rulon grabbed an ankle and dragged the limp form out of the way. He opened the door and stuck his head out. Yohaba was nowhere in sight. Just as he started to panic, he heard her voice on the landing below, soothing a neighbor and apologizing for the racket.

Ten minutes later, Rulon had What's-his-name tied to a chair in the dining room with strips from an old sheet Yohaba had donated to the cause. The man looked to be a little taller than Rulon and about fifteen years older. His already dark complexion seemed even darker because of his two-day growth of beard. Rulon still pegged him as Russian, but he wouldn't know for sure until he heard his accent. His thick eyebrows met in the middle. One eye had started to swell badly, and there was a trickle of blood around his crooked mouth. He wore a black leather jacket, dark jeans, and a pair of soft-soled brown shoes. He looked to be in good shape for his age. Rulon searched him, and, along with the gun, he'd been carrying a wicked little knife, a cell phone, cigarettes, a lighter, and a wallet with a Swiss driver's license that Rulon assumed was fake. He had the look of a professional with resources.

Rulon moved the dining room table up against the wall and out of the way and sat opposite the man on another of the dining room chairs, his back to the kitchen. Yohaba was in the adjoining living room, sitting on a patched-up brown leather couch with a pillow on her lap and a clear view of the proceedings. While Rulon was tying up the bad guy, she'd worked on getting her apartment back together. She had everything under control except for pieces of a busted vase that still lay like a broken-toothed smile on the living room's wood floor. The Russians were thorough, Rulon had to give them that, but with Yohaba's minimalist lifestyle, there wasn't much to trash.

The place was Bohemian bare, decorated in earth-tones, second-hand, non-matching furniture, and a seven-foot carved giraffe for a hat rack. In one corner was the only concession to modern living: an open laptop and attached printer on top of an IKEA self-assembled desk. Nearby was a gray metal roller chair pushed up against the wall. The apartment had an open floor plan, but the small windows rendered the space dark and moody, even with the lights on, a typical feature of budget-friendly student housing.

What's-his-name started to stir, and Rulon gave him a playful slap to speed up the process. A minute later, a gleam of intelligence shone in the man's eyes. He looked around and checked Rulon out. He flexed his hands and grimaced, looking down at his bruised and swollen fingers. He tested his bonds and appeared to accept the fact that he wasn't going anywhere. His eyes focused on Yohaba.

"Where's the other guy?" he asked her in thickly accented German. He was definitely Russian.

"What other guy?" she asked.

"The ape who got me with the door."

"Sitting in front of you," she said.

He looked at Rulon. The words, "You've got to be kidding" hung unspoken in the air.

"He's pretty tough for a fat guy," said Yohaba, rising to Rulon's defense. "And you got off lucky. You should see what he did to your buddies."

"A berserk fat man, they said. Now I believe it." He laughed a short little laugh, then winced and flexed his jaw.

Irritated, Rulon said, "Let's change the subject. What's your name? Your driver's license says Dmitry. Should I call you that?"

"Why not?"

"What do you want with the girl?

"We want to find something."

"Yes, a trunk, we know."

Dmitry paused for a moment, assessing this new reality, wondering how much more they knew. "It was supposedly owned by Einstein." He nodded toward Yohaba. "She's his great-great-granddaughter. What's wrong with her face? Did my men do that? They were told not to hurt her. We're not barbarians."

Yohaba jumped off the couch and threw the pillow at him, along with a steaming pile of invective. "You *liar*," she snarled. "One of your brutes also punched the lights out of a friend of mine.

You're *worse* than barbarians. Just wait until you see what Rulon's going to do to you. Show him your hammer, Rulon. You ever try to walk on a compound fracture, Dmitry? You know what that feels like? Go on, Rulon. Show him what you can do."

Rulon stood up quickly, causing his chair to fall backwards. He reached under his jacket, and Dmitry stiffened when he saw his expression. "Don't torture me," he said quietly.

Rulon looked at him in disgust. "What planet are you from?"

"What are you going to do?" he asked.

Rulon pulled out a cell phone. "I'm calling the police. Maybe it's cool where you come from to break into someone's apartment and trash it and then ambush them when they come home, but I'm pretty sure it's against the law in Switzerland." He started to dial.

"No, no," said the Russian. "Wait, please. Let's talk. I have nothing to hide." He looked at Yohaba. "She's just a girl. We don't think she knows much, but she may know something. We just want to know the next step. "

"I want to know about the trunk," said Rulon.

"We don't know anything," Dmitry answered.

"He's a liar!" Yohaba yelled. "Don't let him off the hook. They know plenty." And before Rulon could stop her, she took a quick step over to Dmitry and slapped him hard across the face. "*And* they like to slap girls," she said. She reared back, looking to land a punch, so Rulon jumped in and grabbed her.

"You're going to hurt yourself," he said, pushing her back to the couch. "She's had a bad day," he said to the Russian after he picked up the chair and sat down again. "But this is how we're going to work this. I'm not going to torture you, but I'm not going to play games either. Answer my questions, and you'll walk out of here. Don't, and we leave you here tied up until the police come. We'll know if you're lying. One mistake, and I dial the police."

"They told me you're American. Your German is very good."

Rulon acknowledged the compliment with a slight nod. "First question," he said. "Your comrades were asking about a number. What was that all about?"

"I don't know anything about a number. Nobody said anything about a number."

Rulon sighed and shook his head. He'd wanted to get at least something out of this guy. He pulled out his phone and started dialing.

"Wait!" Dmitry cried. "Slow down. I swear, I never heard anything about a number. What did they say?"

"They asked me about the number one eighty-two," Yohaba said. She explained to him the German-English homonym thing. "I took it to be a code or a combination to a lock."

"No. You got it wrong. Einstein told one of our agents a riddle about one fish eating two. It was one ate two. One fish ate two others. We don't know what it means, but we never thought of it as a number. But maybe that was the riddle."

"How did you know about the trunk?"

"What does it matter?" Dmitry replied.

"It matters, that's all you need to focus on," said Rulon.

Dmitry shrugged. "There was a report. It was lost for years. A long time ago, when Einstein was dying, one of our agents posed as his long-lost daughter, and he told her to find a trunk that had secrets. He was practically delirious at the time, but because he was Einstein, everyone thinks the trunk holds the secrets of the universe. And now we are running around like idiots.

"He said his daughter could find it. That's why we're here—to talk to one of his descendent daughters. We're just making sure we—how do you Americans say it—leave no stone unturned. It's probably nothing. We get sent on these wild goose chases all the time.

"Look," he said, turning to Rulon, "I don't know who you're working for, but this is not a matter of national security. There is no need for heroes. You'll run around just like us if you start looking for this trunk after fifty years."

"He doesn't work for anybody," said Yohaba. "He just came into the store to buy a computer bag. You got creamed by a civilian chubby boy. Just a regular Joe American. How does that make you feel?" She winked at Rulon, but he was still annoyed by the "chubby boy" comment.

Dmitry looked at her with forbearance. "You really believe that? You are a little girl."

All right, I might forgive him the earlier insult, Rulon thought before saying, "I'm making up another rule. You either tell us something we haven't already heard, or I'm calling the police. You're wasting my time."

"How should I know what you already know?"

"That's your problem, comrade."

Dmitry wriggled in his bonds. "Let me loose."

"No," said Rulon.

"Can I have something to drink?"

"No."

"Toilet?"

"No."

Dmitry clenched his teeth over the pain of his broken fingers, swollen eye, and rearranged jaw. When he regained control, he sighed. "This whole thing is stupid and unnecessary and has gotten completely out of control."

Rulon sat quietly. He looked over at Yohaba. She was playing with an earring, seemingly disinterested.

"Okay," Dmitry said. "Let me think. They only briefed us once." He closed his eyes and tilted his head back. After a few moments, and with his forehead furrowed in concentration, he began to speak. "Einstein said there were three men who knew about the trunk and that they would share the profits with his daughter. He said he felt guilty about the atom bomb, that everyone missed the obvious—something about getting a higher yield from the bomb. That's probably why my government is so interested. He kept saying 'Please.' He also said, 'She is coming back. When she does you will need the trunk. Elsa and the trunk were with the stars.' He talked about his second wife Elsa a lot. He said she was coming back to Geneva someday. We assumed he meant Geneva, Switzerland. His brain was gone. Only a crazed commissar could take this junk seriously."

Dmitry sat there for another half minute. Finally he opened his eyes. "He was obsessed with billiards at the end, saying things about slow shots curving sooner. Stuff like that. Nonsense. He said 'please' a lot. I mention that again only because that came up twice in the briefing. He was crazy at the end. He also said everything was with the stars or among the stars, something like that."

Dmitry shrugged. "That's all. If that's not good enough, then call the police."

Rulon was just about to take him up on his offer when he noticed Yohaba had gotten up and was sitting on the roller chair in front of her laptop, typing away. He started to say something to Dmitry, but then he heard the printer starting up, and he turned to Yohaba. "If you have homework to do, we can leave."

"Let him go," she said, oblivious to Rulon's sarcasm. She didn't even bother to look up. "We'll never learn anything from him anyway. Just let him go."

Rulon was puzzled by her sudden change in attitude, but this was going nowhere. He stood up and cut Dmitry free with the knife he'd taken. "Wrap your fingers with one of these strips," he said. "Then scram."

Dmitry rubbed his wrists and then reached for one of the scraps of material on the floor. While he wrapped his fingers he asked, "Can I have my gun and knife back, please?"

Rulon just stared at him.

"At least my cell phone, then?" Rulon obliged. "My wallet?" Rulon tossed him the wallet and his pack of smokes before he could ask for them too.

"Just don't light up in here," Rulon warned. "By the way, I took five hundred francs from your wallet to pay the girl for the mess your boys made and the broken coat rack. I'm sure your boss will understand." He expected Yohaba to react to this, but she just typed away, not paying attention.

Dmitry shrugged. "Just more paperwork." He checked his wallet and took a hard look at Rulon. "You are a professional. Yes? If you're interested, I could offer you some work."

"I'd rather have a kidney removed," replied Rulon.

Dmitry tried to laugh but again grabbed his jaw and grimaced. He limped toward the door. As he reached for the doorknob, he turned and said to Yohaba, "Sorry about the mess. I'll put it in my report that you got hurt. Someone will be punished."

Yohaba looked up from her laptop. "I got slapped all right, but the guy responsible looks worse than you do. His slapping days are over. Right, Rulon?"

"I was aiming for the gun, but he moved," said Rulon sheepishly. He always felt bad after the adrenaline wore off.

Dmitry touched his eye and winced. Then he was out the door.

Rulon turned to where Yohaba stood at the printer. Their eyes locked, and for the first time, Rulon had a difficult time reading her expression. *What now?* he asked himself. While he watched her, she appeared to come to a decision.

"That's twice today you saved me," she said. She crossed the room and put her arms around Rulon's neck and wriggled up close, pressing her body firmly against his, almost melting herself through his clothes. He was totally caught off guard. He pried her hands from behind his neck and pushed her away but didn't let her go.

She stood there, very still, making no effort to break free. Her hands felt small in his. The feel of her lean, lissome body had short-circuited his senses, and its lingering recollection was so strong it was as if they hadn't separated.

She looked up full into his face, her green eyes dancing. She brightened into a smile, making it clear what she wanted. Rulon stood there, feeling caught, as if between two doors, knowing what the right decision was but slightly tired at having to make it again. Down deep, though, he knew he didn't have a choice. This is how he chose to play his life, and doing anything else would be a betrayal.

But still, he watched her and marveled—not the first time in his life—at the power of a woman and how adept some of them were at wielding that power. He was struck by the contrast between Isabella and Yohaba. Isabella was like a fly fisherman working a fish and played the game as confidently as he'd ever seen it done. Yohaba was a fearless frontal assault.

Yohaba looked at him with the submissive confidence of a woman who knew her way around men, and she must have seen something encouraging in his eyes, because at that moment she tugged easily on his hands and softly said, "C'mon."

In some unspoken way, they were now officially saying hello—not so much by the physical approach she had just initiated but by what they now saw in each other's expression.

He also knew, if she were half as savvy about men as he judged, that she would sense the contradiction between the message in his eyes and what he was about to say with his lips. But that was the way it was going to be. The decision having been made, the internal pressure building in his mind dissipated inadvertently through his hands.

"Ow," she said, "you're hurting me."

"Sorry," he said as he let go. "But don't ever do that again, or you're on your own. Do we understand each other? And by the way, in real life, that's how women get pregnant."

"Just the stupid ones," she said.

"Whatever you want to believe. Just remember—one more move like that, and I'm out of here."

"All right, all right, I got it," she snapped, angry now, surprised and crestfallen, the heat and connection of the moment instantly broken. She turned away, embarrassed, and walked clear across the room to the window. He watched her as she stood there, staring outside and absently twirling a strand of her long auburn hair. He wished he could see the reflection of her face in the glass, but the angle wasn't right. After a minute, she touched the window with the palm of her hand. "You're not like Ivan," she said, still looking out the window. "And by the way, nothing ever happened with him. Or the others. Don't let the looks fool you."

"That's your business," he said firmly. "Just drop the whole thing."

Rulon went back to the dining room and sat down. Wherever they had just gone together, they were back now, each alone with their own thoughts. She wandered over to the desk, and he watched her. She was a wild little filly—almost the opposite of Isabella's chic styling and class. Definitely not his type. Well, he didn't mind the long auburn hair streaked with red, but the nose ring was just plain painful to look at. She had a mouth that begged for a bar of soap. And she was skinny as a branding iron. And he didn't like tattoos. Another turnoff.

He couldn't see her taking care of kids. But she had a nice body, a flat stomach barely covered by her short, tight shirt, and big eyes that looked up at him with the innocence of a doe . . . he shook his head to clear it. His dad used to say that birds will land in your branches, but whether they build a nest is up to you. He snapped back to reality. Yohaba now stood by the computer desk with her back to him, pulling something out of the printer.

"What have you got?" he asked.

"Look at this," she said, her voice filled with wonder and excitement. She seemed back to her old self. "Just look at this. I'm a chip off the old block, it turns out. She handed him some sheets of paper. She crossed the living room again and held the paper in front of his face. "Think I'm right? That Geneva is ground zero?"

He grabbed the paper and read it. At first nothing made sense, but that quickly changed. By the time he got to the second paragraph, his stomach was flipping, and his thoughts were like a cattle stampede. It was a Wikipedia entry. Einstein wasn't saying please. He was saying *Palisa.* Palisa was a nineteenth century astronomer, and 182 Elsa was an asteroid. And suddenly he knew, just as clearly as if Einstein had reached across all those decades and told him personally, that the asteroid was going to hit Geneva someday, and whatever was in the trunk was the only thing that could stop it.

"Yeah, you might be right," Rulon said, still looking at the page, overpowered by what he just read. *But how on earth can someone make a prediction like this—all the way down to which city will be hit?*

8

"EVERYTHING SHOULD BE MADE AS SIMPLE AS POSSIBLE, BUT NOT SIMPLER." —EINSTEIN

YOHABA AND RULON GLARED AT EACH OTHER ACROSS THE dining room table, the apartment still smoldering from her verbal napalm strikes. The fight had been short but vicious, but she was calmer now, and he'd picked up the chairs he inadvertently knocked over as he stormed around the room.

The table was to be the level playing field over which they'd save the world and negotiate their personal truce. She'd made it clear she wasn't meekly going away and leaving it up to him. Their lives were inexplicably thrown together for at least a short time. Though neither of them made mention of the irony, it was obvious to both of them. They were two people who, under different circumstances, would have had nothing to do with each other. But now, despite their differences in religion, background, and moral judgment, they were bound together by their humanity.

Yohaba wanted to light up, but Rulon prevailed upon her to wait. To his surprise, she agreed—a concession he appreciated. After the initial shock wore off, Rulon's conviction that the world was doomed gave way to an equally clear realization that there must be some other explanation. It was crazy. This would have to be confirmed.

They had so many questions. How did Einstein know that 182 Elsa was going to collide with Earth? Were calculations that precise even possible back in the 1950s? And Palisa lived in the late 1800s. What was the connection there? Why did Einstein know about it when no one else did? Why was it was such a big secret? Why didn't he tell the world? No, this was shaping up to be something on the scale of a *Da Vinci Code* hoax. Mentally and emotionally, it was as though Rulon had jumped into the freezing North Fork of the Payette River and was now cold and calculating, right down to the bone. Clearly, this couldn't be happening. But Yohaba disagreed, hence the fight.

"What are you thinking?" asked Yohaba in a conciliatory tone.

He broke off his reverie. "I'm thinking we need to get this confirmed one way or another. I'll turn this over to some folks in the government and see what they come up with."

"Which government? Yours, I suppose."

"Of course. We've got the resources. If it involved banking, chocolate, or yodeling, I'd turn it over to the Swiss. Do you have a problem with that?"

Yohaba rolled her eyes. "First of all, Rulon, Switzerland is my country, but I've lived in Germany as well, so I'm not as blinded by nationalist loyalty as some people in this room. Let's just think this through. Einstein was my great-great-grandfather. I owe him this. And by the way, the trunk is mine if we find it. Remember, he gave it to his daughter."

"No, he gave it to someone he *thought* was his daughter."

"He gave it to his daughter, he just happened to tell the wrong person."

Not a bad answer, thought Rulon. "Okay. But let's save the world first and then decide who gets the royalties."

"This has nothing to do with royalties," she said. "You're not seeing the big picture." Rulon noted a change in her. She sounded mature, and for an instant he almost didn't recognize in this mature, logical woman the pouting, emotional chick he first encountered that morning. Or the one who had just made a pass at him. Or the one who had just exploded.

"Why were you so emotional when we met this morning?" he asked, abruptly changing the subject but needing a better read on her character before they went on. At his question, her face went introspective.

She said, "You can blame my father. He got me hooked on math when I was just a little girl. When you came into the store, I was doing homework and having trouble. It's the one thing in my life I've always been good at. When things go badly, I get in my own little cave with my physics. It's cheaper than therapy. But when I can't figure things out, I get frustrated and think, what am I good for? I'm sure you have something in your life like that too. Your work, perhaps?"

"My anchors are my faith in God and my family. But work is important too. You have to be good, but you have to be good for something. Yeah, work counts."

"Are you married?"

"No. Never had the pleasure. By family, I'm talking about my father and brother, and I've got a million cousins, and three out of four grandparents are still alive. My mom died when I was eight."

"I'm sorry. My mother and father died in a car crash when I was ten. I don't think I ever forgave them. Maybe we have the same needs but just fulfill them differently."

Rulon wasn't ready to concede that point quite yet, but he was willing to push on with the conversation and think about it later. Most likely she'd have to get back to school or work in a few days, and he'd be pursuing this alone. But that thought was immediately negated by a premonition that he was going to be stuck with her, and at some point they would have to come to terms with their different approaches to life.

"Maybe, but tell me, what part of the big picture am I missing?" he asked.

"What do you think is in that trunk?"

"Well, I know what you think—something that will save the world. Something that will stop Elsa."

"Like what?" she asked.

"I don't know. A bomb. A laser. A death ray. He was Einstein—it could be a time machine for all I know."

"I think it's a bomb. Do you remember what Dmitry said about yields? Einstein signed a letter in August 1939 encouraging the US government to develop the atom bomb. He did it because he didn't want the Nazis to get it first. That would have been catastrophic. But then when he saw the results—what happened in Japan—he always regretted it. He always said it was the greatest mistake of his life. Maybe he thought that if he could use that power to save the world, it would make up for things."

"You're exaggerating, right?" said Rulon. "You don't mean this asteroid could actually destroy the world, do you?"

"Yes. That's exactly what I mean," she said. "This thing is a monster. Elsa is twenty-seven miles across." Rulon looked down at the *Wikipedia* printout and saw that she was right. She continued. "That would be unbelievable. Even though a lot of it would burn up in the atmosphere, still, a lot would get through—probably . . . twelve miles across when it hits."

"How big was the asteroid that destroyed that Russian forest?" he asked.

"The one in 1908? Probably no more than fifty yards in diameter."

"What?" Rulon exclaimed in surprise. "That can't be right. How about the one in Arizona? Meteor Crater."

"You mean the Barringer Crater. A little bigger, but still under four hundred yards."

"Are you sure?" he asked, in serious doubt that she had her facts straight. "That has to be too small. I've been there. The crater's huge."

"A five-yard asteroid releases as much energy as Little Boy, the bomb that took out Hiroshima. About fifteen kilotons. The comet or whatever it was over Russia was ten to fifteen megatons."

"What do you mean *over* Russia?"

"Well, it never left a crater, so some people think it was a comet that skipped off the atmosphere, dropping some of its chemical mass on the Earth, which ignited in the air as it heated coming in. But whatever it was that leveled the Tunguska forest, it exploded five miles in the air and blew down eighty million trees over almost a thousand square miles. It was about as big as the hydrogen bomb the Americans detonated in the Bikini Atoll in 1954, but smaller than the hydrogen bomb the Russians set off in 1961 in the Novaya Zemlya archipelago, the one called Kuzka's Mother. That one was fifty megatons. But even that's nothing compared to a decent-sized asteroid hitting the Earth."

"How big was the asteroid that killed the dinosaurs?" Rulon asked, fascinated.

"Maybe six miles across," said Yohaba. "It released the energy of 100 trillion tons of TNT and created the 110-mile-wide Chicxulub crater in the Yucatan Peninsula."

"What would twelve miles do?" he asked, not wanting to let go until he had his worst fears confirmed.

"I don't know exactly—these calculations don't scale linearly—but I once had to do a calculation for a three-mile asteroid, and it came out to ten million megatons and left a crater sixty miles wide. That's about 200,000 times bigger than the biggest hydrogen bomb ever detonated And if it hit the ocean, it could go to the bottom of the Marianas Trench and still penetrate the crust. The debris thrown into the air would blot out the sun for months, and billions of people would die, just like the dinosaurs. I'm telling you, scary doesn't even begin to cover it."

"I'm still amazed you managed to connect the dots on all this."

"It just clicked. I told you I was smart. When I saw *Deep Impact* and *Armageddon,* I went nuts for a while and read everything I could on the subject. Plus, at that time, I had math teachers trying to make the physics real. They assigned us projects every other month, making us calculate yields and trajectories on asteroid hits and all that good stuff. I just got into it. That's probably why my brain focused on asteroids when you were talking to Dmitry. When he said 'out among the stars,' I just went there. I had heard of Palisa too, and I knew how they named asteroids. It just clicked."

Rulon whistled. "I saw those movies too, but I wouldn't have figured it out in a million years. You're one smart cookie."

She blushed at the compliment, and Rulon marveled. A few minutes ago, she was ready to slug a Russian agent, and now she was blushing. Rulon caught himself warming to her slightly then quickly pulled in the reins.

She continued. "Maybe Einstein reveals the secret of the higher yield because we need a bigger bomb to destroy Elsa. Maybe that was his way of making up for the letter. Maybe he wanted to salvage something good from it."

"We can 'maybe this' and 'maybe that' all day," Rulon replied, "but whatever is inside that trunk, it's better that we get it instead of the bad guys, don't you think?"

"If we knew who the bad guys were. Do you know them when

you see them, or do you just assume America's always the good guy? You think that after Iraq, there's no controversy about that?"

"The nut was gassing his own people and had started two unprovoked wars in his region. There was some justification."

"So, knock *him* off," said Yohaba. "One person. Instead, you throw the whole country up in the air like a deck of cards. And do you think anyone is smart enough to know how all the pieces are going to come back together again?

"Was it good for India and Pakistan to split? Gandhi was a great man, but did he really serve India best by getting the British thrown out? Cecil Rhodes was a jerk, but do you think the Zimbabweans wouldn't rather be ruled by him right now? When you set out to change a country, there are too many variables." Yohaba went silent for a few moments before continuing more slowly. "Actually, we're not that far apart. Going in there maybe wasn't the worst thing in the world, but the way you handled it afterwards was horrible. You tore the country's institutions apart. You didn't understand the consequences of what you were doing."

"Not true," said Rulon. "The people who tore that country apart were the ones who blew themselves up in markets, police stations, weddings, and funerals, who wiped out entire families and who planted road-side bombs. Where are you going with this, anyway?"

"I don't want America to have the power to make a bigger bomb," she said. "I don't want *anyone* to have it. But if one country were to have it, I'd prefer it were the Swiss. They've managed to stay neutral in two world wars. They only have one agenda, and the world likes them for it. The Swiss would never start a war or destroy the world. It would mess up the banking system. Let's find it and give it to the Swiss."

Yohaba leaned forward, her long hair dangling over the table. There was an honesty in her voice and eyes that Rulon found very convincing. She wasn't pleading to win the argument as much as she was pleading for a cause that was bigger than herself. She was pleading on behalf of a principle, a principle that Rulon happened to share: that humanity should be a stronger bond than nationality and that all were children of God and brothers and sisters in the same human family.

He looked at Yohaba and realized that here was a deeper person than he first judged. When he looked at her now, he realized he hardly noticed the nose ring or tattoos. Instead he saw an honest person who was maybe a little lost about some things but who overall had a code and was trying to live by it. Now she was caught up in something she never intended but was facing up to her responsibilities. He respected her for that.

"If we are going to find the trunk on our own," he said, "we can't take forever to do it. We don't know when the asteroid is going to hit. It could be tomorrow, or in a year, or in a hundred, but we can't take a chance by delaying too long."

"Agreed," said Yohaba. "But I don't think the impact is too soon. They can track asteroids now and plot their courses. If one had a chance of hitting us within the next few years, they probably wouldn't advertise it, but the astronomers would know. I have a friend who is really plugged into the astronomical community. He is floating down the Amazon right now, but he'll be back in a week, and we can ask him then. In the meantime, let's go looking for the trunk together."

Rulon considered her idea. Technically, he was unemployed. His reseller job was little more than a hobby, and he could call his own shots. If he took off a week or two, no one would mind. The head boss, who knew his true situation, would assume he was off on an OCD assignment somewhere. Yohaba's idea made sense.

Patriot that he was, Rulon also believed that the military-industrial complex was real and that a lot of people in that organization were patriots of a different sort, having given their pledge of allegiance to a green flag with a dollar sign in the middle. Now that he thought about it, he didn't want them to have a bigger bomb either.

"I can give it two weeks," he said. "We search for the trunk for two weeks on our own. Technically I'm not working for the US government right now, so there's no conflict of interest. But if we don't find it in two weeks, we turn it over to someone bigger than us. Agreed?"

"Who?" asked Yohaba. "I vote for Switzerland."

"Maybe no government at all," Rulon said. "I'd feel more

comfortable if it was in the hands of the general public."

"What can the general public do?" asked Yohaba. "They can't build a rocket or a nuclear bomb. They don't have access to reactors and labs, and they certainly don't have the budget."

"Look," said Rulon, "you sold me. We can't give it to the United States. But if you think there is another country out there that I trust with that power more than the American government, you're crazy. No country in history has done more good for more people than America or has better principles.

"Right after World War II, the United States was the only country in the world with nuclear weapons, and we had the army that beat the Nazis in western Europe and the Japanese. If we wanted to, we could've conquered the world right then and there. No one could have stopped us. From my way of thinking, we've *had* the power and have managed not to misuse it. We've passed the test of history.

"Maybe Iraq wasn't the best idea in the world, but do you really think the world would better off with China or Russia . . . or Switzerland as the world's great power? I don't think so. No. I'm not trusting Switzerland or any other country with this. This is too risky."

"Then who?"

"I don't know, but the answer will come. First we have to find the trunk."

Yohaba paused and looked down. "How strange," she said under her breath.

"What's that?"

"How fast a life can change. Do you mind spending two weeks with me?"

"We'll need rules," he said. "You know what *numero uno* is?"

"I think I have a good guess," said Yohaba. "But just so you know, I don't do one-night stands." She caught Rulon rolling his eyes. "No, don't you dare give me that look. I meant to say, 'I don't do one-night stands, except with men who save my life.' But no one has ever saved my life before. And besides, I wasn't thinking of you as a one-night stand."

"A simple 'thank you' would have worked."

"I did say 'thank you.' Remember?" He started to interrupt. "Let me finish," she said. "The important thing is I feel I can trust you. But don't let that go to your head because I also think you and I are going to have lots of fights. And anyway, you're not my type."

Rulon wasn't quite sure what she meant by all that, but he was willing to let it slide as long as she agreed to keep to the rules. They needed to get going. Dmitry surely had reported in by now, and the Russians would be looking for them. They needed Yohaba for answers and Rulon . . . for revenge. Suddenly, letting Dmitry go didn't seem like such a smart idea.

Rulon said, "Yeah, whatever. Let's saddle up. Pack light. We may not be back for a few days."

***

Princeton Hospital, New Jersey, April 1955—The room was sparsely furnished in the institutional colors of a faded picture. Only a chair in one corner, a metal bed, and a small side table with a lamp. On the table was a large, much-read book on billiards. On the window sill, a lonely fish swam languidly in a glass bowl. In the bed, an old man lay dying. A middle-aged woman in a plain brown dress and white pill box hat stood over the bed, telling him the painful story of her life.

"You abandoned me," she said as she leaned over the bed. "Why did you give me up? Why did you never come looking for me? I was your child."

"I can't give you an answer," said the old man, his words drifting up weakly like smoke from an ash heap. He paused to assemble the words of his confession. "If you really are my daughter, then you must understand. We had to give you up. We didn't know we would marry someday. Your mother hated me for a time. I hated myself. And now I am dying. Tell me, what can I do for you?"

"Do you have papers you haven't published? Something you could give me that I could publish for you, so you would never be forgotten."

"Possibly. What did you say your name was?"

"Lieserl," she sniffed as a tear rolled down her cheek. "I'm your little Lieserl.

"Ah, yes, my little Lieserl." He smiled faintly. "Maybe you are my daughter. Why else would you be here? Did you come all the way from Switzerland to see me?"

"Yes, all the way from Switzerland."

"Then listen carefully," he said in a much stronger voice. "I am dying. Someone else was supposed to be here by now, but they are late, and you may have to do. But first, tell me . . . 'Do you know why a slow massé shot curves sooner, even though a harder shot spins faster?'" When she looked at him blankly, he asked, "Have you never played billiards?"

"No," she answered, perplexed.

"Dare I trust you with my joules then?" he asked, and his shoulders shook weakly at his favorite joke.

"I don't want your jewels," she said.

"But you want my trunk."

"A trunk?" she asked, her eyes alight with interest. "Does it have secrets?"

"Secrets? Yes, terrible secrets. But perhaps first, before I tell you where it is, we should establish your pedigree." When she gave him a quizzical look, he asked with a smile, "I would expect a daughter of mine to be good at riddles. Are you good at riddles?"

"I . . . well . . . I . . . ," she stammered.

"Never mind," he said, "We will find out." Nodding towards the window, he asked, "You see my friend swimming nicely?"

"You mean the fish?" she replied with a quick glance at the fishbowl.

"Yes. He used to have a brother and a sister," said the old man. "But one ate two. And now he is all alone. One eight two. Are you listening closely? You never met your stepmother. Do you know her name?

"Elsa," said the woman.

"Good. Good. Remember, this is supposed to be a riddle. My rivals at the academy said I wasted the second half of my life looking for the great unifying theory, but I didn't. I studied astronomy among other things, and I became interested in something called a computer. I had access to one from the American military. It helped me fill my trunk with the most beautiful numbers. And it helped me solve the mystery of . . . of . . ."

"What mystery?" she interrupted, hardly able to contain her excitement. "Tell me."

"Of billiards," he said. "A most fascinating pursuit. Open the book"—he waved a hand at the side table—"and take out the photographs." Between the pages were eleven similar, slightly blurred, four inch by six inch photos in black and white, all taken from the same perspective, looking down on a billiard table swarming with dozens of billiard balls, the shadow of a ladder plainly visible across the table.

"So what?" she said, disappointed after studying the pictures. "This isn't making any sense."

"This is a riddle," he said. "One my daughter can solve." He sat up slightly and tapped her smartly on the forehead with his finger. "Think," he ordered. The effort cost him; his face went white, and he collapsed back on the pillow. He took several deep breaths and moaned, "Palisa, Palisa, Palisa. Elsa was such a fine woman. Now she is out among the stars, but she will be returning one day, won't she?"

His eyes were wide and pleading. He grabbed the lapels of the woman's dress and pulled her closer. "Why that beautiful name for such a terrible misfortune? Palisa, Palisa. Why Elsa? But when she returns, the world will need my trunk. Listen to me: Elsa is out among the stars and so is my trunk. That's where you will find them both." He sank backwards, exhausted. "You have to find both. If you find Elsa, you'll understand why the trunk is so valuable."

He closed his eyes. After a few moments, he said, "If you are my daughter, you will find it. And if you are not, then, well, my old socks will just have to go unwashed, and it will all be in the hands of my stars if they ever get here. I must rest now. I am very tired."

The woman replaced the photos in the book and forgot about them. The room was quiet again. She sat there for a moment longer looking at his peaceful, sleeping expression and then walked out. She needed a smoke. As she walked down the hall, she didn't notice the two well-dressed men in their mid-thirties, each with identical brown leather briefcases, the kind a scientist might carry, standing at the nurse's station.

The old man wasn't asleep, but he was exhausted. Had he said too much? He searched his feelings and felt no regret. This too was part of the great plan, he was sure. And maybe she *was* his daughter. He thought about that. *No*, he decided. *She was much too handsome.* He hoped his young stars would reach him in time. Maybe all three, if Leonard could take time off from school. When they got here he would tell them everything and set things right. No riddles. His memory must not fail him now. It has been such a problem lately.

Just then he heard a knock. "Come in," he said and then gasped as a sharp pain, the sharpest yet, impaled his heart, arching him off the bed.

Outside the hospital, a young man leaned against a street lamp, nonchalantly smoking a cigarette. He wore a gray, slightly baggy, double-breasted pin stripe suit and a matching fedora set at a jaunty, Frank Sinatra angle. As the woman in the brown dress walked up, he straightened and asked, "Well?"

She grabbed the cigarette out of his mouth and took a long drag. "He left me his trunk. The old goat left me his trunk. I'll bet it's filled with his unmatched socks and the hair brush he never uses. I thought for a second we had something, but he's delirious."

"You look like a wreck," he said. "It must have been quite a performance."

The woman pulled a small mirror out of her handbag and dabbed at her smeared mascara with a tissue. "The old coot," she said between wipes. "If he just could have stayed conscious for five more minutes." The man reached to take back the cigarette, but she pulled away.

"Maybe the trunk's got something valuable in it," he said.

She gave him a withering look and said sarcastically, "What genius keeps the secrets of the universe in a trunk?"

"Probably the same genius who can't match his socks, Comrade Soboleva."

9

"TWO THINGS ARE INFINITE: THE UNIVERSE AND HUMAN STUPIDITY; AND I'M NOT SURE ABOUT THE UNIVERSE."
—EINSTEIN

"YOU REALLY DON'T KNOW WOMEN VERY WELL, DO YOU, cowboy?" said Yohaba. "No decent girl would go for having another woman join her on her second date."

"Isabella isn't any girl," said Rulon.

They had just gotten off the 89 at Frankental and were walking up the long, steep, paved path to his apartment. He wanted to pick up the BMW, so he would have it for his date with Isabella. Yohaba still wore the same faded jeans, but she had changed into a brown leather jacket with a red cashmere scarf and a Red Hot Chili Peppers T-shirt so tight it could have fit a five-year old. Over her shoulder she carried a gym bag with some extra clothes and toiletries. Smart girl, she'd left her gaudy handbag behind.

"If she goes along with this, she's a non-carbon life form."

Exasperated, Rulon stopped and turned to her. "If I didn't need you to save the world, I'd dump you in the Limmat." He looked straight at her when he said that, and he saw that he hurt her. A wave of guilt washed over him. He looked down and took a deep breath to calm himself. Then it struck him that the brat was playing his emotions like a violin.

"Look," he said, "you're an attractive girl. You don't need me to tell you that. But you're not my type. And I'm not yours. Where I grew up, the bulls had the nose rings, not the girls." *Dang. Hurt her again.*

She recovered quickly and inched a little closer than he was comfortable with. He wished she wouldn't do that. "How did you ever control the girls, then?" she asked, looking up into his face with those big innocent eyes. He wished she wouldn't do that either.

"The girls didn't need controlling," he said. "They were brought up proper. With morals.

"Look, about earlier, it's not about not wanting to or being afraid. People who act like you do always think that. For me it's a religious thing. It's about what I believe and who I am. If I ever broke that rule, well, you wouldn't recognize me. I'd be changed, and not for the better."

"There's no need to preach," she scolded, aided by a colorful burst of profanity.

"Then don't act like you need an explanation," he growled. They stood there on the path up to his apartment block and let those final words die off. They turned together and started walking again. "And while we're on the subject, I don't like it when you swear. I find it jarring."

To his surprise, she answered, "If it offends you, I'll try to control it."

After a few more paces, the now-serious Yohaba said, "We're on a quest together, aren't we? To save the world? How many people can say that?"

"To some degree, every couple can say that," he said.

"Did you just say we're a couple?"

"No."

"Hold my hand."

"No."

"Why not? Am I fat?" she asked.

Rulon yelled, threw up his hands, and exploded.

When he was done, Yohaba said, with a sly smile on her face, "I wish you wouldn't swear. I find it jarring."

Rulon stopped walking and started to say something, but it came out as an incoherent stammer. He abruptly turned and stomped up the hill, huffing like an angry buffalo. She caught up to him easily, and they continued side by side, her long legs keeping pace with his, gym bag and all.

"Here, give me your bag," he said gruffly.

"No thanks, I've got it." She laughed. "No way I'm letting you work off your guilt."

"I don't feel guilty in the least," he said. "Why should I feel guilty about anything? Heck, I saved your life twice today, lady."

"That was hours ago," she replied.

They walked on in silence—Yohaba thinking about saving the world and wondering if Rulon thought she was fat and Rulon thinking about how she had felt pressed up against him back in her apartment.

"Were you really a cowboy?" she asked after a minute. "Aren't you a little big?"

"I grew up on a ranch, plus I was the Idaho Cowboy's Association bull riding champion for two years before I went to college. I didn't quite fit the profile, but yeah, I was a cowboy."

"I've heard about bull riding. It sounds dangerous." And then she added, her eyes wide and teasing, "In your case, I'm sure the bulls must have been huge,"

He caught her drift. "I was a little lighter at the time. But, yeah, they were big enough."

"Did you ever break anything?"

"Nothing serious."

"What does that mean, nothing serious?"

"Broken ribs. Collar bones and arms. Stuff like that. Collapsed a lung a few times."

"What did your family call you when you were growing up?"

"They called me Rulon. My name. Why?"

"Didn't you have a nickname?"

"No."

" 'A much-loved child has many names.' You've never heard that saying before? You rode bulls and nobody could come up with a nickname for you. Why, right now I can think of half a dozen without breaking a sweat."

"I'm sure you can. And, by the way, I haven't forgotten you called me Strudel Boy in front of your boss."

"Sorry. Didn't you say you have a brother? What did your brother call you?"

"Yes, I have a brother. Tyler. He's seven years younger. He used to call me Jiminy."

"As in Jiminy Cricket? Did you chirp like a cricket when you were a little boy?" She was getting a kick out of this.

"No. He just knew it bugged me. He's warped. What can I say?"

"Were you his conscience? Did you use to tattle-tale on him and get him in trouble?"

"No, I used to *save* his butt. That was my full-time job when I was growing up. It still is when I'm back home."

They continued to talk as they walked up the hill, a surprisingly friendly conversation for having just had an argument. Her voice was in the alto range, and except for when she was giving him a hard time, it wasn't bad to listen to. Smooth as butter melting over a warm biscuit. A few times he caught the slightest trace of a British accent. But then there was that Oriental-sounding name, Yohaba. Puzzling.

Eventually they turned silent as the hill got steeper. The path led straight up the hill past several terraced rows of apartment blocks. His was in the second-to-last row, nearly at the top of the hill. He could walk it in ten minutes if he wasn't stopping every few feet to argue with someone.

Fifty yards from his block, Rulon's normal paranoia kicked in. It suddenly occurred to him that by accepting Dmitry's compliment on his German, he'd all but admitted he was American. A rookie mistake. Could they have tied him to the consulate? And if they did, could they have found out where he lived that quickly? Not likely, but they'd find him soon enough. After all, they were motivated. He couldn't take that chance.

He'd learned over the years that revenge was a big motivation in his business, even among people who considered themselves professionals. You hurt their friend, and they'll come off the reservation to find you. That's why violence was usually a lousy first choice. It was necessary sometimes to forestall an immediate, short-term negative consequence or for self-defense, like it was today, but it always ended up complicating things in the end. It started to bug Rulon again that he let Dmitry go. On the other hand, maybe it earned him some heavenly brownie points. He had to assume the Russians were waiting for them, even though it was unlikely.

As he reached the last point on the hill from which they could stay hidden, he stopped and told Yohaba to stay put. Once she was settled, he continued on for another dozen yards, staying in the shadows until he reached the last line of bushes and trees. He now had a clear view of his apartment complex across the street. He waited there for a good ten minutes, watching. He could feel Yohaba seething with impatience behind him. She whispered his name every few minutes, but he kept waving her off. After a few more minutes, he was satisfied and walked back to her.

"I'm going to mosey over to the garage entrance. It looks clear, but stay put till I've checked it out. I'll bring the car over."

"I never realized being a spy could be so boring," she said.

"You're joking, right?"

"Yeah," she said and let out a merry little laugh.

He smiled, and, not for the first time, the thought struck him of what a trooper she was. She'd been through a lot in the last few hours. And the way she went after Dmitry when he was tied up, he just had to laugh.

"You've got a nice laugh," she said. A compliment? What was she up to now? Then before he could say anything, she asked, "How's your chest?"

He'd forgotten all about it. Rulon stretched his arm over his head then reached under his vest to rub the injured pectoral. It had been a small caliber pistol, and the silencer would have lowered the velocity even further. He wouldn't be doing any bench presses for a while, but it felt surprisingly good. He knew he'd see a bruise when he took his shirt off, but he'd been through worse. "Fine," he said.

He told her he'd be right back and went after the car. Five minutes later, he drove up to where the path met the street and threw the door open. She scampered up the hill and jumped in.

Before he reached third gear, she was already checking out the dashboard controls. "What's this?" she asked as she hit the button for the passenger seat heater. "Ooooh, bum-bum warmers."

"You know your way around Beemers," said Rulon.

"It's pure instinct. Never been in a 3-series before. You should really call your girlfriend first. You don't want to spring me on her."

"You only say that because you don't know Isabella. Once I explain the situation, she'll understand."

"Were you raised by gerbils? As soon as she sees me, she'll be like a werewolf when the moon rises. She won't be able to help it. I bring it out in normal women. I'm the enemy. It's instinctual in the species. Trust me. You need to call her."

Reluctantly, Rulon reached for his cell phone and hit Isabella's speed dial button. She picked up right away. "Hello, Isabella," he said, "it's me." He told her as much of the truth about Yohaba as he could. She didn't know about his other day job, so he left out the gory details. Not surprisingly, Isabella had a few questions.

* * *

Twenty minutes later, Yohaba and Rulon were sitting at opposite sides of a table in Desperado Restaurant, waiting for their drinks. Rulon was in an ugly mood. "I already told you once," he said irately. "I'm not repeating the story again." It was dinner time, and the restaurant was filling up. They had been lucky to get a table. The place was swirling with tobacco smoke.

Rulon had been there so often that no matter how smoky it was, and no matter how foul his mood, the rhythm of the place was soothingly familiar. Over the years, the fake adobe walls and plastic cactus plants, rather than seeming cheap and intrusive, had become part of the ambience for him. And to sit at a table, savoring a decent enchilada and listening to country western music and the mixed growl of native Swiss Germans, well, that was about as good as it got as far as he was concerned.

But today, he was still drained from all the drama. Some of the scenes from the luggage store fight still lurked in his mind. He didn't like hurting people, but he was glad to be alive. On some level, he was singing with life. That's how it always was afterwards. But when he spoke to Isabella, she blew up over Yohaba and canceled their date. In fact, she had hung up on him.

"I know, I know," said Yohaba, "but when she asked what I looked like, tell me again what you said."

"You were sitting right next to me! You heard everything. All I said was that you were a little younger than me, tall, thin, and that your hair's long. What's your point?"

"What else did you tell her? There is a lesson in here for you."

"I mentioned your nose ring," he said. "I couldn't leave that out." Yohaba motioned with her hand as if to say, *C'mon you're almost there.*

"I told her about your tattoo."

"Yes, go on. Think."

"And I said you had green eyes."

"Bingo."

"Bingo? Your eyes *are* green. What of it?"

"*You* noticed *my* eyes. Don't you see?"

"You've lost me," he said, just as the drinks arrived.

After the first sip, Yohaba started up again. "I have just one more question, and it's not about Isabella," she said. Despite the disclaimer, Rulon went immediately to DEFCON 3.

"Fire away," he replied wearily.

"You are in Zurich," she said, "the most cosmopolitan of cities, and yet you take me to a Mexican restaurant. I'm not complaining. Just curious."

"I'm glad you're not complaining. Where I come from that might be considered looking a gift horse in the mouth. And don't make this sound like a date."

"Are you comparing yourself to a horse?" she asked, ignoring his "date" remark. "That doesn't say much for your self esteem."

"No. It's just an expression. I was referring to the dinner." She had him on the back foot again.

"They serve horse meat here? Is that what you are saying?" she asked with a poker face, and he thought maybe she was being serious. Some American expressions didn't translate well.

"No, no, no. This is a perfectly reputable place. I eat here all the time." He looked around. This place wasn't so bad. Was it?

Yohaba kept pushing. "My grandmother always said that you shouldn't judge people unless they're men. And men should be judged by where they take you to dinner."

"My dad used to say . . ."

She rushed in and with a mocking look finished the sentence for him: "Son, you are a cheapskate with no sense of culture." She cocked her head to the side and looked at him with her large oval eyes. She raised a single eyebrow. "Am I right?"

Rulon felt himself rapidly losing control of a situation that up until a minute ago couldn't even be considered a situation. "No. You got it wrong. My father speaks very highly of me . . ."

She broke in again with a laugh. "You're lying. Your father probably calls you 'Rulon the traitor' because you live in Switzerland. I'm sure he's terrified you're going to marry a Swiss girl. Imagine if you came home with me."

That last comment ignited a horrifying image in Rulon's mind.

"If I came home with a Ubangi tree worshipper, he'd take it better. He misses me. He's afraid he's going to die, and I won't be there. Truth is, he's promised not to die until Boise State wins the NCAA football championship, which I—"

She cut him off again. "Boise State? Never heard of it. Which I suspect means he will be living to a ripe old age. Yes?"

"I hope so," he said, not caring to debate Boise State's prospects with someone who didn't know football. "He has the constitution of a water buffalo." He made a show of looking around. "I wonder where Werner is," he said to no one in particular when he couldn't spot his regular waiter.

"All right, you don't want to talk about anything. But are you really that dense? About the eyes, I mean. I want to talk about it again. I think this is really about me. I think you're sending me a signal."

Rulon was suddenly exhausted. Yohaba was driving him crazy. He closed his eyes and pinched the bridge of his nose in a vain attempt to suppress a headache.

"I know what you're getting at about the eyes," he said. "It was stupid of me to mention it. But I notice things. It's part of my training. Don't read anything into it."

Just then his cell phone rang. When he answered and heard the contrite voice on the other end, his mood immediately improved. "Hey. I'm glad you called back," he said. "Yes. Yes. Of course. Great. You won't regret this. See you soon."

He hung up and reached for his drink. His headache was gone.

"Well?" asked Yohaba, bursting with curiosity.

He was enjoying this. "Oh, that was just Isabella. She's sorry she hung up on me. She wants to join us for dinner after all."

Yohaba leaned back in her chair, balancing on the two back legs, sipping a glass of Pellegrino. "And you fell for it," she said, placing her glass emphatically on the table. Leaning forward, she pointed at him with her fork and said in a conspiratorial tone, "There is something fishy about this gal, Rulon. Have you heard about the reptile theory? Half the world's leaders and movie stars are shape-changing lizards. Well, if she shows up here in a good mood, I think she's one of them."

"Aha," Rulon said, leaning forward too. "Now who's got the fangs out? You've never even met her. And please don't tell me you really believe in that stuff. I suppose Armstrong didn't walk on the moon."

"It was a movie set in Arizona."

"But there are flying saucers from outer space?"

"They're actually from the center of the Earth."

"Or that Oswald didn't kill Kennedy?"

"Check out the Zapruder film. The killing shot came from the grassy knoll."

"Okay, that one I believe," he said. "But this has nothing to do with what's happening right now between you and me in this restaurant. The fact is you were wrong about Isabella, and I was right. She's coming to dinner with both of us. Handle it."

"No, *I'm right.* She's not normal. How long have you known her? You've been on what, half a dozen dates?" Rulon looked down and didn't answer. Yohaba gave him a savage look. "Rulon, don't tell me. You've only been on one date. One—" she looked for a safe word "—*dang* date! See? Now you've got me using that stupid word! Okay, fine. Don't believe me. You'll see."

"What are we going to do about the asteroid hitting Geneva?" asked Rulon.

"Don't try changing the subject. We're talking about your love life, Rulon. Next to the world ending, this is the biggest thing you've got." Fortunately, just then, Werner came over to take their orders. Rulon let him know they were expecting one more person and asked him to bring another liter of mineral water.

The interruption lasted long enough for them to get off the subject of Isabella. They shifted to the asteroid and what few facts they had. The more they talked, the more Rulon could feel his original certainty returning. As crazy as everything sounded, it sounded crazier when he tried to twist the facts in a different way. Maybe Einstein was wrong, but Rulon was convinced that at the very least, Einstein must have believed he was right. Since this was Einstein they were talking about, he had to take him seriously. Plus, even if Einstein was wrong about Elsa, that didn't mean there wasn't something important in the trunk. Something the Russians shouldn't have.

In the middle of trying to put the pieces together, Yohaba announced she was heading for the restroom. Rulon shifted mental gears and watched her leave. She moved freely with her arms akimbo and her feet slightly splayed, a bit like Charlie Chaplin. Not the most feminine walk in the world, but distinctive, like her. He filed away that Chaplin comparison for the next time she called him chubby.

When Yohaba came back, she announced a desire to talk to her grandmother who lived near Bergün, a small town in the Graubünden canton, southeast of Zurich in the mountains near St. Moritz. Rulon agreed. He wanted to find out if she knew anything about the three men Dmitry had talked about. What if Einstein had given them the trunk? If so, where was it now? And what had they been doing with it all these years? Or maybe they had passed away, and now it truly was lost.

There were so many possible scenarios. Maybe Yohaba's grandmother knew something her mother had told her. Maybe there was a diary or a letter. A shiver of dread ran through Rulon. Maybe the Russians had already visited the grandmother and talked to her. He asked Yohaba when she had last talked to her grandmother, and she said four days ago. He told her to call her now.

Before she could dial her own phone, Rulon's rang. It was Isabella again. She was outside and wanted to talk to him face-to-face before she came in. He had no choice but to agree. This situation with Isabella was getting very complex. Rulon got up to meet her.

"If she threatens to blow herself up, call her bluff," Yohaba advised.

"Call your grandmother," he said.

Isabella was waiting outside on the sidewalk. "Well, you got here fast," Rulon said when he saw her. He smiled. "I'm glad you came. You look great." She was dressed in a knee-length, rust-colored raincoat with a dark brown scarf wrapped loosely around her neck. Her black hair shone under the street lights. Her eyes were a deep, beautiful blue. All that was missing was the smile. She didn't move forward for a trio of greeting pecks, so he kept his distance.

"Even for a mystery man, this is pretty unusual," she said, her voice low and grave and her eyes looking down, unsure. "I wanted to talk to you first, face-to-face, before I came in." She looked directly into his eyes. "This is the weirdest second date I've ever been on. Is this an old girlfriend?"

Rulon reached out and firmly grabbed both her arms. "No," he said, returning her steady gaze with an unwavering look of his own. "I never met her before this morning. This is strictly business. As soon as you see her, you'll know she's not my type."

"But you said she was in trouble. What does that mean? And come to think of it, let me look at you." She stepped back and looked him up and down. "You're fat, mister. You've put on thirty pounds in two weeks. What have you been doing?"

Rulon liked this girl, so he played her straight. He opened up his jacket and pulled the Know-foam pillow out from under his bullet-proof vest.

"Mystery Man, why are you wearing a pillow under your jacket?"

"I wear it so people will underestimate me," he said. "It's part of my job."

"We work for the same company, Rulon. If I go into work Monday and have to wear one of those under my blouse, I'm quitting. Just so you know."

Rulon opened his mouth, but no sounds came out. If this relationship were to go anywhere, this was the moment of truth. He leveled with her. "I only work for Portal part time. It's a front. They get favors from my government in return for letting people like me work there. I'm a security specialist for a company called Office Crimes Division." He told her a little more about the work he did—not too much—and related a slightly more detailed version than his earlier account of rescuing Yohaba from Dmitry. It took him about fifteen minutes to explain what was going on and to answer her questions. And even then, he didn't mention anything about 182 Elsa, the end of the world, or the fight at the luggage store. He decided getting her to accept Yohaba would be enough for a second date.

While they talked, a picture flashed through Rulon's mind of Yohaba upstairs, ordering liters of wine, and he was anxious to get back.

"And all this time, Rulon, I thought you were just a nice guy." Isabella said this sadly, and this made him sad. He hated to disappoint people. Fumbling for words, he managed to blurt out his old tried-and-true response.

"I am a nice guy. Just a different kind of nice guy," he said. She didn't even crack a smile. The look in her eyes was like a knife through his heart. "Let's go upstairs," he said with more enthusiasm than he felt. "I'll introduce you to Yohaba. She's a character."

Rulon hooked his arm through hers and led her to the door of the restaurant. "She's Einstein's great-great-granddaughter. Smart. Don't let the punk stuff fool you. Wait a second." He let go of her arm and replaced the pillow under his vest. "There," he said, shoving the pillow around until it fell in place.

Isabella poked his stomach. "Why is it so hard?" she asked.

"That would be my bullet-proof vest."

"Mystery Man," she said, with a sigh and a shake of her head. "After this we're going to have to go back over everything we talked about on our first date."

Rulon took her arm again. "As long as it has the same happy ending," he replied. Rather dashingly, he thought. When they reached the top of the stairs, he turned to her. "Now, everything is cool, right? No hard feelings?"

She told him to relax and in they went.

Yohaba was sitting at the same table with an empty wine bottle in front of her and a half-full glass in her hand. She swayed like a drunken pirate on a rolling ship. Sometimes Rulon hated being right.

He walked up to her with a no-nonsense expression on his face. "I hope you brought money because you're paying for that wine."

She looked up, and her bloodshot eyes were a perfect complement to her right cheek, which was still a little red and puffy from getting slapped earlier. "What kind of gentleman are you?" she said with a pronounced slur. "Don't look at me like that. You ask me out on a date and then leave me sitting here by myself for half the night. What did you expect? Besides, I got the cheapest wine on the menu. The least you can do is pay for it."

Yohaba looked over at Isabella and offered her a wobbly hand. "Hello, you must be Isabella. I was kidding about the date. Rulon isn't my type. He wears a pillow under his bullet-proof vest." Rulon looked at her in amazement. He didn't think it was possible to get drunk so quickly. He made a mental note never to introduce her to Magnus.

"Too late, darling," said Isabella, flexing her claws. "I already know about the pillow and the vest. Tell me something I don't know."

"He whacks people with a big hammer. Hits them on the legs mostly, unless they slap girls and have a gun, then he whacks their hands instead. He's a real gentleman." She teetered unsteadily in her chair and swung her wine glass around as she talked.

Rulon stood there, stunned. Isabella turned to leave, so he grabbed her arm. "Yohaba has a strange sense of humor. And she is obviously too young to be drinking. Here, let's sit down and sort this out. It's been a long day, but let's stay focused on why we're meeting." He pulled out a chair for Isabella, and she reluctantly sat down.

"Since when did this become a meeting?" she asked.

"I'm going to be sick," said Yohaba. "Rulon's right. I can't hold my wine. But I'm not drunk, I'm allergic." She pushed her chair back and placed both hands on the table to steady herself. "I'll be right back." She pointed at Isabella. "Don't you leave on account of me. And keep an eye on the brute." Then she headed off in the direction of the restroom.

After she was out of sight, Isabella turned back to Rulon. "Rulon, you've got to be kidding. It's like I don't know you at all! What can you possibly see in her?"

Rulon really liked Isabella and everything they'd shared during their first date, but the time had come to make a decision. Government secrets he would never reveal, and certain details about his job were off limits too, but in all of this, he really wasn't working for anyone at the moment.

Billy Ray Cyrus played in the background, and someone had turned down the lights. It felt like the right moment to him.

"I can't dump her because an asteroid is coming to destroy the world, and I need her to help me find a trunk that used to belong to Albert Einstein. There is some kind of secret inside that is supposed to save everybody." Rulon's dad always said that honesty was the best policy. But then he also used to say, "Sometimes, son, you don't know when to shut up."

Isabella didn't miss a beat. "I've known a lot of Americans, Rulon, and this is not an American sense of humor. This is more British."

"I'm telling the truth."

"Perhaps Scottish."

As per his usual routine, he sat in a chair facing the door. A couple walked in, but nothing about them registered a concern, and he dropped them off the radar. He looked around to see if anyone was listening.

"How can I prove it to you?" he asked.

Isabella thought for a moment. "You're getting me back for our first date, aren't you? I was a little rough on you, wasn't I?"

"No, no," he protested. "You were wonderful. I had a great time."

"What did she mean about the hammer, about hitting guys on the legs?"

"It puts them down, but it isn't life threatening. It's really humane if you think about it."

"Oh my . . ." gasped Isabella, and then she caught herself and dropped into a whisper. "Are you telling me she didn't make that up? Are you crazy?"

Werner came by and filled their glasses with Pellegrino. They turned down his offer of more wine. "Isabella," said Rulon. "I think you and I have something to offer each other, but unfortunately you are with me on the single strangest day of my life. I've been in three fights and shot in the chest; only my bullet-proof vest saved me. And I busted up some Russians who were trying to beat information out of Yohaba about this Einstein trunk thing. You saw her face. I'm not making this up."

Rulon had a soft spot for women, but at some point, they had to either take him as he was or go lasso themselves another bronc.

Isabella looked at him. He couldn't tell what she was thinking. She played with the clasp of her purse, and it looked to him like she was deciding whether to leave or not. He tried to read her face but had a hard time. He didn't like where this was going. Just then, Yohaba came back.

She dropped into her chair like a sack of old shoes, her elbows on the table and her face buried in her hands. "Sorry everyone. Don't let me drink ever again. It was only half a liter. I wasn't kidding when I said I'm allergic. I didn't mean to shoot my mouth off." She moved her hands slightly apart and peeked through them. "Are you guys still friends? Do you want me to leave?"

Isabella answered a resolute "no" at the exact same time Rulon answered a resolute "yes." Isabella said she wanted to hear Yohaba's side of the story. And now that Rulon thought about it, he couldn't wait to hear it himself.

Yohaba looked at Rulon, and he nodded. She then told Isabella her story with humor, even the part where Rulon was shot. Rulon couldn't help laughing over it, though it wasn't so funny to him when it happened. And then he spoke up about Yohaba smacking Dmitry and made a pretty good story of it himself. They stopped just long enough to order dinner.

Isabella asked lots of good questions. She wanted to see the hammer, but Rulon had left it in the car. He did give her a peek at Dmitry's gun, though, and the knife, and that seemed to satisfy her. A little material corroboration never hurt.

While Rulon had been outside with Isabella, Yohaba had managed to call her grandmother between gulps of wine. She said that when her grandmother was in one of her dingbat moods, she wouldn't know a Russian if he came in guzzling vodka and singing a babushka love song. Still, after talking with her, Yohaba was sure the Russians had visited. How many power company repairmen ask to see the attic and then stay for two hours drinking hot chocolate and talking about Einstein? That's all Yohaba could pry out of her. She was convinced they would have to go visit her in person if they wanted to learn more.

Dinner arrived, but the conversation never faltered. After the initial shock wore off, Isabella seemed to actually enjoy herself.

By the time they were done eating, the restaurant was near closing but still full, and Isabella knew everything. The question of whether or not they were telling the truth never came up again.

Somehow, in a way Rulon couldn't quite put his finger on, having Isabella there was a good balance for Yohaba. She seemed to bring out Yohaba's mature side, while Rulon had only been successful in bringing out something else. And he was starting to learn something else about Yohaba. Whatever her weaknesses were, she was an honest person and an excellent observer. Isabella was good too. She asked the kinds of questions he would have asked. Almost like she'd had training.

"I just have one more question," Isabella said when Rulon paid the bill. Her tone caused Rulon's guard to go up. "When do we get started looking for this trunk?" She looked at them both with a little smile, but her eyes were set, and he wondered why she wanted to be a part of this. His hopeful heart suggested that maybe it had something to do with him. He looked at Yohaba, and they both gave a small shrug. He turned back to Isabella and suggested they start by visiting Yohaba's grandmother in Bergün, and everyone agreed.

Yohaba and Isabella were soon lost in their own world, talking and laughing about whatever it is that women talk and laugh about. Rulon leaned back in his chair with his thumbs tucked into his belt loops, feeling like he'd just won the grand prize at the rodeo. *And Yohaba thought it couldn't be done.* But now this little doggie was all nicely tied up, the horn had sounded, and Rulon was strutting back to the chute with his spurs jangling. Yup, he felt mighty proud of himself. As soon as he got Yohaba alone, he was going to rub it in.

Rulon looked over at the girls and smiled, but they were chatting away, and for the moment he was forgotten. He was just about to say "saddle-up" when a warning bell sounded in his head, and he did a quick scan of the room. He had just felt a draft and the restaurant door was slipping closed. Someone had just walked out. But no one had walked past him, and the chairs by the tables between him and the door were all filled. Someone had stuck his head in the door and then quickly left.

The subconscious is a marvelous thing and should oftentimes be trusted. Most people notice it when they are leaving their house and have a nagging sense they've forgotten something. Rulon closed his eyes and tried to let his subconscious do the work. After a moment, a thought, like the most delicate of bubbles, popped to the surface. In his peripheral vision, he had seen a man with a butterfly bandage over one eye. Dmitry! It had to be. But how? A tracer on the car?

The Russians would've had to place the tracer before Rulon got back to his apartment, but they wouldn't have had time. Maybe Dmitry waited around and followed them. No, Rulon would have spotted him. A partner? Someone Rulon missed? Yes. But why send Dmitry to verify Rulon was in the restaurant and risk being spotted? Why not the tail? Maybe they thought Rulon had spotted him . . . or her. No. There was another reason.

All these thoughts went through Rulon's mind in an instant. Then it hit him, the bug was on him. He went through his pockets and even before he reached it, he remembered Dmitry's lighter; the one he'd confiscated when he searched him, the one Dmitry didn't ask for back.

Rulon caught Werner's eye and he came over wiping his hands on his apron. "There are some people outside I don't want to see," said Rulon. "Is there another way out?" The two girls got quiet.

"Herr Hurt, what have you been up to?" asked Werner with a worldly grin. "One of these people wouldn't happen to be married to one of these ladies, would they?"

"Werner, if I stop eating here, this place will go out of business, so if you want to save a customer and your job, help us to leave without being seen. Can you please check all the exits for me? See if anyone's waiting?"

"But, of course, Herr Hurt," he said, leaving with a smirk.

"What's up?" asked Isabella.

"They found us," said Yohaba.

"Who's they?" asked Isabella. "You mean the Russians?"

"Shhh," said Yohaba. "Rulon's thinking. Hey Rulon, after what you did to them, I'll bet they brought a bus load of their buddies with baseball bats this time. Don't you think?"

"They probably came to apologize," he said. He told them there was nothing to worry about; this was kid's stuff. He handled these kinds of situations five times a week. Inwardly, though, he was worried, especially with the girls around. Werner came back just then and gave him the news.

"I think they must want to see you very badly, Herr Hurt, all the exits are covered."

10

“I do not know with what weapons World War Three will be fought, but World War Four will be fought with sticks and stones.” —Einstein

There are some problems that weren’t covered in the manual, but this wasn’t one of them. The solution was simple. Call the police. If it were Rulon by himself, he’d have taken his chances with a direct confrontation. No sense getting entangled with the local constabulary if he didn’t have to. But not with the girls around. Without a second thought, he pulled out his cell phone and dialed 117, the Swiss equivalent to 911. Unfortunately, his cell phone wasn’t working, and neither were Yohaba’s or Isabella’s. The tell-tale crackling told him they were being jammed.

He asked Werner if he could use the manager’s landline. Werner took him into the back office. *Hmm . . . no dial tone there either.* Okay, they’d disabled the phone lines too. But “problem” is just another word for “opportunity.” Rulon asked Werner to pop over to one of the nearby businesses, call the police, and have them send over a squad car. Werner scurried off, and Rulon returned to the table.

When Rulon got back to his chair, Yohaba was gripping a flatware knife like she was priming for a fight. “Planning on buttering someone?” he asked, trying with only moderate success to keep the amusement out of his voice.

“You don’t have to be so dismissive,” she said as she tossed the knife on the table. “I was only trying to help. Did Gary Cooper sneer at Grace Kelly when she tried to help?”

High Noon was one of Rulon’s favorite flicks. But was she serious? Did she really think she was going to help? He still didn’t know what to make of her, but if nothing else, the girl had grit.

He told them about the phone and joked that the restaurant probably hadn't paid its phone bill.

Ten minutes later, Werner returned with his report. All the phones in the nearby businesses were also dead. Rulon was miffed. He said to Werner, "I know the Swiss are more into quality than customer service, but doesn't the phone company send out technicians when an entire neighborhood loses connection?" Werner shrugged and assured Rulon this was very rare. The girls had been following all this with growing alarm, but Rulon was getting more and more irked. It dawned on him that he was trying to avoid a meeting that simply couldn't be put off. Time for Plan B.

"You guys are getting out of here," he told the girls. He assumed this team was after him and not Yohaba. If they were after Yohaba, they wouldn't be snatching her at a restaurant. It was too public. But revenge? Against him? That was enough motivation to do something reckless. He gave Yohaba the keys to the car, and she assured him she could find her way back. "Just go to my apartment and wait for me," he said. "There's food and something to drink in the fridge and two spare bedrooms if you want to sleep."

The girls chattered like magpies, asking lots of questions, but he wasn't listening. Yes, yes, he'd be all right. He just needed to talk to these guys and work things out. He asked Werner to take Orlando, another waiter, and escort the girls to the car. As a precaution, Rulon had one of the waitresses take Yohaba into the back and whip up a little disguise. Yohaba returned wearing a kerchief and an old pair of sunglasses. Then followed a touching farewell scene reminiscent of *The Empire Strikes Back*, and in a different situation Rulon would have milked it to the max. But he was all business now. In fact, he was feeling a bit reckless. Man, was there nothing sacred anymore? This was *his* Mexican restaurant.

It was raining buckets outside, so the waiters grabbed their umbrellas and hustled the girls out. After they left, Rulon was thirsty. He was also hungry again. He looked around for another waiter so he could order a Sprite and a plate of nachos.

While he sat there waiting, he thought about Dmitry and wondered what he was up to. He pictured him standing in the cold rain, miserable, and wondering what the heck was taking Rulon so long.

The image made him laugh. By the time the restaurant closed, it would be five degrees colder outside, and Dmitry and his pals would be frozen. Rulon needed every edge he could get. *Let them wait.*

* * *

Dmitry was cold and stiff. The doorway of the now-closed Kebab-Haus restaurant just down the street from the Desperado wasn't the best place to hang out. He'd gotten tired of sitting in the white communications van that was disguised as a phone company's tech vehicle. The wind slashed icy rain against his legs. By his feet was a single mashed-out cigarette. He stared at it and thought about lighting another, but after the beating, he'd taken, a cigarette was too painful to hold let alone inhale. Normally he was a chain smoker, and this inconvenience was particularly galling.

And it was all thanks to the fat American. A few minutes ago, Dmitry had taken a chance by sticking his head in the restaurant door, but he needed to make sure the fat man was still there, and nobody else on the team knew what he looked like. Rulon. A strange name. Sounded like a cowboy.

Dmitry had his three henchmen covering the exits. They had worked for years with Yuri and the team that had botched things up at the luggage store—that same team that was now in a hospital pinned, casted, tractioned, and stuffed with painkillers.

Dmitry stayed in contact with his team through wireless earpieces and throat mikes. It was Rulon they were after. Yohaba could wait. The mission to find Einstein's trunk could wait too. It was a joke anyway. *Screw the orders*, thought Dmitry. *This is personal.* The plan was to do this by the book, but you could never tell who was going to lose it once the action started, especially if the fat man decided to resist.

Dmitry's ear phone buzzed. It was Yuri from the hospital, wanting an update. After Dmitry gave his report, Yuri offered a word of advice. "If he shows the hammer, shoot him. Do not take chances with this guy."

Dmitry remembered how Rulon had let him go. "There isn't going to be a shooting. He never used a gun. This will be a proportional response. We'll take care of it."

"If he pulls out the hammer," said Yuri, starting out quietly before erupting, "you shoot him in the head!"

"No," said Dmitry evenly. "No shooting. If he's dead, he won't remember the lesson. I'll call you when it's over."

Without waiting for a response, Dmitry switched frequencies. He thought about what Yuri had said. The three agents Rulon had tackled in the luggage store had all been armed, making them fair game. All had violated orders by getting rough with Yohaba and her friends. To some extent, they had it coming—not that it changed anything as far as what was going to happen to Rulon.

Dmitry's one eye was swollen almost shut and decorated with a small bandage. He also limped and had two broken fingers. *But,* he reasoned to himself, *I was the one who ambushed him in the apartment. He just happened to come out on top.* Rulon had stayed within the rules and so would he. They'd bust this guy up, and then everyone would be happy. Well, maybe not Rulon.

This whole Einstein operation was a screwup from the beginning. There were too many civilians involved and, as usual, too much pressure from the top to resolve things quickly. The Einstein mystery had sat dormant for fifty years, and all of a sudden they wanted resolution in three days. Typical.

But this he knew how to do. A simple catch and release. A white cloth, a bottle of chloroform, and the fat man will be taken into the nearby Hönggerberg forest and worked over. Dmitry pulled the tracking monitor out of his pocket and verified Rulon was still there. Yes, the cigarette lighter was still transmitting clearly from Rulon's pocket. Eight yards from the front door. Three yards from the rear west window. *Well, enjoy yourself, my flabby friend. After tonight, you won't be enjoying much for a long time.*

Dmitry shuffled around in the doorway to keep warm. He pictured Rulon sitting on the kitchen chair in Yohaba's apartment. Though he was fat around the middle, the rest of him looked pretty solid. Dmitry considered that and shrugged. Strange body type. But this Rulon was an okay guy in Dmitry's book. He still had to pay the price, though. Those were the rules.

The earpiece came alive. "Two women are leaving with a couple of guys," said the man by the entrance. "One of them could be the chick from the luggage store. They're heading right toward you."

"Do you see the fat man?" asked Dmitry anxiously.

"No. These guys look like waiters. They're probably heading for a car or the tram stop. What do you want us to do?"

"Wait. I see them," said Dmitry. "Let them go. I'm tracking the girl a different way, and we'll pick her up tomorrow. It's the American we want."

Dmitry adjusted his cap and put his hands in his pocket. The night got colder and wetter. His knee was stiffening up. He shifted his weight from one leg to the other to keep limber, but after a few minutes, he gave up and returned to the shelter of the van.

* * *

Three hours later, the last of the patrons had left the restaurant and the sign on the door read *Geschlossen*. The staff had all left together fifteen minutes ago in a good mood. Dmitry was certain the fat American was still inside. It was 12:30 a.m., and the restaurant had been closed for half an hour. For what he hoped was the last time, Dmitry stood in the Kebab-Haus doorway and watched the rain pour down. He got everyone on the earphones. "What do you want to do? Do we go in or keep waiting?"

"I'm freezing," one of the men said. "Let's go in." The others agreed. Dmitry told one of them to stick his head inside and see who was still there. The man reported back five minutes later that there was a single, nerdy-looking fat guy sitting at a table in the middle of the room. No one else was there, not even the waiters.

"It can't be him," said the man. "He sort of matches the description, but there's no way this was the guy that took out Yuri's team. No way."

"It's him," said Dmitry.

* * *

Rulon waited, knowing that the end game to this little skirmish was about to play out. The girls were safely away. The restaurant was empty except for him. All of the restaurant's five remaining staff were in a bar down the street, presumably whooping it up, thanks to Rulon's 300-franc donation. He had told them to come back at 1:00 a.m., promising the place would still be in one piece when they did.

Rulon sat at a table in the middle of the room facing the door when the Russians made their appearance. There were four of them and they came in fast. As they did, Dmitry nodded, and one of them peeled off, heading for the kitchen. The other two came straight for Rulon and, keeping a safe distance, planted themselves in front of his table. Dmitry lagged behind. When he caught up, the two guys moved aside. The next thing Rulon knew, Dmitry was standing in front of him looking all business.

Everyone looked edgy except Dmitry. He seemed as calm and in control as Rulon was trying to fake. The other men's eyes darted to every corner of the restaurant looking for threats. Each of them except Dmitry had one hand held stiffly near his waist, a sure sign they were packing. The guy on the right carried a small white hand towel. *Chloroform*, thought Rulon.

"Hello," said Dmitry.

"Hello," said Rulon.

The man who had gone to check out the kitchen took his place on Dmitry's right side, nodding an all-clear as he did so. Then the four of them moved a little closer to the table. Rulon did a quick assessment and concluded that these were no pilgrims. One of them had had his nose broken and badly reset. Another had a scar across his neck. The third was younger, barely in his twenties. He looked mean and eager to earn his stripes. All except the young guy had the look that you only get after a hundred bar brawls. A look that, despite their shifty eyes, was dull and thuglike from having had one too many cognac bottles smashed over their heads.

Their stiff body language told Rulon they were struggling to control the adrenaline. Yes, Dmitry's three thugs looked set to explode. Rulon further sensed that they had already performed whatever psychological rituals they practiced to turn off their inhibitions to violence. They were ready to rock.

Only Dmitry and the young guy made eye contact with Rulon. He was sure that said something about their intentions. It occurred to him that the two men who wouldn't meet his eyes intended to murder him. These guys weren't martial arts specialists. They were brutal thugs who knew their place in the world and accepted it.

Rulon tried to read their faces and sensed they were clenching down their anger. He knew immediately that this was personal for them. These were all big men—the size of strong safeties in the NFL. Not as big as Rulon, but tough. Could Dmitry control them? He'd taken Dmitry's measure back in Yohaba's apartment and was betting that he could. Rulon tried to look calm, but at that moment, the words of his father never rang truer: "Rulon, my son, Custer was an idiot. You too."

Rulon leaned back with his arms draped casually across the backs of the chairs on either side. These particular chairs weren't like the others in the restaurant. They were made of heavy wood like the table and weighed a good twenty pounds each. Nothing he couldn't manage but heavy enough to raise a knot on someone's head. The table looked like it was made of timbers from Old Ironsides and had taken three men to carry. It wasn't normally set in the main restaurant area. Orlando and Werner had helped him carry it in from the overflow room along with the chairs. Though it was thick and burly, he wasn't counting on it to stop a bullet.

On the table in front of him but far enough away that he couldn't reach them easily were the gun and knife he'd taken from Dmitry earlier, plus his own Colt. He was taking a chance, he knew, but he'd been in this league for eight years, and he thought he knew how the game was played. Russians had certain rules, and responses to threats were usually proportional. If he'd been dealing with some of the old Eastern Bloc countries, he'd have had a gun in each hand and the knife between his teeth.

As it was, he scratched his stomach for effect, and adjusted the nerdy, black, non-prescription glasses he was wearing, all in an attempt to make himself look as benign as possible. With no protection from the government, he could very easily end up in jail—make that prison—over what had gone down this afternoon. Then who would save the world? Plus, he was really ticked at these guys.

Dmitry stood at the opposite side of the table. He looked around casually before focusing his eyes on Rulon. Since that afternoon,

Dmitry had changed into a waist-length black leather jacket zippered up the front and a pair of rough dark corduroy trousers. He now wore a gray, wool flat cap on his head. "Surprised to see me?" asked Dmitry. As he spoke, he pulled a pair of leather gloves from his jacket pocket and tried putting them on. His broken fingers made it impossible, and after a few inept tries, he put the gloves away again. He fixed Rulon with a threatening glare.

"Not as surprised as I was the first time," said Rulon.

"Earlier today, when I offered you a job, I didn't know the details of what happened in the luggage store. Now that I know, I'm rescinding my offer."

To Rulon's surprise Dmitry spoke English. *Some of these clowns don't speak German*, he concluded. They must have been flown in for a special occasion. Not that it mattered.

"With all your recent openings, can you afford to be so picky?" asked Rulon.

"In your case," said Dmitry, "it's your impending medical condition that makes you unemployable."

Rulon ignored the threat. "Speaking of work, I notice one of your guys is carrying a white towel. Is he looking for a job as a waiter? I could put in a good word here. Does he have experience?"

"Will you come with us quietly?" asked Dmitry casually, ignoring the jibe. The men around him were like Dobermans straining at a leash.

"I am disinclined to acquiesce to your request," said Rulon.

Now, this would be a tough answer to decipher even for some native English speakers, so it was no surprise to Rulon that a rather long silence ensued. But to his amazement, the man on Dmitry's right, the one who had checked out the kitchen, quietly said in a thick Eastern European accent, "Geoffrey Rush, *Pirates of*—"

"Shut up, idiot." Dmitry hissed. Rulon acknowledged the correct answer with a nod.

"Well?" asked Dmitry

Rulon raised his hand. "Hold off for a second." A silenced automatic suddenly appeared in the hand of the man to Dmitry's left. He pointed it directly at Rulon's head. *Okay*, Rulon thought, *you're fast*. He looked at the gun in feigned amusement. "You gonna shoot me? Here? Then what? Kill the staff if they come back early? Talk to him, Dmitry."

Without taking his eyes off Rulon, Dmitry said something in Russian. His partner hesitated briefly before slipping the gun back into his shoulder holster and adjusting his jacket to cover the bulge. "You're coming with us. One way or another," said Dmitry.

Rulon slowly and deliberately got half-way up from the chair and reached toward the weapons on the table. Instantly Dmitry's three thugs all snapped into a crouch with their hands on their guns, ready to draw.

"Had you snortin' there, didn't I, boys?" said Rulon, smiling innocently. He completed his move and wiped the weapons off the table like he was brushing flies away from a salad bowl. The only sounds in the restaurant were the weapons sliding across the floor and banging against the far wall. "No weapons," he said. "We settle this like gentlemen. Fairly. Just you four against me."

Dmitry took his cap off and wiped his forehead with the back of his hand. "Nobody roughs up our boys and gets away with it. They're in the hospital, and they'd like to share a room with you. Where's the hammer?"

Rulon slowly held his jacket open as if to say: *See? No hammer.*

Dmitry leaned over the table to verify. "Nice vest. If we see the hammer we're using guns, and we'll be aiming for your head."

When the inspection was over, instead of putting his arms across the chairs again, Rulon dropped them on his lap.

Now was the time to unleash his awesome powers of persuasion. "You're playing this all wrong," he said. "Your guys were thumping people and threatening a girl with a knife and acting like a bunch of Neanderthals. I had a gun, and I could have used it. But I just wanted to help the girl. Heck, I got shot in the chest. I'm the one who should be mad. By the way, how are your guys doing?" This last bit was said with the most sympathetic look he could muster. He was still hoping he could talk his way out of this.

"Badly. They want you dead. But I intervened. We are not all Neanderthals."

"This isn't a shooting situation," said Rulon, pressing on with his counterargument. "You're a professional. If there's a shooting, life gets tougher for all of us. What did you tell the hospital staff?"

Dmitry shrugged and then responded with his signature short, harsh laugh. "We said they were moving a piano and it fell on them from a second story window."

"And they bought it?" said Rulon, incredulous. One of the goons started yelling, and Rulon thought for a second that the time had come, but Dmitry yelled just as loud and the goon reluctantly backed off.

Dmitry continued. "We've had an understanding with them for a long time. They pretend to believe what we tell them, we pretend we like to overpay. We'll take you there when this is over."

Rulon asked, "Which hospital?" When Dmitry gave him a puzzled look, he said, "I just want to make sure it's covered on my medical plan." Dmitry laughed again but then grew serious.

"No more talk," said Dmitry. "Will you leave quietly?"

Rulon was about to roll his shoulders but caught himself. It was a reflex, but to an experienced opponent, it could also be taken as a signal that he was getting ready to rumble, and he wanted to throw off the most non-threatening vibes he could. He hoped that with the nerdy glasses, stomach pillow, and calm manner would make them the slightest bit overconfident. He also hoped that since they'd been standing for hours in terrible weather, he'd have an added advantage.

"First, tell your guys to throw their guns away like I did," he said. "I don't want any accidents." Up until now he'd been stalling to let their adrenaline drain off, but he realized he'd made a serious miscalculation. If anything, they were winding up tighter, and they were probably thawing out as well. He suspected a couple of them were high on something. Would they even feel his punches?

"You are some joker," said Dmitry gravely.

"I have to know you won't kill me," said Rulon.

Before Dmitry could answer, Quickdraw exploded with a stream of Russian. "This is taking too long! He comes or we waste him!"

The guy with the towel produced the bottle of chloroform. Prodded now by one of his men and caught up in the excruciating tension of the situation, Dmitry started to lose it. "Are you leaving quietly?" he screamed.

Finally, Rulon thought, *the cracks are starting to show.*

"Yes," said Rulon without raising his voice. He sat there, waiting patiently for the right moment, knowing it would come. Then, like a curtain rising over a darkened stage, he saw the final act begin. Dmitry's eyes flickered away from him for a split second. In that same instant, Rulon sensed the others focusing their attention on Dmitry. Time to rock.

With a bellow loud enough to freeze everyone in their tracks, Rulon grabbed the edge of the table and with every ounce of his strength and the quickness of his hammer-throwing days, he flipped the table into Dmitry and the two other men close enough to be caught by its length. It lifted all three of them right off the floor. Dmitry took the table square in the chest. The man had no reflexes.

Rulon especially wanted to get Mr. Quickdraw. But, as fast as Rulon was, the guy still managed to get his automatic out just as the table hit him. Rulon heard the spit of a silenced round whiz by his ear, causing his combat juices to really surge.

In the blink of an eye, Rulon was all over the one thug still standing—the young, mean-looking guy. He previously sensed that this yahoo was strong but slow, possibly still numb from the cold, and the least experienced of the four. Rulon's instincts turned out to be right. The guy was still processing the scene, his mouth wide open but no sounds coming out, when Rulon grabbed him by the face and threw him on top of the overturned table.

Rulon then took a flying leap and landed on the whole crazy mess with both feet. He jumped up and down like a kid on a trampoline. Hands reached up trying to grip his thighs and feet, but he kept jumping. He heard bones snap. *More job openings,* he thought grimly. A face appeared, and he kicked it hard enough to split the uprights from fifty yards. A gun appeared in a hand, and he kicked it away. Strange sounds reached his ears—roars of anger, pain, and alarm—but he kept jumping.

Somehow, two of the men fought their way to their feet. Rulon jumped off the table and grabbed two of the heavy chairs. He whirled them like windmills, and both men went down like a house of cards.

Rulon kept windmilling his way right over the top of the whole muddle of bodies and furniture—applying a little elbow grease to the situation, as he liked to put it—and then over the top of the other guys now desperately trying to disentangle themselves from the table. Eventually, the heap stopped moving. Rulon's personal motto was the fight's not over till the groaning stops. When finally all was still and quiet, he put down the chairs and bent over with his hands on his knees, sucking air.

"What a great sixty-second workout," he said to no one in particular.

While he was still bent over, Orlando, Werner, and the rest of the restaurant staff came back from their happy hour. They stepped around the overturned table and gathered around Rulon with their mouths open. He spun them the best cover story he could—one he hoped they could say with a straight face if the police arrived—that these guys were trying to move the table, and the clumsy oafs had dropped it on themselves. *Stick with what works.* He told Werner the name of the hospital Dmitry had given him and asked him to call an ambulance. Rulon knew they didn't believe him, but being a regular customer had its advantages.

The staff all pitched in, and they quickly got the table upright. Only two of the men were completely knocked out. Dmitry and Quickdraw were conscious but had trouble focusing. Rulon searched them all for weapons, retrieved the gun he had kicked in the skirmish, and collected the weapons he'd flung earlier, dropping what he found into an onion sack Werner provided along with the bottle of chloroform. He paused briefly over the knife before deciding to keep it.

He went back to each of the men and made sure the fractures were under control and that there was no excessive bleeding from compound fractures or head wounds. He next shifted the two that were knocked out into a recovery position—on their sides, one leg bent and head tilted so the air passage stayed open. At Rulon's request, Werner brought some ice, plastic bags, and towels. Rulon went to work making everyone as comfortable as possible until the ambulance arrived.

When Dmitry was reasonably coherent, Rulon propped him up against the bar and crouched down next to him so they could face each other. It was then he got his first good look at Dmitry's face. It wasn't pretty. A flicker of guilt flashed through him, but he immediately reminded himself that they probably had something much worse in store for him.

Rulon's actions had been in self-defense, but when was this cycle going to stop? At some point, one side was going to have to take their licks and decide not to retaliate. But that scenario was highly unlikely, since up until now, one side had taken all the licks. Rulon was sure that in their minds, the ledger couldn't be closed until there was at least some measure of balance. He sighed. Talking to Dmitry was probably a waste of time, but he gave it a try anyway. After this, the closest he'd get to Dmitry would be the receiving end of a hollow-point round from two hundred yards.

"This whole thing was pointless and unnecessary," Rulon said. "When one side is just doing its job and enforcing a certain civility in a situation involving a young woman, no one should take offense." When Dmitry just stared at him, Rulon continued. "Hey, I'm the one who got shot at the luggage store. I could have given you a lot more trouble. And I thought I showed reasonable restraint at Yohaba's apartment. Let's stop the overreacting, okay?" Rulon carefully shifted Dmitry's position and turned his head for him so he could see his buddy, who was now passed out on his back. "Even Quickdraw over there took a shot at me, and I didn't take it personally."

Rulon couldn't tell how much of this Dmitry was buying, but he felt he had common sense on his side. The left side of Dmitry's jaw was significantly swollen. Probably broken. Talking was painful, so Dmitry nodded slightly, and Rulon took that as a sign of understanding. He'd always felt that being reasonable and fair was the best argument.

Ten minutes had elapsed since the fight started, and Rulon was anxious to leave. He certainly didn't want to be there when the ambulance arrived and have to answer a bunch of questions. He noticed that Dmitry was sweating profusely and that his face was looking worse. Rulon yelled to Werner to bring more ice.

Rulon talked to Orlando and Werner and the rest of the staff before he left, just to make sure everyone had their stories straight.

He piggy-backed on Werner's earlier insinuation and allowed him to pry out of him that, yes, this had all been a scuffle over a woman. As implausible as it sounded to Rulon, they bought it, and their opinion of Rulon went up a few notches as a result.

After everyone dispersed, Rulon pulled Werner aside and gave him the weapons sack along with a fifty-franc note. Without him even having to ask, Werner said he'd take a swing by the river on his way home. Rulon gave him a hearty slap on the back and sent him on his way.

Looking around one last time, Rulon was pleased with what he saw. As promised, the place was still in one piece. No furniture or glassware broken. At his request, the wait staff had moved everything breakable before Dmitry and his boys made their appearance. The only casualty had been his phony eyeglasses—busted beyond repair. It suddenly hit him again what a raw deal it was being laid off. OCD would be hard-pressed to replace him. The last thing he did before leaving was to toss Dmitry the cigarette lighter tracking device. Then he left quietly, just like he said he would.

Rulon walked downstairs feeling pretty chuffed. He'd handled a difficult situation quite efficiently. It wasn't nearly as ugly as the luggage store had been. That place had been totaled. Just then, the thought hit him that he couldn't wait to see the girls again and immediately saw a red flag. He'd thought of both girls and not just Isabella. How did Yohaba manage to worm her way into his thoughts?

Once outside, he stood in the rain, exalting in being alive. There is no greater short-term feeling. He flipped up the collar of his jacket against the rain, dug his hands deep into his pockets, and started walking home. Except for that thing about the asteroid hitting the Earth, he didn't have a care in the world.

* * *

Inside the restaurant, Dmitry fumbled with his cell phone, trying to punch in a number with his mangled fingers. The ensuing conversation was painful and muffled, and the other party had a hard time understanding what he was trying to say. Finally, Dmitry managed to make his point through the searing pain of his broken jaw.

"Use the rest of the team," he was told. Dmitry, near exhaustion, with a concussion headache, broken jaw, two broken arms, and a crushed ankle, bit out the message that there was no "rest of the team."

"Then I'll send in some help from Vienna."

No, that wasn't what Dmitry wanted.

"Amsterdam then?" No.

"Prague?" No.

"Look," said his regional supervisor on the other end. "Either we have a bad connection or you have a sock in your mouth. But, in any case, we don't seem to be communicating."

The pain in his jaw was a regular marching band of agony whenever he tried to speak. He steeled himself against the searing ache and managed in between breaths to slowly but clearly form the words he wanted to say: "I . . . want . . . the brothers. The three Serbians."

11

"ANYONE WHO HAS NEVER MADE A MISTAKE HAS NEVER TRIED ANYTHING NEW." —EINSTEIN

RULON DIDN'T MIND WALKING HOME IN THE RAIN. IT GAVE HIM time to process what he'd been through, though fully unwinding, he knew from experience, would take a few days. The girls were waiting for him. He felt good about that. He picked up the pace, but oh, was he tired. Only three blocks from the restaurant and he was already running on empty.

The rain fell harder. He welcomed it and prayed the drenching would wash away the unseen stains that crowded his soul. Violence, no matter the reason, left a mark. He let the water douse him and stream down his collar, soaking him so thoroughly that he couldn't have been wetter if he'd been thrown in a pool. He was conscious of very little except the pounding rain and the steady cadence of his footsteps.

Three fights in ten hours. His jaw hurt. He wondered who punched him. Or maybe he'd hit himself while swinging the chairs. He had the bone structure of a rhinoceros, or so his dad liked to tell people. Where Rulon got it from, he had no idea. His father, while tough as old shoe leather, was not a big man. His mother was Irish and not big at all, but pretty, with red hair. In the right light, Rulon's short, light brown hair also looked a little red. His dad liked to joke that he was adopted, but the red hair was proof enough he wasn't.

His knuckles were scraped, but not too badly. He generally went for body shots when fighting with his fists, just to keep from busting up his hands. His chest was doing okay from the bullet he took that morning. It had been the first time he'd ever tested the vest in the heat of battle. He made a mental note to write a letter of appreciation to Turtleskin, the manufacturer.

No, what bothered Rulon most was that his right shin ached. He must have banged himself as he flipped the table, but he didn't remember doing it. *Surprised the heck out of them with that table stunt, that's for sure.*

By now, the elation Rulon had been feeling was gone. All that was left was the usual post-combat depression like a black fog in a hollow. It was then that he wished more than ever he was married, to feel the sweet comfort of a woman's embrace, to be able to talk about things he could never discuss with a man.

Rulon had almost quit OCD right after his first really violent assignment. It had ended in a bad fight in Berlin that there was no getting out of. Without telling anyone, he visited the department psychiatrist a few weeks later. She told him that the problem was with an operative's training. It was all focused on getting agents ready to do violence, but almost none of it was spent teaching them how to deal with the psychological aftereffects. She had said it was a rare person who didn't have some strong emotional reaction afterwards. She said that with his profile, if he ever found himself not feeling guilty, the time had come to think about quitting.

He reached his row of apartment blocks and walked to the end, making a short, right turn onto a bush-lined footpath that took him to the front of his building. He was looking down, lost in his own thoughts, when it suddenly struck him how irresponsible he'd been. He'd walked all the way from the Desperado without looking back even once. For all he knew, there was a battalion of *Spetsnaz* following him. To make up for it, he decided to do a full circle around the apartment block and double back to see if he could surprise anyone.

That thought lasted a whole second before it vanished entirely. Just in front of the entrance to his building, he saw Yohaba, huddled under the doorway overhang, smoking a cigarette. She turned quickly at his approach, her long auburn hair flaring out behind her as she spun. Their eyes met, and even through the rain, there was no disguising the light in her face when she saw him. The sincerity of it warmed Rulon right through his rain-soaked clothes and applied a healing balm to the brutal memories of the day.

"Hey, shouldn't you—?" he began, intending to tease her about it being past her bedtime, but he was stopped in mid-sentence when she threw down the cigarette and took a half-dozen determined steps and caught him in a surprise embrace. They stood there in the rain, her arms around his neck and her head turned sideways against his shoulder. At first he was slow to react. Then, without really thinking about it, he closed his arms around her strongly enough to lift her to her toes. It was all right. They'd been through a lot together today.

"I was worried about you," she said over the rain, close to his ear, her voice a husky deepness. Then lifting her head to look at him but holding all the tighter, she said angrily, "You're crazy. So crazy. You don't listen to anyone but yourself. You don't call. You walk home in the rain. You don't answer your cell phone."

"I turned it off. For tactical reasons."

"They didn't come to apologize, did they?" she asked, her voice quieter now but even more serious. She let go of him, and Rulon immediately felt a chill.

"Not initially," he said, "but they were real sorry later."

"Are you hurt?"

"No."

"Let me look at you," she ordered, pulling him into the light of the doorway. She looked him over and made sure his stomach pillow was properly centered, giving it a pat for good measure when done. Then she squeezed his arms a few times to see if he'd wince. "Let me see your hands," she said. She held his palms up for inspection and then turned them over. "Your knuckles are a mess."

"Where's Isabella?" he asked, trying to change the subject. Immediately Yohaba backed away, and the atmosphere got cold enough to snow.

"The princess is probably powdering her nose," she said from within the dryness of the entrance way. "Would you get in here?" she ordered irritably, pulling on his sleeve to get him out of the rain. "Listen, we need to talk about her. Now do you understand what I was talking about?"

"No," he said. "I thought you two were getting along great. What happened?" He thought things over for a second. "Did you start a fight?"

"No, I didn't start a fight. How could I? She is so nice," she said with a sarcastic snarl that would have done a cougar proud. "I'm not sleeping in the same house with her. I'm telling you, the girl is trouble."

Now Rulon was angry. "Your problem is you've only hung around people as dysfunctional as you. You can't stand being in the same room with someone who is normal and mature."

"Well, you and I seem to be spending a lot of time in rooms together!" she yelled. "What does that tell you?" Through his fatigue, it sounded like an insult. He started to huff. *Man, she can push my buttons.* They glared at each other, and both sensed at the same time that things were escalating out of control—something neither of them wanted.

"We need to talk," she said, suddenly calm. Rulon braced himself. "I spoke to Ivan, and he and the boys are okay. He says thank you, and I didn't even have to twist his arm for him to say that. He's really not a bad guy. And by the way, you didn't have to throw him into the piano. He's all muscle, but his bark is worse than his bite."

"Whatever," said Rulon, not caring to get into an argument over what a nice guy Ivan was. But he was suddenly curious. "So, what is the story with the store anyway? What were you guys up to?"

"Don't ask me," she snapped. "I'm not a rat."

"I think you just answered my question," he said.

"No, I didn't," said Yohaba, her eyes narrowed and angry. "You don't know anything about anything. I'm not involved; that's all I'm going to tell you."

"There's a second confirmation," he said, feeling good about finally scoring a few points. "They're being watched. That's why I came to the store in the first place. They're up to something. I was supposed to check them out."

"Those idiots," said Yohaba, shaking her head in disgust. "But why tell me? What's to stop me from calling them and telling them to beat it back to Bulgaria?"

"Wouldn't bother me if you did—as long as they gave up their source in the States."

"Fine," she said, simply and sincerely. "That's what I'll tell them."

Again, Rulon was touched by her implicit trust. He worked in a world where trusting someone, even people on your own side, was not something you did lightly. And yet, she trusted him to keep his word on this. He would, of course, but how could she be so sure? They'd only known each other since that morning.

With the luggage store issue settled, he thought the argument about Isabella was behind them, but as they went through the vestibule door to the elevator, the subject came up again.

"Now listen, Rulon, before we go upstairs, I just have one more thing to say about the show pony." She looked him in the eye. "I know I'm coming across as catty and jealous, but, I'm telling you, something isn't right. If she had any real affection for you at all, she'd be ripping my eyes out by now. I mean, look at me," she said, gesturing toward her obvious assets. "I'm serious competition here, Herr Hurt, in case you haven't noticed." She paused for effect. "Just watch her," she warned. "That's all I'm asking."

"Oh, don't worry," Rulon said agreeably. "I'll be watching her." She gave him a look, but he ignored her. They took the elevator upstairs in silence.

As they entered his apartment, he immediately looked to his right and saw Isabella sitting by his computer desk in the dining room. At the same time, he caught her snatching her hand away from the phone with the speed of a chameleon's tongue. His brain did a double take at her obviously guilty maneuver, but before he could comment, she rushed over.

"Are you all right?" she asked, breathless.

To be welcomed with such enthusiasm by two beautiful women in the space of a few minutes—*Did I just classify Yohaba, the girl with the nose ring and tattoo, as beautiful?*—was more than a tongue-tied cowboy could handle. He stood there practically speechless, managing only a few mumbled responses to her questions.

But after her initial enthusiastic greeting, he realized something was missing. No hug. His wet clothes hadn't stopped Yohaba from rushing into the rain and hugging him, but Isabella couldn't hide her pained expression when she saw how wet he was. The obvious solution was to change his clothes, so he called a time-out and ran off to his bedroom after directing Yohaba to one of the spare bedrooms so she could do the same.

While he changed into dry clothes, he thought about Isabella and the phone and wished he could shrug off his immediate suspicion. So what if she was using the phone. But that wasn't the issue. She had clearly acted guilty.

Once he had his shirt off, he got his first look at the bruise left behind by the bullet he'd taken to his vest. It was black and orange and the size of a small saucer. He'd been lucky. A few inches higher and . . . he pushed the thought out of his mind.

Five minutes later, everyone was back in the living room, the two women on the couch and Rulon on the floor with his back against the radiator. With everyone comfortable, he gave them a PG rendition of what had gone down at the Desperado.

Throughout the story, he noticed Yohaba staring at his stomach and realized she was having trouble getting over the difference without the Know-foam. Isabella however, wasn't near as distracted, having never seen him wear the pillow before tonight. For Yohaba's sake, he offered to put it back on, but she just laughed and waved him off. Women had always been a mystery to him. Now that he was so close to two such beautiful specimens, he found himself intoxicated with the sound of their voices and the graceful flow of their movements.

Rulon hadn't forgotten about Isabella and the phone, however. When he was finished with his story, he claimed he couldn't stand the mess and walked over to the desk to straighten up some papers. He purposely tapped his fingers on the phone buttons just to see if Isabella would react. He sensed her tense eyes following his every move. *Interesting*, he thought, *but still not conclusive.* When he made as if to pick up the receiver, she was at his side instantly, clucking over his busted-up knuckles and easing herself between him and the desk. It wasn't that he minded being close enough to smell her perfume, but given what he'd recently been through, his preservation meter was dialed up to maximum sensitivity. Anything out of the ordinary registered as a threat.

He let himself appear distracted by her offer to make them some tea. A few minutes later, he was sitting on the floor with a steaming cup of blackberry herb tea, flanked by the two girls.

Isabella and Yohaba seemed to get along great. Knowing how

Yohaba felt about Isabella, he considered this a minor miracle. Or maybe it was a sign of how adept women were at disguising their feelings. The phone thing kept bugging him.

A little while later, he sent the girls off to raid the refrigerator and took the opportunity to steal a quick look at Isabella's cell phone in the outside pocket of her purse. It was out of power. He had wondered why she was using his land line, and now he knew.

Around 3:00 a.m., the girls started yawning, so he wrapped things up by laying out a plan for the next day. He had already decided they should stay together for the night. The situation was dicey, and he wasn't sure they had seen the last of the Russians. Plus, it was really late, the trams weren't running, and driving Isabella home wasn't worth it. Between Yohaba and himself, they had enough sundries for Isabella to get by for one night. If she needed something for tomorrow they could always stop by her apartment on their way to Yohaba's grandmother's house.

Isabella was part of the team now. He guessed it was partly because she wanted so badly to come. If he were honest with himself, it was also because he wanted her around. For one thing, he wasn't entirely comfortable traveling alone with Yohaba. It wasn't because he didn't trust her. It was because he didn't trust himself. Also, he hoped that Isabella's interest in coming was really more about being with him than about solving a fifty-year-old riddle. He assigned each of the girls to their own bedroom, grateful that the agency had such a huge apartment, by Swiss standards, with lots of extra furnishings and linens. Once they were situated, he retired to his own room and closed the door.

Once in bed, he lay there in the dark and listened to the murmur of the girls' voices as they talked in the hallway bathroom opposite his door. They sounded like two sisters. He was pleased about that; he always liked to see people getting along.

But, now that he was alone, he had to admit that Isabella's behavior with the phone still bothered him. Why it had sent up such a red flag, he wasn't sure. Maybe it was because the natural thing for her to do would have been to say, "I hope you don't mind I used your phone, I had to call—whomever."

She could have been calling her roommate—she said she had

one. Or her mother in South Africa, which Rulon wouldn't have minded either. Maybe it was her forced nonchalance afterwards that kept the warning bells ringing. Or maybe Yohaba's warnings were getting to him, and he was starting to build things way out of proportion. He considered that possibility for a minute but decided Isabella was definitely hiding something. Rushing over to him when he was by the phone only confirmed his suspicions.

After the girls closed their doors, he waited a few minutes before getting out of bed and heading for the kitchen for something to eat. At least he wanted it to appear that way. He opened and closed the refrigerator a few times and rattled some silverware just for effect. As an afterthought, he grabbed a package of frozen vegetables out of the freezer for his bruised chest. In the midst of the controlled racket, he stepped over to the phone. It took pushing just a few buttons to see the call history. Satisfied but stunned, he walked back to his room and settled into bed, a bag of frozen peas on his chest, staring at the ceiling, sleep now impossible.

OCD had set him up in this expensive apartment but then tried to save money by buying the cheapest phone they could find. It had a feature where he could see the call history, but it wouldn't tell him if the displayed number was an incoming or outgoing call. This meant that even if Isabella had been on the phone, he had no way of knowing if she had made the call or just happened to answer. He wanted to give her the benefit of every doubt. Yohaba might think that he knew nothing about women, but even he knew that accusing someone of conspiring to kill him could ruin even a well-established relationship, let alone one that was only two dates old. He needed proof. So he waited a few minutes. Right on time, he heard a sound.

He would have thought that after a day like today, everyone would be asleep in seconds. Rulon had his reasons for staying awake, but what was this little night owl's excuse? One of the bedroom doors was opening, and he had a good guess as to whose it was and why. He quickly got up and listened at his own door for a moment before opening it a crack. There was the soft sound of stockinged feet retreating toward the far side of the apartment. Then a light from the dining room bounced around the kitchen to glow faintly down the hallway. A long pause. Then darkness again, soft feet surreptitiously returning, a hand on the doorknob, a furtive look backward, a bedroom door quietly closing.

Rulon stood there for a moment, pondering the significance of what he'd just seen and then backed up and sat on the bed.

While icing his chest and with one eye on the alarm clock, he waited a full five minutes before stealthily repeating his earlier foray down the hall and through the kitchen to check again the call history log. As he suspected, the number he was most interested in had been deleted. Retracing his steps, he stopped to make sure the apartment door was locked from the inside and removed the key he normally left in the lock for that purpose. No one was getting in or out tonight.

Back in his bedroom, he locked his door as well. Like a bad moon rising, his paranoia cast a new but depressing light on everything he'd seen that day and on every one of his previous conversations with Isabella. His Colt was still in its shoulder holster hanging in the closet. He took it out and checked the action, chambered a round and set it on the side table next to the bed. He suddenly remembered that Freya was still in the car. He considered going downstairs to get her, but he felt exhausted. Given the circumstances, he thought the chances of an attack on the apartment were small.

Once in bed he again considered what he'd just seen. He had assumed all along that the Russians had been tracking them with the lighter. Now he wasn't even sure the lighter had been bugged at all. Going back over the events of the day, he now saw the little clues that he'd missed at the time. He was right about the phone and Isabella's look of guilt. He was right about her wanting to return and delete the number.

Sometimes being right can be a real pain in the butt. *Isabella? No,* Jezebella, *the treasonous wench!* The number she deleted was Dmitry's number, the same number Rulon had memorized when he first relieved Dmitry of his cell phone back in Yohaba's apartment—Spy Craft 101. Obviously, the Russians now knew where Rulon lived and that they were planning to visit Yohaba's grandmother tomorrow.

Rulon's dad used to tell him he was a few clowns short of a circus. But he also used to say, in one of his rare complimentary moods, "Son, you are not only built like a brick outhouse, but you can see through one too, given enough time." Now Rulon knew the score. Tomorrow, all three of them would be in the car together.

But what about Isabella? The Russians had tried several times before to infiltrate Portal. This time they hired an outside contractor from South Africa and sent her in because she was less likely to draw suspicion. Rulon figured he knew how things went down: she spends six months trolling for agents and listening to office chatter, and she finally hears a snippet of conversation speculating about Rulon and his double life. Only four people at Portal actually knew he was an agent: Magnus, Michael, the Zurich office manager, and the two senior partners. She inveigles herself into his department, and the next thing you know they are dating.

What about earlier this evening? Rulon calls up to invite her to meet them for dinner. She turns him down for all the obvious womanly reasons. After she hangs up, she gets a call from Dmitry, asking if she knows where Rulon is. What luck, she tells him. He just called her. She calls Rulon back, says she has changed her mind and wants to meet for dinner. He tells her they're at the Desperado. She keeps him pinned there for several hours while Dmitry puts his team together. And she's tracking Yohaba for them as well. She's thinking Christmas bonus.

Rulon decided he needed a good night's sleep to figure this out entirely. Mercifully, his subconscious concluded that staying awake served no useful purpose. The last thing he remembered was rolling over onto a wet, partially thawed bag of peas and thinking that he really should move it. Five hours later he woke up. It's funny how the subconscious works because as soon as he opened his eyes, he knew exactly what to do.

12

"LOGIC WILL GET YOU FROM A TO B. IMAGINATION WILL TAKE YOU EVERYWHERE." —EINSTEIN

RULON HAD HIS OWN PHILOSOPHY ABOUT WOMEN. MOST OF THE time, a man was better off dealing with a woman through intuition. Logic would get him nowhere. He knew that sounded chauvinistic, but that was the way he saw it. Tricks, traps, and puzzles would get him nowhere with Isabella. The girl was good, and he wasn't ashamed to admit that he wasn't in her league when it came to deceit.

Yohaba woke up first and was in the kitchen cooking breakfast. The smell of bacon wafted down the hall and found its way into Rulon's bedroom and served just as well as an alarm clock. As he got dressed, he reminded himself to act naturally around Isabella. No glares and no references to Benedict Arnold or the Rosenbergs.

When he came into the kitchen, Isabella was there with Yohaba, and fortunately, keeping his mouth occupied turned out not to be a problem. Waiting for him on the table was a six-egg omelet filled with bell peppers, onions, and a half-slab of chopped bacon, plus a healthy helping of *knäckebrot* with some sliced mango on the side. All that was missing was the fried banana, but if she'd done that, he'd have taken her down to the courthouse and married her on the spot.

As nervous as it made him, Rulon realized that his feelings for Yohaba had reached a tipping point. Between the problems he was having with Isabella and now knowing that Yohaba could cook, the nose ring, web tattoo, and smoking habit continued to dwindle in importance.

The girls picked up right where they had left off the night before, but Rulon was quieter than usual. He told them it was because he was tired and banged up, and that got a potato field's worth of sympathy out of both of them.

After breakfast, he did squat thrusts, bear crawls, and a few pushups on the living room floor despite his bruised chest, giving the girls a thrill. Today was Saturday, and normally he'd have gone mountain biking despite last night's rain, but not today. While the girls were cleaning up the kitchen, he did a quick search on Google for some information he needed before tackling Isabella. As usual, Google did not disappoint.

By 10:00 a.m. they trio was heading south on the A-3 toward Bergün and Yohaba's grandmother. Before they set out, Rulon had checked the car for bugs using a handy little device you can't buy at Radio Shack. He set the device on vibrate and kept it in his jacket pocket so the girls wouldn't see what he was up to. This allowed him, while he was checking the car, to also get a reading on them as they stood a few feet away. Sure enough, the bug-checker picked up a signal from Isabella's purse. He assumed the tracking device was in her cell phone, running on a separate, more high-tech battery. He already knew where her loyalties were, but it was nice to have additional confirmation.

On their way out of the city, he performed a number of maneuvers designed to lose any tails. With Isabella sitting next to him, he didn't think the Russians would risk trailing them visually. They were more likely homing in on her cell phone from a distance. But he performed these little ploys anyway, mostly for Isabella's sake. He didn't want her thinking he was on to her.

Again, she betrayed her tactical savvy by commenting on his backtracking and circling before Yohaba did. So far everything was under control. He also moved Freya from the trunk into the space beneath his seat, just in case.

Talking to Isabella right now was risky. He was plagued by the absurd feeling she could read him like a book. So as a diversion, he fired a few scientific questions at Yohaba, just to prime the pump, hoping she'd eat up the silence. She sat in the back seat and cooperated perfectly, oblivious to the nuclear explosion Rulon was trying to control.

Yohaba's long hair was in a ponytail today. Against the chill, she had brought a black North Face down jacket; a dark red, long sleeved turtle-neck shirt; blue jeans; and black Adidas running shoes. Isabella, of necessity, wore the same smart outfit she had on the previous night. Rulon claimed that because of their late start, they didn't have time to stop by her apartment. Still, she managed to look quite stunning, and in spite of everything, Rulon knew he would miss her. Lucky for her, her raincoat was lined with fleece. If things went according to plan, she'd be needing it.

He was reviewing his plans for the day in silence, working through his moves and countermoves, when he became distracted as Yohaba segued onto a different topic. Up until then she had been focused on black holes, making sure they all knew the differences between a Schwarzschild non-rotating black hole, a rotating black hole called a Kerr hole, and an Einstein-Rosen bridge, better known as a wormhole. She'd been on a roll for the last half hour, but then she brought up the subject of nuclear bombs.

"Are you sure you guys want to hear this?" she asked, fishing for a positive response. An image filled Rulon's mind of a cornered Ivan during a slow day at the luggage store, and he couldn't help burst out laughing. Quickly recovering, he assured Yohaba of his interest, and she plunged into her discourse.

"This is really cool stuff," she said. "Feel free to ask questions any time." She was really into this. "Atom bombs can use either uranium or plutonium as an energy source. Both those elements are made up of constantly decaying atoms that are trying to throw off neutrons so they can turn into a simpler but more stable element. Every time an atom falls apart, it releases the energy that had been holding it together, plus a few extra neutrons.

"In an atom bomb, this nuclear material is surrounded with TNT. When the TNT detonates, it compresses the plutonium, whose atoms then reach critical mass. That means that the plutonium is so densely packed from the compression caused by the explosion that every decaying atom can't help hitting other atoms when it shoots off its extra neutrons. These neutrons hit other atoms that are also decaying. Then they throw off their energy, and their extra neutrons hit other atoms, and a big chain reaction takes place. That chain reaction is a humongous explosion with lots of heat and wind."

"How much heat?" asked Rulon.

"Several million degrees at least. It becomes a white hot fireball as hot as the sun. At Hiroshima, all that was left of some exposed people within a half mile of ground-zero were burnt shadows on stones. The blast also created thousand-mile-an-hour winds that sucked up everything that wasn't bolted down into that big mushroom cloud you always see. And remember, it was a really small bomb. No more than fifteen kilotons. There is a reason why the world is so paranoid about nuclear weapons."

"How's an atom bomb different from a hydrogen bomb?" he asked. "Or a neutron bomb?"

"A hydrogen bomb is somewhat similar," she replied, "except instead of using energy from atoms splitting apart, it uses energy that comes from fusing together trillions of deuterium and tritium atoms, both isotopes of hydrogen. That's where the name 'hydrogen bomb' comes from.

"The original design was worked out in 1951 by Edward Teller, a Hungarian-born physicist, and a Polish mathematician named Stanislaw Ulam, while they were both working for the US government.

"What makes atoms fuse together is pressure from multiple atom bombs placed around the bomb core, which explode like the TNT did with the atom bomb, causing immense heat and pressure. That's bad enough, but what makes it even worse is that typically, the casing for a hydrogen bomb is made from uranium. When the hydrogen bomb goes off, it actually turns the casing into an atom bomb of its own. This adds to the strength of the blast while at the same time producing a lot of nasty radiation. A neutron bomb is simply a hydrogen bomb without the uranium casing."

Rulon said, "So, lots of heat and wind but not much radiation, right?"

"Yeah, that's basically it. But hydrogen bombs are in a class by themselves as far as destruction is concerned. The first full-scale hydrogen bomb was code named Ivy Mike and was detonated at Eniwetok Atoll on November 1, 1952. It was over ten megatons, about seven hundred times bigger than the Hiroshima bomb. What do you think of that?"

"I think you're amazing," he said, impressed at the information but more so at the ongoing contradiction between Yohaba's superficial persona and her underlying intellect.

"It weighed about seventy tons," she continued, ignoring his comment. "But by 1960, they were making megaton-sized hydrogen bombs that were eighteen inches in diameter and weighed only seven hundred pounds. In the 1960s, the boys at Lawrence Livermore had developed megaton-sized hydrogen bombs so small that ten of them could fit on the head of a missile. That tells you something."

"If that's the case," Rulon said, "whether we find the trunk or not, surely we have the technology now to blast Elsa out of the sky." He could see her in the rearview mirror, twirling and untwirling her ponytail as she talked.

"You would think so," she replied. "Before Einstein died, the world had already detonated some pretty big bombs but none small enough to be transported by a rocket.

"The yield on the typical bomb is only point seven percent. In other words, less than a percent of all potential energy is released. If you could increase the yield dramatically, you could send a bomb big enough to vaporize the whole thing."

Yohaba and Rulon continued on the topic for a few more minutes but then eventually veered off onto the subject of doomsday movies.

It was the first clear day that week, a stunning blue sky day that made Rulon fall in love with Switzerland all over again. The rain left the fields a dark green and the trees sparkling in the late morning dew.

Rulon got off the A-3 and took back roads down perfectly manicured lanes, past quaint, centuries-old farmhouses, and precisely fenced-off fields. They drove through a forest on a two-lane road that was really only wide enough for a single car. After ten miles, he veered off down a muddy dirt track, a perfect setting for the dirty job he was about to do. He noticed Isabella getting fidgety and expected her to say something, but Yohaba spoke up first.

"Hey, where you taking us, cowboy? This isn't the way."

Rulon made a point of glaring at his GPS unit. "This darn GPS has a mind of its own. It'll get us there. Just sit tight and enjoy the ride." When Isabella joined in the protest, he said, "Look on the bright side. If there is anyone following us, this should throw them off. Just relax." That quieted them down.

As they drove along with Yohaba nattering away, Rulon reviewed in his mind all the evidence he had against Isabella. In the end, he couldn't get around the transmitter in her bag or that she'd erased Dmitry's phone number from his phone. He drove along in stony silence, trying to look pleasant, but with darkness gripping his thoughts. He felt betrayed. His dad used to say, "Son, a good woman is worth her weight in gold, but a bad one isn't worth a pile of skunk bait." Like most of his dad's backwoods sayings, it got the point across, and it was hard to argue with.

When Rulon thought they were far enough away from civilization, he slapped himself on the forehead as if he'd forgotten something and said to Isabella that he'd left his cell phone behind and could he please borrow hers. She replied that her phone was dead, and he assured her that he could charge it in the car. She turned it over to him—it would have been awkward for her to refuse—but he could sense her antennas were up. He didn't mind though. He wanted the cell phone, and he didn't want to have to wrestle it from her later.

Isabella continued to watch him, but he made no attempt to charge the phone. In the stiffness of her posture, and in the way she held onto the door grip, the arm rest, her other arm—anything she could latch onto—he could feel her curiosity turning into apprehension. But she didn't say anything.

It's amazing what a guilty conscience will do. In the backseat, Yohaba was quiet and sitting up straight, the tension in the car palpable in the silence. She caught Rulon's eye in the rearview mirror and mouthed single word, "What?" Rulon shook his head as a warning to stay out of this. Up ahead he saw a good place to turn off. As he started to slow down, he noticed Isabella's hand moving toward the lock-release button on her door. It suddenly occurred to him that she might be armed.

The turnout was a muddy brown patch, cut out of a ten-foot wide grass fringe that sat between the dirt path and a well maintained, wood-rail fence. It was dark and secluded. Overhead, a canopy of trees blocked most of the sunlight. There was thick forest on both sides of the road, and they hadn't seen a car for ten minutes. Perfect. The car came to a gentle stop, and Rulon turned off the engine.

"Why are we stopping?" asked Isabella. He didn't answer immediately but deliberately took the pressure up a few notches by hitting the master door-lock on the center console, making it impossible for anyone to get out.

He felt his heart rate pick up, and he started noticing little things, like Isabella flinching slightly at the sound of the doors re-clicking themselves and her knuckles going white on the arm rest. He had to give her credit—she wasn't giving away much, but he thought he could take a good guess as to what she was thinking.

Up until right then, her little charade was all about charming a hick from Idaho. She had been in control. Now she was in a locked car with a guy who had recently taken out seven of her buddies—taken them out hard. Now she was second-guessing herself, wondering if she misjudged this yahoo, that she didn't know him as well as she thought she did. He could almost hear her brain whirring as she calculated the risk of getting out alive, knowing there was no room for error.

"I never told you," Rulon said quietly, "but last night those guys in the Desperado were coming to kill me. How does that make you feel?"

"What kind of a question is that?" Isabella stammered. "I'm sure it must have been awful." She reached over and casually undid her seat belt, and then, eyeing him cautiously, she edged up against the door, as far away from him as she could. In a feeble attempt at familiarity, she added, "You are the luckiest Mystery Man I've ever known."

"But not so lucky in love," he said. When she made no reply, he continued. "If you hadn't gotten up last night to erase Dmitry's phone number, I would've still had my doubts. You were too thorough for your own good." At that, her eyes lost a bit of their focus, and he could tell she was running through her short list of options. He had one eye on her face and, still concerned she might have a weapon, one eye on her hands.

After a few moments, her brain correctly calculated that the gig was up, and her eyes refocused. "Well, Haystack," she said in a voice as hard as diamonds. "Where do we go from here?"

That Haystack crack was going to cost her. "You get out. Now."

"Won't this make it awkward when you see me at work on Monday?" she asked cattily, looking straight at Rulon and trying to hold his attention with her eyes while her right hand inched its way toward her handbag on the floor.

"Not half as awkward for me as meeting a team of your Russian buddies in an alley somewhere," he said. "Here, let me help you with that." He ripped the handbag out of her grip. She struggled for it more fiercely than he had anticipated, fueling his suspicion that there was a painful surprise hidden in its depths. "Let's see what baubles this little treasure chest is hiding." In mid-rummage, he suddenly stopped and looked up at her. "Should I be worried about mousetraps?" By then she had her back to him and was staring out the window, but with his mousetrap comment, she slowly turned.

One time when riding bulls, Rulon found himself underneath a two-thousand-pound Brahma. The rodeo clowns were doing their job, but they couldn't get him disentangled from the bull, which stomped around, searching for him with its hoofs. Suddenly, in all its thrashing and bucking, its head spun around, twisting at a weird angle, and Rulon found himself staring up into a single, insane, hate-filled, bloodshot eye. This all happened in a split second, but the memory was seared into his brain like a brand. Isabella now had the same psychotic look. And in a strange way, because she was a woman, it was creepier. Her expression only intensified when he pulled his hand out of her bag.

"Look, a girl gun," he said lightheartedly. It was a Bersa 380 with a seven-round magazine, 3.5 inch barrel, and a combat trigger guard. He let her get a good look at it then slipped it in his jacket pocket. "We are going in different directions. Starting now. Adios."

"How am I supposed to get home from here?" she asked, her cloaking device activated and her true nature once again unreadable and businesslike. Though she didn't show it, he was sure she was greatly relieved he was letting her go. He handed back her bag, satisfied that it contained no other weapons or bugs.

He couldn't resist. " 'Frankly, my dear, I don't give a damn.' "

From the backseat, Yohaba whispered, "Clark Gable, *Gone with the Wind*. 1939." Up until that moment, she hadn't made a peep.

"Not now, Yohaba," he hissed. "You're ruining the moment." He hit the door lock and released the doors. Without a word, Isabella got out, indecorously slamming the door on her trailing handbag and then having to re-slam it. The thought came to him that she might have another gun in a thigh holster, and a jolt of fear hit him as he pictured her pulling out a pistol and shooting him through the window. His hand slid under his jacket and gripped the Colt.

Instead, she turned and bent over to look in the window as if she wanted to say something. He lowered it a crack. "Enjoy your little mosh pit loser. I'm sure she'll rock your world," she said with a leer.

"Enjoy your walk home," he responded with a smile and raised the window again. She started to say something but the sound never made it through the glass.

Rulon reached for the ignition button just as Yohaba cleared her throat. "Well, that's one way to leave your lover that Paul Simon never thought of," she said.

He turned around to face her. "So, you liked that?" he asked, unable to disguise his satisfaction at how smoothly he handled the situation.

"Rulon, not only did I like that, but I'm proud of you too," she said, leaning forward over the front seat. At that moment Isabella started banging on the window with her fists. She was yelling for her cell phone. *Yeah, right.* Rulon started the car and drove off, but before he got more than fifty yards away, he remembered something. Slamming on the brakes, he put the Beemer in reverse and drove backwards at a high rate of speed to pull up alongside of Isabella again. He lowered the window.

"Hey!" he yelled. At the sound of his voice, she stopped scraping the mud off her shoe against the fence rail and slowly turned to face him. "I think I've finally come up with a nickname for you. Have a nice life, *Unamanga*." The car fishtailed a bit when he sped off, and the last thing he saw of Isabella was the view from his rear-view mirror, throwing up her arms to block the mud coming off his tires. That last touch was for calling Yohaba a loser.

A few hundred yards down the road, Yohaba told him to pull over so she could sit in front. Once she was settled in the passenger seat and had buckled herself in, she asked, "What was that you called her?"

"Oh, that was a Zulu word for liar. She's South African. I got it off Google this morning."

"So this is how you dump girls in Idaho—you drive them to the woods, throw them out, yell Zulu words at them, and then splash mud on them as you drive off?"

"Pretty much," he said. "What's the problem?"

"Nothing. Just so I know." They drove on in silence for another five minutes. With one hand on the steering wheel, Rulon reprogrammed the GPS to take them to Yohaba's grandmother's house. As they drove, he got lost in thought, thinking of all the better retorts he could have made.

He was in his own world when Yohaba broke his reverie and softly stated, "You're going to make me ask you, aren't you?"

"What?"

"I'm glad you did what you did, but seriously, what on earth was going on back there?"

"I guess I owe you an explanation." Rulon told her the whole story and made himself sound like a regular George Smiley in the process. He told her he had uncovered the 'rampages of betrayal,' as John le Carré liked to put it. She thought he was a genius. He explained to her why he kept the cell phone—so the Russians would think Isabella was still with them and not interrupt their conversation with the grandmother.

She asked to see Isabella's gun, and he showed her, first ejecting the magazine and checking the chamber before he let her hold it. She gave it back, making him laugh when she did an imitation of a gunslinger, quick-drawing two guns, firing off a few shots, then blowing smoke from the barrels.

For the rest of the drive, they passed the time pointing out the sights and telling each other funny stories about their lives. He found out that her name was based on a dream her mother had before she was born. She found out he was related to John Hook, one of the eleven Victoria Cross winners at the British battle with the Zulus at Rorke's Drift. She asked him if the 1964 movie *Zulu* that portrayed Hook as a malingerer was accurate, and he set her straight. The truth was that Hook was in the hospital because he volunteered to stay behind and defend the sick, even though it was a suicide mission. She said such stupid bravery must run in the family. As they drove along, it was as if the ugly incident with Isabella had never happened.

At one point in the drive, he noticed her green eyes filled with mirth and her red-streaked hair, loose and free about her shoulders. The entire effect imprinted a memory on him that even then he could sense would continue to steep and deepen over time. It was at that moment, buttressed by laughter and good feelings, that he knew they had become friends. He was convinced that they had something more to offer each other than a mere physical infatuation. If anything more were to follow, well then, looking back, this is when that would have started, at least for him.

He didn't even try to explain it to himself, but at that moment his train got switched to a different track as far as Yohaba was concerned. He decided then and there that he wanted to get to know her even better, despite their obvious differences and against everything he ever thought about himself and about the kind of woman he thought he would be attracted to.

Rulon liked to drive with his hand on the gear shift, and at one point, she put her hand over his and left it there. He didn't resist or comment, which must have surprised her as much as it did him.

They drove on in silence through the fall colors of a winding, trackless Swiss forest, the leaves on the road resettling after their passing. It had been a long time since he'd been alone with a girl in a car, driving to get somewhere, a little electricity in the air between them, and enjoying the ride. Rulon suspected he wasn't the only one trying to make sense of how far they'd come in just one day—emotionally, that is.

By now her hand had moved to his shoulder, and it still felt right. Rulon looked over at her. She didn't return his gaze but looked straight ahead, her face tanned and slightly freckled, looking sure of herself. But she knew he was looking at her, and she must have felt what he was thinking, because a smile broke out over her face like a dawn over Redfish Lake. Then, suddenly, they were pulling into her grandmother's circular driveway, and it wasn't just the deepening shade of the tall trees that made her expression look dark and troubled.

"You'll protect me, won't you, Rulon?" she asked calmly but seriously once they stopped. "If they come after me again, you'll be there, right? I don't want you to do anything stupid, but I have to know we'll come out of this together."

Her question took him by surprise. She had a way of throwing him off balance. Had she also been imagining a mutual story between them? Without thinking, he blurted, "If they ever come after you again, they'll regret the day they were born." He meant for it to sound like a joke, but instead it came out as a solemn, reckless vow. "I mean, I would give my life to save you," he said, trying to recover with more humor, but he only made it worse, the thickness in his throat betraying his emotions.

"Rulon!" she said with amused alarm. "Am I going to have problems with you now that I'm the only game in town?"

"No," he said, a two-letter word being about as much as he dared speak for fear of digging himself a deeper hole.

"Good," she said. "Because you're not any better now at hiding your feelings than you were in my apartment. Oh, don't think I didn't know. I thought cowboys were supposed to be taciturn."

Rulon looked down at his hands and mumbled something about rule number one still being rule number one. Yohaba reached over and grabbed his chin and made him face her.

"Well, I should hope so," she said, her green eyes twinkling with mirth at his embarrassment. "But I'd hate to be in a car with you when 'rule' number one becomes 'guideline' number one. So, for now, just remember, I'm taking you to see my grandmother, and I don't want you frightening the old bat."

"Look," Rulon said, getting angry now. "What I said just came out wrong. I didn't mean it the way you took it."

"Of course, you didn't," she said amidst gales of laughter. "What did our little two-faced Mata Hari call you? Mystery Man. Well, I got news for you, Cowboy, you're not much of a mystery to me."

Rulon had no idea what she meant by that, but he wasn't going to get dragged into a discussion about it.

13

"THERE ARE TWO WAYS TO LIVE YOUR LIFE—ONE IS AS THOUGH NOTHING IS A MIRACLE, THE OTHER IS AS THOUGH EVERYTHING IS A MIRACLE." —EINSTEIN

YOHABA'S GRANDMOTHER'S TWO-STORY HOME WAS NESTLED deep within a strand of tall, dark pine trees. When Rulon and Yohaba got out of the car, they stood there for a moment in the cool shade. A stone path, about ten yards long, led from the gravel driveway to the front door. The grounds were unkempt by Swiss standards and looked more like a French garden—teeming with plants, bushes, and trees—all wild and overgrown.

The house had a Tudor feel, with brown boards for trim, but it also had two turrets with small windows perched along the top that added a slightly Gothic touch. Several narrow windows at ground level indicated a cellar beneath the house. The home looked to be a hundred years old, maybe older. A large plate glass window, an obvious recent addition, graced the front.

"I should warn you," said Yohaba as they walked toward the house, hand in hand, "she can be a handful."

"Must be genetic," was Rulon's reply.

"Hey, watch yourself," she said, but she gave his hand an affectionate squeeze and added, "I haven't been here for three weeks. When you meet her, you'll understand why. She pretends she likes her privacy, and I go through periods where I pretend to believe her. Let me look at you."

Rulon turned to face her, and she gave him a look like a foreman eyeing a building for demolition. She straightened his jacket, resettled his Know-foam, checked the Velcro on his vest, patted his Colt through the jacket, and peeked into his pocket to see if Isabella's gun was still there.

"Are you sure you have enough weapons?" she asked facetiously. "Where's Freya? Do you want me to get it?"

"No," he said. "For old ladies, two guns are usually enough."

She socked him in the stomach in reply. Just then, her grandmother came charging from around the back of the house like an enraged mother elephant. Her arms were pumping, her loose fitting brown denim shirt billowing behind her while she trumpeted words of outrage at their trespass.

"I changed my mind. Get the hammer," he whispered. Yohaba socked him again.

"Go on! Get, get! You've no business being here. *Schnell. Schnell*," she yelled. "This isn't a place for U-turns or stopping." To Rulon's surprise, she spoke mostly English.

"Gran, Gran, it's me, Yohaba."

The old woman stopped mid-charge and peered at them through a pair of small, round spectacles that balanced precariously on the tip of her nose. In one gloved hand she held a well-used trowel, in her other hand a couple of foot-long stakes, suitable for vampires and trespassers. Upon her head sat a straw hat, held more or less in place by a sash that looped through slits in the brim and tied off in a bow beneath her chin. Her denim pants and shirt looked worn but well cared for.

She reared back as if gathering a second wind but then squinted and said, "Yohaba? Girl? Who's the double-decker bus?" She dropped the trowel and stakes into the deep pockets of her thick canvas apron and wiped her hands on the fabric.

"He's a friend, Gran. He drove me here."

"A friend, you say," she snorted. "I know what that's code for these days."

"Be good to him, Gran," entreated Yohaba. "He's a nice boy."

She looked Rulon up and down. "He looks like *two* nice boys. Has he got a name?"

At that point, Rulon broke in. "The name is Rulon Hurt, ma'am. Pleased to meet you." He stuck out his hand, and she responded with a surprisingly firm grip.

"Rulon. An unusual name," she said with a trace of authentic Swiss suspicion. "Where are you from? You've got farmer's hands."

"Born and bred in the US, in Idaho, ma'am," he answered. "My family owns six hundred acres there. We're mostly ranchers, but we have to grow feed for the cattle. I grew up riding a horse and bucking hay bales."

"Idaho," she sniffed. "I've always wanted to go there. That's where they grow those lovely potatoes. In my garden, I keep a small patch of Dittas. Have you ever heard of those?

"Yes, ma'am. Brown skin, buttery taste. Best harvested around September. Let 'em store for a few more weeks and they should be perfect for shredding up into a fine plate of *Rösti*."

"Well, you have at least one redeeming quality," said the old lady, softening, but not quite ready to let go of her cantankerous attitude. "That's more than I can say for Yohaba's other boyfriends. But, just one thing, Mr. Rulon Hurt from the US in Idaho, if we are going to get along then you need to stop calling me 'ma'am.' Every time you do, I feel a year older. Call me Gran or Granny, same as Yohaba. These eyes don't see so well anymore, but I'd have to be blind not to notice the way she looks at you. Is she pregnant or something? Is that what this visit is all about?"

"*Grandmother!*" yelled Yohaba. "You leave Rulon alone. We came here for something important. Let's go inside. You can sit down with Rulon while I make tea."

Granny peered at Rulon. "See what I had to live with when she was growing up? Bossy thing, isn't she? But we do love her." Granny turned toward the house. "Come in, you two. You're early for tea, but come in anyway."

Once inside, Yohaba veered off to the kitchen while Granny led Rulon into the house proper. As they walked down the hallway to the living room, she hooked her arm through his and affectionately patted his hand.

The living room was dimly lit by light that filtered through the front yard trees, giving the impression of late afternoon even though it was only a little past lunch time. The furniture was old, some of it antique, except for a modern brown leather reclining chair sitting in a corner. Rulon stepped inside, and the wood floor creaked, the sound muffled by the thick fabric of the room's ornate wallpaper and the equally plush upholstery of the chairs and sofa.

"Been meaning to fix that and a million other things," Granny said, still holding onto his arm.

This was a room filled with memories and echoes of late night conversations. It was full but not cluttered. As they stepped further in, Rulon brushed the tassels dangling from a lamp shade on one of the side tables. She led him to the recliner.

"This is where I usually sit," she said as she released his arm, "but I don't think any of my other chairs will hold you."

Before he sat down, he excused himself and sauntered over to the large picture window to scan the yard. He was counting on being safe at least until the following morning, but in his business, paranoia was a sign of good mental health. He didn't like the look of the dark shadows that surrounded the house. You could hide the First Armored Division in those trees. He pictured guys in ski masks and camo darting from tree to tree, surrounding the house before tossing a stun grenade through the front window. That's how he would do it.

By the time he turned around, Granny had eased herself into a delicately carved chair and was watching him. "Not much to see, is there?" she said. Rulon nodded and took his place in the recliner, angling it just a mite so he could keep an eye on the window and front door.

She asked about the ranch in Idaho; he asked her if she was English. It turned out she was Swiss, but her husband had been British. She said that in falling in love with him, she fell in love with most things British as well.

Love is like that, thought Rulon. Before he could comment, Yohaba came in with a tray laden with a traditional tea service, complete with crumpets and set it within reach on the coffee table. She then took her place in the third chair of their intimate little triangle, sitting opposite Rulon with her long legs stretched out and her attractive figure nicely delineated by her snug shirt. *She's a mighty pretty sight,* Rulon thought. And even though he could feel Gran's eyes on him like a hawk's, he couldn't keep his eyes off her granddaughter.

They sat there quietly for a few moments, and then the old lady cleared her throat and dropped a bombshell. "You're here about your great-great-grandfather's trunk, aren't you?" she asked. "Just like the Russians."

Yohaba practically jumped out of her chair. "You knew they were Russians all this time? You lied to me on the phone! You knew what I was looking for and you lied to me!"

"Not really a lie, dear," said the grandmother evenly. "I just wanted to see you. If I told you everything over the phone, you wouldn't be here now."

Yohaba crossed her legs and turned away from her grandmother. The ticking of the hall grandfather clock was clearly audible in the silence. "You still lied to me."

Rulon tried easing the situation with a little humor. "And you said your grandmother wouldn't recognize a Russian if he came in drinking vodka and singing . . . what was that again?"

"A babushka love song," muttered Yohaba.

"That's right. Well, I think you might have underestimated your dear old Granny."

Granny readjusted her position in the chair, sitting up straight with her teacup in one hand and saucer in the other, both close to her mouth, in a vain attempt to conceal her pleased smile.

"It just so happens that I was having a bad day that day," said Granny matter-of-factly between sips of tea. "I'm afraid I didn't really tell them anything. You know how we old people are. They were such nice men, though." When Yohaba still didn't turn around, she added, "Come, child, don't be silly."

With that, Yohaba uncrossed her legs and faced her. "You lied to me."

"Yes, darling, I lied to you. I'm sorry." Yohaba made a face but eventually relented. Gran then told them what had happened with the phony repairmen. As she related her story, Rulon and Yohaba prodded her along with a few questions of their own, but in the end they learned nothing new about the trunk.

When Gran was finished, Yohaba said, "Oh, no. You're not getting off that easily. We want the whole story this time about my great-great-grandfather *and* the trunk. Nothing left out. And I want the truth this time."

Granny took a deep breath. "Don't worry. No one could make

up a story like I'm about to tell you. But—"she paused and looked at them closely—"are you sure you want to hear this?"

"I love all your stories, Granny, you know that."

"That's kind of you to say so, dear. I sometimes think we spend the first half of our life doing things we wish to keep secret and the second half confessing them. Today you will hear things I've never told you before. And you, Mr. Hurt," she said, "you sit there listening so patiently, not missing a thing, with your handgun under your jacket. Did you think I wouldn't notice?" When Rulon didn't say anything, she asked, "Are you a dangerous man, Mr. Hurt?"

"Yes, ma'am," he answered.

The old woman adjusted her glasses and scrutinized him up, down, and through, but he met her unwavering gaze with a steady look of his own. "I believe you, Mr. Hurt. But you're no danger to us, I think. If you take good care of my little girl, you'll be welcome for tea and crumpets anytime. Did she tell you I raised her?"

"No, but I figured as much. I know her parents died when she was still young."

"She told you it was a car crash, didn't she? Did she say anything else?" Before he could answer, she continued. "No matter. When she's ready, she'll tell you. Mr. Hurt, do you know what the highest, truest form of love is?"

"To lay down your life for a friend," Rulon answered automatically, a habit born of childhood Sunday school lessons.

"No, Mr. Hurt. First on the list is to listen to an old woman's stories."

"Yes, Gran, but we can't appreciate your stories if you don't tell them," prodded Yohaba gently.

"That is what passes for a hint with Yohaba. Are you paying close attention, Rulon? This could save you a lot of trouble in the future." Granny put her head back and closed her eyes. "I'm stalling. Can you tell?"

"Yes," said Yohaba. "But I'm not letting you off the hook."

And so with a deep sigh and a troubled glance at both of them, Granny proceeded to fill in the missing pieces to the story of Einstein's trunk.

It began in 1902, when Einstein, while living in Switzerland, had an illegitimate daughter with Mileva Maric, the woman he later married. The child's name was Lieserl, and she was given up for adoption as soon as she was born—given to one of Mileva's friends in Serbia, far from Einstein's disapproving mother. But Lies-rl's new parents were surprisingly progressive and told her when she was twelve about her adoption and who her real father was.

She led a wild and adventurous life up until she was twenty-six, when she too had a daughter out of wedlock. Contrary to how her real parents handled things, she kept the child and sent the young man packing instead. She eventually moved to Switzerland. The child was Granny.

"But now, child," said Granny, focusing on Yohaba, "I'll trust that your maturity and love for me will mean you won't be too judgmental."

"Gran, I promise you that there is nothing you can tell me that will shock me."

"Remember that, my dear, when the time comes. Now, where was I? Oh, yes, we moved to Switzerland. I was young then, but I remember my mother becoming obsessed with learning everything she could about her real father. But she never tried to contact him, until one day, when she was thirty-three years old, she wrote to him, posing as an admirer."

Granny put one hand over her heart and the back of her other hand against her forehead, affecting a swoon as in a silent movie. "Such an admirer he never had. I think initially it had quite an effect on him, for I don't think he ever told his second wife Elsa about her. He divorced Mileva back in 1920 and by the time Mother started writing him he had remarried—Elsa, his true love. But, strangely, as far as we know, he never told her about Mother's letters. And Mother never once revealed their true relationship. I never quite understood why. I suppose the Swiss part of her saw it as too much of an intrusion into his life.

"One day, years later, my mother arranged to meet him, still as the admirer. It was 1944. She flew to New York, and they met at a restaurant in Brooklyn called *The Little Garden*. She was fifty-three and brought some of the letters he'd written her over the years. It turned out it was her age that attracted him. He had never forgotten his abandoned daughter, and here was a woman exactly his daughter's age, willing to communicate with him. He simply enjoyed writing to her and sharing his work. It was as if he needed to prove that he could be a father to someone his daughter's age. Quite touching, really."

"Where were you, Grandma, when all this was happening?" asked Yohaba, leaning forward and brushing a few strands of hair from her face. "You must have been twenty-seven at the time." By now, Yohaba had pulled her chair next to Rulon's, and they were holding hands again.

"I was in the restaurant with them," answered Granny. "Albert wanted to meet me too, and so my mother took me along. About an hour after we got there, three men showed up. Two of them were much older than me, but one was much younger, a mere boy, really. It turns out your great-great-grandfather was trying to set me up. He was hoping one of the two older men would marry me. It sounds sweet now, but at the time I was horrified. At least initially.

"Now, I'll spare you both the lurid details, but I ended up having a baby by one of those men. When I realized I was pregnant two months later, I married Basil, your step-grandfather, I suppose you would call him. I told him everything before we were married. He was a special man.

"Now, I'm sure you've figured this out already. The baby was your mother. And Albert referred to those men as his three stars. One of them is your true grandfather, and based on what those two Russian men were asking me, and based on what you said, I'll bet those protégés of his were the men he gave the trunk to before he died."

There was no other sound except for the ticking clock and the clinking of china as Granny sipped her tea. At the words, "The baby was your mother," Yohaba gripped Rulon's hand with a strength he didn't know she had. Now Yohaba sat there, leaning back, quietly processing the revelation. She could barely remember the man who all her life she thought of as her grandfather. He had died when she was four. A kind smile and the sweet smell of his pipe tobacco. That is what she remembered most.

Rulon sat there not believing their luck. Only a few questions needed to be answered, and then this case was a wrap. He posed the first question after a suitably respectful pause. "And do you know their names?"

"Well, I should know at least one of their names, don't you think?" Grandma teased, looking at him over the tops of her glasses.

"No offense, Granny," he said. He waited a few polite beats, but the old woman wasn't forthcoming, so he bluntly urged, "Can you tell us the names, then? We need to know."

"Grandma!" said Yohaba. "Stop teasing Rulon.

"Sorry, dear. It's just that your friend looks so earnest. I couldn't resist tweaking him. Bring me my scrapbook. The blue one next to the bed." A minute later they were all sitting on the couch together with Granny in the middle and an open scrapbook on her lap.

Granny gently flipped the cover and the book opened to two pages displaying five faded news clippings, and a few photographs of Einstein. One photo showed Einstein in front of a restaurant, in the company of three men and two women. "This is me," said Granny proudly, pointing to the younger of the two women in the picture. "Beautiful, wasn't I, Rulon? Makes you wonder how I stayed single all that time."

"Yes, you were beautiful," he said. And he wasn't just being polite. She was regally tall like Yohaba and had the same facial contours and confident posture.

"Which one is he?" asked Yohaba.

Granny gave a resigned sigh. "Oh, I wasn't looking forward to this. Rulon, close your eyes." He obliged. Then he heard her say, "This is him."

There was a long pause, then Yohaba gasped. "*Grandmother!*" she exclaimed in genuine horror. Rulon heard the sounds of the scrapbook transferring from Granny's lap to Yohaba's. A few more moments of silence ensued, resoundingly broken by, "A *priest*?"

It took every ounce of his self-control, but somehow Rulon kept his eyes shut.

"I was afraid something like this would happen," said Granny with irritation. "Oh, open your eyes, Rulon. I don't know why I bothered."

The first thing he noticed was the expression on Yohaba's face. Her lips were pursed, and she stared blankly ahead. The scrapbook was back on Granny's lap. Rulon looked at the picture again. It was grainy and faded, but now that he was looking for it, he could plainly see the telltale splash of white under the coat collar of the man on the far left.

"Now I know where Yohaba gets her nose," he said, trying to lighten the atmosphere. At that, Yohaba got up off the couch with a huff and began pacing back and forth.

"My grandfather is a Father . . . I-I mean a priest," she said heatedly, stopping in front of her grandmother. "My entire family history is a web of lies!" Having made her point, she went back to pacing.

"No, no," said Grandma, "it's not that sordid. He was a Jesuit scholastic teaching at Fordham University. He hadn't taken his vows yet."

Yohaba stopped her pacing and demanded, "He looks like a baby. How old was he? Tell me the truth."

"Come sit down first." Yohaba plopped back down on the coach and hunched over with her elbows on her knees and her chin resting on her hands. Granny put her arm around her and stroked her hair. "Don't be mad at me. It turned out all right in the end. What a blessing you and your mother were, rest her soul. What would I have done without the two of you in my life?"

"But did you have wait to tell me all this in front of Rulon? He already thinks I'm weird enough."

"Well, to be fair, you were the one that blurted it out." Yohaba sniffled. Rulon grabbed a tissue box from the end table and handed it to Granny.

"No crying, dear," she said. "You promised you wouldn't be shocked. Would you like to hear the rest of the story?" She took a tissue and dabbed Yohaba's tears.

Trying to be helpful, Rulon said, "Give her some math to do. That will snap her out of it."

Granny glared at him for an instant but persevered with her explanation. "The man was going to leave the order anyway. I think for him, the whole ordeal was like Cortes burning his boats." At that, Yohaba let out a groan.

* * *

The scrapbook was now on the coffee table, and Yohaba's head had found its way to Granny's lap. Slowly and gently, Gran rubbed Yohaba's brow. Rulon sat quietly, watching a scene he was sure had been repeated many times since the death of Yohaba's mother. In a strange way, it seemed like a sacred moment.

"We were both as innocent as goldfish about the whole thing," said Grandma with a giggle. "To answer your question, he was twenty years old and already had his Ph.D. in computer science, one of the very first. He later chaired the committee that produced the report titled, oh I forget. Read it for us, will you Rulon, dear? It's in the article about that Gore fellow."

Rulon took the scrapbook off the coffee table and did a quick scan. " 'Toward a National Research Network.' Hey, listen to this: It's what influenced Senator Al Gore to introduce the High Performance Computing Act of 1991. It's what essentially got the Internet going big time. Well, I'll be horn-swoggled." He looked up and said to Yohaba, "What do you think of that; you've got the bloodlines of a Kentucky Derby winner."

Still resting on Granny's lap, Yohaba turned her head. "I guess that means if we have children, they'll be Nobel Prize winning sumo wrestlers."

The girl had a habit of saying things that left Rulon both mystified and tongue-tied.

"I'm not fat," he said pleasantly. Then the implications occurred to him of what he'd objected to in Yohaba's statement and what he had tacitly accepted. He noticed Granny and Yohaba looking at him oddly and decided to beat a graceful retreat by offering to make some more tea. He left for the kitchen with the scrapbook under his arm.

While waiting for the water to boil, he went through the old album and put together the story of the three shining stars from articles, pictures, and little notes written in the margins by Granny in a penmanship style so precise it almost looked typed.

The three amigos were Michael Ferris, thirty-eight; Leonard Steenberg the Jesuit, twenty, both computer scientists; and Simon Whitehouse, a thirty-five-year-old electrical engineer. One note in particular caught his eye. On October 10, 1954, seven months before his death, Einstein and his three stars had met on the campus of the City College of New York, where Steenberg, a full professor at Fordham, was a guest lecturer. At that meeting, the note said, they discussed an undertaking that was "bigger than the Manhattan project."

Within ten years of that meeting, the three scientists had collaborated on the discovery and implementation of packet switching. Soon Whitehouse developed the first packet-switched network, ARPANET. After that, it was only a matter of time before the development of the Worldwide Web and Internet. Later, Whitehouse also founded Metricom, the first wireless Internet company. Ferris, the other older gentleman, had worked on Britain's nuclear program during World War II.

As for Steenberg, he later chaired the famous committee that influenced Gore's legislation. In fact, as one of the head scientists at CERN, he was the mastermind behind the world-wide web, and more recently, he had helped design the GEANT, the pan-European multi-gigabit research network. He also started the European Very Long Baseline Interferometry Network, a group of fourteen radio telescopes that carry out astronomical observations. His design enabled those fourteen telescopes to mimic a single telescope thousands of miles in diameter. The guy was a regular Leonardo da Vinci. But of most interest to Rulon was the fact that of Einstein's three stars, only Steenberg, Yohaba's grandfather, was still alive. He was seventy-five years old and, at one time, he lived in the Geneva area, a mere three-hour drive from Zurich. With any luck, he'd still be there.

Rulon lifted his eyes from the scrapbook. Things seemed too easy, but sometimes life worked that way. The kettle had boiled and turned itself off ten minutes ago. All was quiet in the living room. Deep in thought, Rulon happened to look through the kitchen window toward the BMW. As he did, a movement in the dim light caught his eye, and suddenly he was at full alert.

In the semi-darkness, he saw someone walking around the car, pulling at the passenger door. A single figure, but he knew there had to be more. He had hoped it would take longer for them to react to Isabella being out of the picture. She'd made it to a phone quicker than he expected. He pulled out the Colt, quietly chambered a round, and removed the safety. He had a sick feeling in his stomach that there was going to be a gunfight, and he wondered how fast the police could get to Gran's rural property. He pushed through the kitchen's swinging door into the living room.

"Where's the phone?" he asked. His cell phone was in the car. He did his best to sound nonchalant, but there must have been something in his tone that sounded a warning. Yohaba slowly lifted her head off Granny's lap and sat up.

"What is it?" she asked, a tinge of fear in her voice.

"We've got company outside," he said grimly. She read his expression and then her eyes moved to the gun hanging at his side. She quickly turned to Granny.

"Where is he? Is he in his room?" she asked, slightly panicked.

"I thought he was," said Granny. Then she looked at Rulon. "Don't do anything rash." With that, Yohaba and Granny rushed to the back of the house. Then came the sound of doors opening and slamming. A moment later Yohaba came rushing back with Granny in her slipstream.

"How many people did you see?" asked Yohaba breathlessly as Granny rushed off to another part of the house.

By now Rulon was peering out the large front window from behind the curtain. He said, "Just one. What's up?"

"I've got an older brother. He's very curious, but he's harmless. He's not in his room. It's got to be him." She started to go outside, but Rulon grabbed her arm.

"Whoever he is, he's in the car now," he said. "Take a look from here. Tell me what you see."

Yohaba cupped her eyes to see through the window glare. "It's him," she yelled. "Grandma, it's him." She headed for the door, but he stopped her again and said, "No, me first."

Gun in hand, Rulon led the way outside. Granny caught up to them halfway along the path. When they reached the car, Yohaba's brother was sitting in the driver's seat, fooling with the buttons.

They all three stood in the deep shade around the car, the brother still oblivious to their presence. Yohaba grabbed Rulon's hand.

"Welcome to the nuthouse," she whispered.

"Stop that, Yohaba," hissed her grandmother. "It's not his fault." Granny opened the car door, and the man didn't react. By now he was fooling with the turn signals, flipping them left and right, on and off.

"Come on now, Alex," said Granny. "You know you don't belong in there."

"This is a BMW 320i," he said. "It takes regular unleaded and has a top speed of 153 miles per hour. Weighs 4,200 pounds. Has a 3.2 liter engine and the highest rated GPS on the market. Who does it belong to?"

"That would be me," said Rulon.

Alex got out of the car and immediately put his hands in his pants pockets. He was a few inches shorter than Yohaba, maybe five-five if he stood up straight. Perhaps one-twenty soaking wet. His slacks and shirt were impeccably ironed. His blue eyes were clear, but he wouldn't make eye contact. Rulon held out his hand, but Alex ignored it. He didn't look mentally handicapped, but there was definitely something strange about him. His eyes constantly shifted.

"Sorry. I've never been in one before," he said in a voice so soft Rulon had to strain to hear. "Are you my sister's new boyfriend?"

In a flash, Rulon thought of all the possible answers and all the trouble they would get him into. He took the path of least resistance. "Yes," he said.

Yohaba sidled up closer and whispered, "You take a lot for granted, cowboy," but she gave him an affectionate squeeze all the same.

"That's a Colt .45 caliber Gold Cup Trophy, isn't it?" Alex asked.

Well now, Rulon thought, *the man knows his hardware.*

Alex continued: "Five-inch match-grade barrel. Eight-round magazine. A competition automatic." Rulon was downright impressed. Then Alex said, "The safety is off. Don't you know how to handle a pistol?" and Rulon's good feelings evaporated.

Rulon started to say something, but Yohaba squeezed his arm to stop him. Rulon shrugged the whole thing off, safetied the piece, and holstered it. After all, the guy was right.

"Are you a cop?" Alex asked.

"No," he said, "but I'm licensed to carry a gun."

"Hi, sis," said Alex, ignoring Rulon and focusing on Yohaba.

"Hi Alex," responded Yohaba without enthusiasm.

"Why doesn't this car have an internal trunk release?" he asked, turning his attention to the car again. At that point Granny intervened and shuffled everyone inside.

* * *

The sun was on its downward arc. Isabella was cold, hungry, and exhausted. Jimmy Choo high heels were not made for walking down country roads. Over the last two hours, she had resolutely hiked five miles in her stylish red pumps until a heel snapped.

Now she rested against a tree with the offending heel in her hand. She flipped it lightly a few times then threw it with every ounce of her strength at a group of cows on the other side of a nearby fence. It hit a cow on the side, and the cow didn't even blink; he just continued on with its patient ruminations. While completely absorbed in this pastoral metaphor for cosmic indifference, Isabella reached absently into her purse for her gun, but caught herself when she remembered where it was. The memory whipped her into a cold, blind fury that she focused like a laser on a certain red neck, in-bred, hillbilly farm boy named Rulon Hurt.

She pushed herself off the tree and stomped off, taking ten unbalanced steps before stopping again. Teetering awkwardly on one foot, she reached down to snatch off her good shoe. Letting out a mighty scream, she ripped the heel off of that one, too. She'd gone only a few more steps before suddenly turning and hurling the second heel viciously in the direction of the oblivious cows.

Isabella stood there with her hands on her hips, breathing heavily. Her second throw hadn't even cleared the fence. Her sweaty, disheveled hair flopped over her face like a sheep dog's, and she flipped it back so she could see. Last night, Dmitry had told her through his broken mouth that he'd slipped the leash on the three Serbian brothers. If only she could be there when they found Rulon. But then, they always made videos. She'd bring the popcorn. The thought of revenge drove her legs like pistons as she slipped and slid her way toward a farmhouse up ahead.

14

"I AM CONVINCED THAT HE DOES NOT PLAY DICE."
—EINSTEIN

THE NEXT MORNING, AFTER BREAKFAST, RULON SPENT SOME one-on-one time with Granny around the handmade rough-hewn kitchen table, coaching her on what to say if the Russians came back again. His advice was to just act batty and pretend to mistake them for long lost relatives.

Lesson complete, he started to get up, but she asked him to stay, saying she had something important to discuss. He was in a hurry to get back to Zurich, but it was hard to refuse, especially when she grabbed his arm and wouldn't let go. She'd already been out in her garden that morning. There was dirt under her fingernails, and she was wearing her thick gardening apron.

"It's about Yohaba," she began, her voice so low he had to lean closer to hear. At this point she also craned her neck to look down the hall. "She'd kill me if she knew I was talking to you about this." When she said that, Rulon started fidgeting a mite, resolving at the same time to hightail it out of there at the first mention of the word *feelings*.

"Oh, settle down," she said, grouchy and irritated at his obvious discomfort. "I'm not going to ask you what your intentions are with the girl, for heaven's sake. Just listen. I see the way she looks at you." She shook her head slightly, closed her eyes, and sighed; the expression on Rulon's face was proving a major obstacle. After a few deep breaths, she opened her eyes and forged onward. "You probably can't tell, but that's because you haven't known her as long as I have, and you haven't seen her with other men. She is incredibly loyal to the people she loves. And she has a code. She's just like you that way. So please, don't think she is so different." Rulon didn't say anything, but Granny had his full attention. She was losing a little of her self-control. She'd been annoyed before, but now her face was roiling with emotion.

"That's all I wanted to say. Oh, I could say more. I could tell you that she loves you fiercely, but I think you already know that. But promise me one thing: promise me you'll protect her, no matter what. You're strong, and I'm not asking this lightly. Can you do that for an old woman?" Her eyes brimmed with tears, and she trembled as she urged the promise upon him.

Rulon didn't hesitate. "You have my word," he said. She squeezed his arm hard. He smiled at her, and she tried smiling back but then just broke down, deep sobs racking her body. He took her in his arms, not saying a word.

They sat there for a good minute, and then Granny got up quickly and wiped her eyes with her sleeve. "No fool like an old fool, right, Rulon?" she said, taking off down the hallway.

Rulon went in the opposite direction, out the front door to the car. The bug checker was in the glove box, and he took it out and did a check. Still clean. Yohaba joined him just as he was finishing up. A few minutes later, Granny and Alex came out, and everyone said their good-byes.

This time, Rulon took a more direct route back to Zurich. He was pleasantly surprised to find no one following them. Soon after they started out, he dumped Isabella's cell phone into a garbage truck parked on the side of the road, figuring that would lead any pursuers on a merry chase.

Despite having gone to bed reasonably early, Rulon hadn't gotten much sleep. Before Yohaba said good night, she told him that he and Alex would be sharing a room and then casually mentioned that Alex had Asperger's Syndrome. When he asked her what that was, she patted his cheek and said not to worry—he would be an expert by the morning. "Just don't let him talk your ear off," she said and kissed him lightly on the cheek.

Sure enough, Alex yakked for hours. He chatted on about Russian serial killers, the migratory patterns of butterflies, and why Newton was the greatest mathematician of all time. Rulon would've told him to pipe down, but he didn't have the heart, and besides, he was kind of interesting.

"Alex really likes you," said Yohaba, breaking their companionable silence. On her lap was her grandmother's scrapbook.

"What's the problem?" he asked. "He seemed a little strange, but not crazy."

"Asperger's is hard to understand," she said. "He's a genius, but very impractical. He can't hold a job. He can't plan. He has difficulty feeling empathy for other people. He eventually gets in fights with anyone who isn't as smart as him, which is everyone. Even at the university, he makes the professors feel like morons. He can be extremely cruel to people sometimes without meaning to. He just says what he's thinking. Some days you think he could be designing the space station, and other days he can't brush his teeth. I think he's getting worse as he gets older."

Rulon asked, "Does he believe reptiles rule the Earth?"

Yohaba looked at him and smirked. They had been holding hands again as usual, his hand on the gearshift, her hand on his. "No," she said emphatically. "And neither do I, for your information."

"So you think they are only partially in control?" asked Rulon, keeping it light.

Instead of rising to the bait, she turned serious. "You think I'm weird, don't you?" She removed her hand. *Uh-oh.*

"Yeah, pretty much," he said. "But that doesn't mean I don't like you." *Where was she going with this?*

"Why?" she asked. "Why do you think I'm weird? Be serious. I want to know. And don't tell me it's the nose ring or something superficial like that."

Rulon pretended to be thinking hard. "It's the nose ring," he finally said. When she didn't laugh, he tried to recover. "No. Seriously, I'm used to it by now. But since you mention it, is it about getting attention or just about being rebellious?"

"Some guys think it looks good."

"They only say that because they think it's a sign you're easy." The look on her face told him he'd said the wrong thing, and he immediately started backpedaling. "Come on, you've been around. Who were these guys telling you it looked good? How many of them tried something afterward?" Yohaba turned away and nervously bit her lip.

After a few miles, she turned back to him. "Then how come we like each other so much if we're so different?"

"I think you like me because I bailed out your bacon a couple of times. Women are programmed to go for Alpha males. They want protection."

"Some women, maybe. But I like you for more reasons than that. Why do you like me?"

"Your have wide hips," he said drily. "Good for birthing man-child."

Yohaba smacked the dashboard and shouted angrily, "Can't you just be serious for once?"

Rulon let out a deep sigh. "Why?" he asked. "Why talk about this stuff?" To him this was like pouring lemon juice on a paper cut.

She turned in her seat belt so she could face him better and pleaded, "Please, Rulon. Just tell me. I know you don't like my nose ring. Most guys think I'm hot, you know. But as soon as they find out how smart I am, they run away. Everybody thinks I'm weird."

"They're idiots," he said, angry that someone would hurt her. He thought about what he was going to say next and then sighed again. "Are you sure you want to hear this?"

She nodded eagerly.

"Okay then. I don't know why I like you."

"That doesn't even make sense," she said softly, looking away again.

"What more do you want?" he snapped. He hated these conversations Trying to define a relationship never ended well. "Okay, fine. You're honest and brave and adventurous. You're funny. And you're smart. I like all of that. And you're beautiful. I'm not blind, okay? You're beautiful." He took his eyes off the road to look at her and saw that she was crying. He searched his feelings. What *did* he feel about her? The two of them were so different. She sat there crying so softly he could hardly hear her. He noticed her shoulders shaking, and his heart broke.

"Please don't cry," he said, scrambling desperately for the right words. "I'm thirty-one and not married. Where I come from, that tells you a lot. You think you know me, but you don't. I told you my mother died when I was young. I have problems trusting women." Yohaba started to say something through her tears, but he cut her off. "No, just listen. Can you do that for me?" She nodded, sniffled, and wiped her eyes with the back of her sleeve, just like her grandmother. He waited until she was done. "But there is something about *you* I trust. When this is over, I'd like for us to spend time together. I think we connect. The truth is, I think of you as a friend. Maybe that sounds funny coming from a guy, but it means a lot to me. And I don't mean 'just a friend. Do you understand what I'm saying? I'd like to see where this goes."

"Me too," she said through her sniffles and a few last tears. She looked at him with swollen eyes and a brave smile. His heart was in his throat, and maybe he should have said something more, but the words didn't come. Ten miles down the road, her hand found his on the gearshift. He felt good again. Actions always speak louder than words.

15

"SOMETIMES ONE PAYS MOST FOR THE THINGS ONE GETS FOR NOTHING." —EINSTEIN

A FEW MILES OUTSIDE OF ZURICH, YOHABA TOLD RULON ABOUT the car crash that killed her mother and father. It turned out Alex had been driving. Her parents could never accept that he wasn't like other boys. He had very poor motor coordination, and despite his amazing intellect, Yohaba said he didn't have the common sense of a fence post.

One day, when he was seventeen, their parents took him out along a country road, trying to get him comfortable with driving before he actually took his official lessons. From what the police said, the car hadn't gone two hundred yards with Alex behind the wheel before it crashed into a tree at high speed. There wasn't a single skid mark. Alex almost died too. Sometimes Yohaba wished he had.

They arrived in Zurich about noon. It was Sunday, and Rulon felt bad about missing church. He took the back streets to his apartment, taking his time because he was still trying to decide if going there was a smart thing to do. They came through Meierhofplatz just a block from the Desperado, and he was struck with a Pavlovian desire for Mexican food. He gave it a miss, though, as he didn't like to eat out or shop on Sunday if he could help it.

Going back to the apartment would be tricky. He had to assume it was being watched. But on Sundays in Zurich, most people were at home or outside with their kids. And he figured the Russians would have to be pretty stupid to try something in broad daylight. He kicked the idea around for a few more minutes and decided to take a chance.

They came slowly up Reinhold-Frei Strasse. He parked in an

open patch of ground by the field connected to the next-door grade school. From there he could view the entire length of the street as well as his apartment block. He and Yohaba sat together, watching for a few minutes. She tried to entice him into cutting short his surveillance by offering to cook a meal once they were inside, but he wouldn't budge. Finally, deciding it was safe, he told Yohaba the rules: Stay in the car. Stay alert. Honk if she sensed trouble. Wait for him to come back.

The sun was shining—it was a beautiful day. He walked along the gravel to the street. A nearby tree provided convenient cover. He stood behind it for a few minutes, nonchalantly watching and waiting. OCD had originally chosen this apartment block for a lot of good tactical reasons. There were several exit and entry points, good lines of sight, good counter-surveillance vantage points like this tree, and plenty of nosy neighbors. And when it wasn't lunch time like it was now, lots of kids played outside, which meant lots of parents wary of strangers. Also, it was hard to make a hit here and get away cleanly; there were too many twisting, narrow streets, plus two annoying speed cameras between his block and the main road. Rulon wasn't foolhardy enough to let down his guard, but he felt reasonably satisfied that coming back here was low risk. During the next few minutes, he performed his usual efficient reconnaissance routine and then returned to Yohaba.

He found her reading the BMW's driver manual. He tapped on the window, and she rolled it down. "Hey, I thought I told you to stay alert in there," he said. "I'm going up to the apartment to check things out. I'll be back in ten minutes."

The underground garage was a good way to enter the apartment block undetected, so that's where he headed. He slipped his key into the keyhole atop the three-foot stanchion just outside the garage and watched as the wide, creaky door slid slowly open. He stepped inside and waited for the motion sensors to turn on the lights. Behind him, the garage door slowly and noisily closed.

Just before it shut, though, he heard the revving of an engine and tires crunching gravel. Then the door closed, and he stood there in semi-darkness. *Nah, can't be.* But life on a ranch taught him to take nothing for granted, so he waved his hand in front of the overhead sensor and triggered the door opener. As soon as the door slid open a crack, he slipped outside, not really expecting anything, but ready nonetheless.

The driveway was lined with bushes on either side, obscuring his view until he could get past them. He double-timed back to the elementary school and was relieved to find the Beemer still there. He wasn't going to be satisfied, though, until he had a clear shot of Yohaba. As he walked toward the car, he couldn't see her yet. A ripple of anxiety shivered through him. Maybe she was bent over, looking through the glove box for something else to read. He swore under his breath. He had told her to stay alert. He picked up the pace. He was ten feet away now. Eagle talons sunk through his stomach. Still no Yohaba. He panicked and ran to the car. For a split second, he thought he saw her smiling at him through the glare of the windshield, but the image quickly dissolved. She was gone.

The passenger door was ajar, and the driver's side window was smashed, leaving a thousand glass fragments on the floor. Granny's scrapbook lay open on the seat. Rolled up in one of the cup holders was a sheet of paper. He grabbed it and read the hastily scrawled note. It said that he was to come alone to the tower at the top of the Uetliberg at 3:00 p.m. or they would do unspeakable things to the girl before killing her.

Rulon stood there, stunned. He was used to playing in the big leagues. He'd steeled himself over the years to dishing it out but also to taking it, if it ever came to that. But this was different. He looked at the empty seat where Yohaba had been and pictured her struggling. He pictured the men and what they must be like.

He immediately knew he would go to the tower and trade himself for her if there was no other way. Then the words of the note came back to him, and something snapped inside him. In a volcanic instant, he went white hot.

And then the adrenaline kicked in.

They think I'm heading up to the apartment. They think I won't be back for a few more minutes. They'll take it slow past the speed cameras. I can catch them.

He jumped in the car and drove like a wild man. He tripped off both speed cameras going over ninety through a twenty zone. He could get thrown in prison for driving those speeds in Switzerland, but he never even blinked. By the time he was on the main road, he was doing a hundred and ten. What kind of car would they have? If Yohaba was in the trunk, how would he know which car?

He drove on the wrong side of the road up Regensdorferstrasse, trying to spot a car with at least two men inside. He pictured men like the ones from the Desperado. He pictured them laughing at her while she cursed them as they held her down. He didn't even know which way they had turned. He was going on pure instinct.

Going four times the speed of the cars around him, he swung into the wrong lane to pass a white Volvo station wagon and saw oncoming traffic up ahead. He saw they had a place to turn out and just figured they'd do the right thing. As he sped up to the Volvo, he caught a glimpse of auburn hair in the cargo area. Was that Yohaba lifting her head? They were headed into the Hönggerberg forest. Was that really her? He had a nanosecond to decide.

At that instant, the driver of the Volvo saw him, and his eyes went wide in recognition. He started to brake. In his previous life, Rulon had ridden bulls for money, been a national class hammer thrower, and a collegiate finalist Greco-Roman wrestler. But none of those skills held a candle to how he could shoot. He was hell-on-wheels with a gun. In an adrenaline-charged flash, he drew the Colt and shot the driver through the window, dead square in the center of his forehead. It was the best shot of his life.

Cars spilled off both sides of the road. Rulon fishtailed all over. In his rear-view mirror, he saw the Volvo bounce off a few trees and then roll to a stop in a thicket a few feet into the forest. He did a quick U-turn and floored it back to the banged-up Volvo.

He came out of the car with his gun drawn, extended in front of him at chin level in a two-handed grip. The surviving thug was already out. He had Yohaba in front of him as a shield, one beefy, hairy forearm around her neck, shaking her like a terrier shaking a rat to get her under control. In his other hand he had a gun pressed hard against her head. Her eyes were big, and her mouth gaped open, the terror plainly visible on her face. Rulon kept walking toward them without saying a word. The guy was taller than Rulon by a head, dressed all in black, and had one big, ugly, unshaven mug.

"I swear, I'll kill her!" the man screamed in High German. His face didn't look right. It was mangled and contorted with fear and anguish. Tears and blood streamed down his cheeks. Rulon kept walking toward him and stopped five yards away.

"You killed my brother, man!" the Serb cried. "You killed my brother! I'm going to kill you, man! Put the gun down, or I'll kill the girl right in front of you!" He wrenched Yohaba's head back. She tried to say something, to tell Rulon no, but the words were strangled out of her.

Rulon waited for the guy to get it out of his system. Then in a quiet rage, he said, "You just saw what I did to your brother just now. You really think I can't make this shot?" The guy's eyes darted to Rulon, the Volvo, and the other stopped cars in panic. "I have an idea," Rulon said evenly, wanting the man to believe he had a way out of this. "*You* put *your* gun down, and *I* don't kill *you*." He gave Rulon a slightly puzzled look, and Rulon roared at the top of his lungs, "Now! Or you die!"

The man dropped his gun like it burned his hand and released Yohaba, letting her slump to the ground. Rulon advanced. Yohaba was on her hands and knees coughing. The kidnapper backed up, slowly at first then faster and faster. Rulon yelled, "*Halt! Jetzt!*" and the man froze. Rulon walked towards him, the Colt pointed at his head.

When he was within arm's length, Rulon paused for a second. The kidnapper's left eye was ruined, and the rest of his face was bleeding from a dozen small cuts, some very deep. From glass fragments or his brother's bone chips, Rulon had no idea, and he didn't much care.

Up close, even through his disfigurement, the man's face told a story of a lifetime of abuse and cruelty. But whatever swaggering bravado he previously had was gone. Now he was on the receiving end, and it didn't feel so good. Where did they find these people?

Rulon motioned with his gun, and the man got down on his knees. He pleaded with Rulon not to kill him, totally incoherent, mixing languages and blubbering, the sounds seeming to reach Rulon's ears from far away. Rulon's furnace was still roaring. He put the muzzle of the gun against the guy's chest and pushed him onto his back. Everything slowed down. Rulon planted his foot on his chest, pinning him to the ground.

For three days now, Rulon had been sparing people, and it had gotten him nothing but trouble. And now he'd crossed a line he'd hoped never to cross. He'd killed a man. The brother clutched at Rulon's foot and closed his sobbing eyes, but tears still bubbled through. It was going to take more than his useless tears to save him. The hammer came back on the Colt.

As these thoughts spun through Rulon's head, and as he pointed the gun at the kidnapper's chest, even he didn't know where those cosmic tumblers were going to stop. In the midst of his hesitation, he caught a whiff of Yohaba's perfume mixed with the smell of the discharged gun, a strange blend he would never forget.

From far away, he heard a woman's voice. "Come on, Cowboy. Stampede's over." Then there was Yohaba at his side, pulling on his arm. "It's time to go home. Come on." He shrugged her off and continued to stare menacingly down at her kidnapper. She came right back. "Don't, Rulon. Please don't. Not because of me." She was pleading now, pulling with all her strength. "Rulon, it's Sunday," she yelled. "You won't even *shop* on Sunday."

For some crazy reason, her words got through to him. The floodgates opened, and his mind swamped with the old Sunday School lessons he'd grown up with and that his dad had hammered into him over the years. *Vengeance is mine. With what judgment ye judge, ye shall be judged. Live by the sword, die by the sword.*

That didn't mean he was letting the guy off the hook. He grabbed him by his greasy hair and pulled him half off the ground. Their eyes locked for a long second, then he told him, "I don't want to ever see you again." Rulon let the words sink in. As the implication of what he'd said slowly hit him, a visible look of relief animated the brother's face.

He got to enjoy the experience for only a second, because Rulon buffaloed him viciously with the Colt, laying the barrel hard and flush against his head just above and behind his left ear. He went immediately limp. When Rulon released his hold, the man hit the ground like a sack of grain. At that point, out of habit, Rulon ejected the old clip and replaced it with a full one from his jacket pocket. He holstered his gun and took a deep breath. He looked up and wanted to breathe in the entire sky, anything to put out the fire within.

Yohaba came up and put her arms around him, stroked his head, and whispered, "I knew you'd come. Look what they made you do."

Never taking his eyes off the unconscious man at his feet, Rulon said harshly, "I didn't want to lose you." She reached up and kissed him softly, touching his lips in a way that told him she was his. He had one arm around her waist, and he pulled her close in reply, telling her that was okay with him.

Bright sun shone through the trees, and whether it was the warmth of the sun making Rulon feel good or some feeling for him that he felt rising out of Yohaba, he didn't know for sure. He just knew it felt good. He closed his eyes, faced heavenward, and took in a deep breath. His fire at last had burned itself out.

16

"ANY MAN WHO CAN DRIVE SAFELY WHILE KISSING A PRETTY GIRL IS SIMPLY NOT GIVING THE KISS THE ATTENTION IT DESERVES." —EINSTEIN

DESPITE THE EMOTIONAL DRAIN, RULON'S TACTICAL SENSE hadn't deserted him. "Gotta skedaddle," he said to Yohaba. When she looked at him puzzled, he said, "Scram, vamoose. You know—cops."

"But you were in the right. You were saving me."

"It'll all get cleared up eventually, but it's better this way for now. Trust me." He didn't want to face the cops until the consulate was blocking for him.

He grabbed the unconscious brother by an ankle and dragged him through the mud and pine needles back to the Volvo. He propped him up next to his dead brother in the front seat, a present for the police. He went back to retrieve the dropped gun, picking it up carefully with his handkerchief so as to not leave prints. Its disassembled parts got thrown in the back seat. It had been exactly six minutes since he shot the brother.

Almost as if they appeared out of nowhere, he was suddenly conscious of people across the road, standing beside their cars watching. A few of them were on their cell phones. One guy called over to Rulon and asked if he was the police. Rulon yelled back in Schwyzerdütsch that this was a hostage situation and tried to imply he was the police without actually saying so. He wanted to stop any interference without chalking up another felony.

Traffic moved slowly on the road in both directions. Flares were out. There had been other accidents, and Rulon was truly sorry. He hoped no one was hurt.

As they walked back to the Beemer, he sensed Yohaba starting to sag, so he scooped her up and carried her in his arms. While holding her, he glanced back at the Volvo and the dead man slumped over the steering wheel. A few minutes ago he was alive. What choices had he made in life to bring him to this end? An arrogant thought—*he chose to mess with me and came out second best.* But Rulon quickly rejected that. Certain rules governed all life, and eventually those laws catch up with everyone without exception. He was grateful, but he knew this was one scene that would be hard to shake. Knowing himself, he feared what was coming.

When he reached the Beemer, he laid Yohaba gently in the passenger seat and buckled her in. She'd been walking fine, so he knew there couldn't be too much wrong with her. Nevertheless, before he got in the car, he checked her over for injuries. She touched his cheek as he did so and looked up at him with slightly glazed eyes and smiled wearily.

"You done good, cowboy," she said, the exhaustion evident in her voice. "You take good care of me. I'll be all right. I'm sorry I'm such a baby. I'm just feeling a little weird right now, that's all. I've never seen anyone shot in the head before."

He remember how she had jabbered like a magpie after the luggage store, but now she was quiet. This was a few notches tougher. He worried she was going into shock, but she assured him again she was okay. Her color looked good. He reached for her carotid artery and felt her pulse. It was strong.

Rulon knew that unless a person was used to it, witnessing a violent death, especially at such close range, can be a terrible shock. No matter how nonchalantly people reacted in the movies, in real life most people are unsettled for days, and some never get over it. He finished examining Yohaba. As far as he could tell, she was unscathed—on the outside. They drove away at a normal speed.

He thought about ditching the car but rejected the idea for now. New license plates would serve just as well. He thought again about turning himself in. But he rejected that too—for now.

Rulon knew he should contact Magnus. In fact, he wondered why Magnus hadn't called when he was first laid off. When Magnus found out he'd killed a guy, Rulon knew what he'd say. About some things, he was so predictable. But not about everything. *What would Magnus do in this situation*?

Rulon had a flash of inspiration. He should visit Dmitry in the hospital and work out a truce. But first he needed a new set of license plates.

Ten minutes later, Rulon was driving his blue BMW, a common enough car in Switzerland, but with plates he'd swapped off a Volkswagen Jetta parked at a trail head just off the forest road. They headed for the south side of the Zurich lake to the hospital Dmitry had joked about sending Rulon. He was willing to bet his last paycheck that's where Dmitry was.

But after just a few minutes, Rulon couldn't help pulling over so he could kiss Yohaba. Before he knew it, they were pulling apart in mutual surprise and breathing hard. *Man,* he thought, *even BMWs don't accelerate that fast.* He looked at her, and she looked back, shaking her head ever so slightly, reminding him that he didn't really want to do this. He sat there looking at her while his reptilian brain and his moral side struggled for control. He reached out and gently rubbed her cheek with the back of his hand. She didn't flinch, and all the time her eyes never left his.

Finally, Yohaba let out a sigh. "What I do for love," she said. She took his hand and placed it firmly on the steering wheel. "Just drive, you idiot."

17

"PEACE CANNOT BE ACHIEVED THROUGH VIOLENCE; IT CAN ONLY BE ATTAINED THROUGH UNDERSTANDING."
—EINSTEIN

HOW DO YOU KNOW IF SOMEONE REALLY LOVES YOU? OR IF someone is trustworthy enough for you to love in return? Rulon had often asked himself those questions and decided that in the end each person had to find his own answers. For him, the answer to the first question came down to sacrifice. He knew if he found a woman who was willing to sacrifice herself, and he didn't necessarily mean sacrificing her life or anything else so dramatic, but if she was willing to sacrifice a need, a goal, or even something she wanted because she knew it was important to him, well, that's what real love was all about. And if she helped him be a better a person, that meant she was trustworthy enough for him to love her in return.

Experience had taught him that all romantic relationships were a complicated mix of physical attraction, friendship, common goals, and the relationship a person had with their parents. He knew her morals were different from his—he'd known it since that afternoon in her apartment.

But she also knew him better now. And while he was a normal, red-blooded man, Yohaba knew and respected that the man he wanted to be was one who lived a moral life. She had reminded him of that a few minutes ago and even helped him to live up to that principle when it wasn't really what she wanted. More than anything she could have done, that convinced him they had something good and right to build on. This was a woman who loved him and who was safe to love in return. At least, that's how he saw it.

He was alive, and he was grateful for that. And he had Yohaba. How this was going to end, he had no idea. He had just killed a man to save her and most likely ignited a war that would only end with more deaths. But, at the moment, he felt richly blessed.

Up until now, Yohaba hadn't told him what happened when they first grabbed her, and he hadn't asked. He figured she'd been through enough and that she'd get around to telling him when she was ready. Sure enough, just before they pulled into the hospital's underground garage, she started spilling the beans.

"I honestly had no idea where they came from. The first thing I knew, they'd smashed the driver's side window. They caught me completely by surprise. They dragged me from the car like a rag doll. Once they got me in the Volvo, they threatened me with all sorts of things if I gave them any trouble. I always thought I was tough, but those guys weren't human."

Even though she was safe now, with Rulon sitting next to her, just the mere thought of being in their power, knowing they could do anything they wanted, caused her to shake and tremble. She cried a little on his shoulder as they sat there. Her story elicited a different reaction from Rulon, however, and he felt his earlier anger sparking to life again.

He tactfully decided this wasn't the right time to tell her all the things she had done wrong. This wasn't her world. How could she be expected to know? But he promised himself he'd teach her to shoot someday and review with her what she should have done. In the meantime, he took Dmitry's wicked little knife out of his pocket and gave it to her.

"What's this for?" she asked.

"To use on me if my amorous feelings start to take over again," he joked. At that she burst into tears. "Oh, Yohaba, I was kidding!"

She quickly pulled herself together. "It's hard for me too," she said. "That's all." Then she reached behind his neck and pulled him to her, and they kissed a long, soft kiss. It was these soft kisses that were killing him. "It's been a tough day," she said after they separated, her voice choking with emotion. "A really tough day." She looked at the knife in her hand. "If those guys ever get me again, I'm using this on myself."

"Don't make jokes like that!" he said, his anger directed both at her and at the men who caused her to say such a thing. In a more subdued tone, he added, "I'm not letting you out of my sight from now on."

They had just started to lean into another kiss when his cell phone rang. It was Magnus. He was calling on what Rulon referred to as the red phone—the second cell phone he always carried that no one but Magnus knew he had.

"I'm surprised you're still able to answer your phone. Where are you now?"

"I'm in a hospital garage," said Rulon.

"Checking in or out?"

"Neither," he said. "Just visiting."

"Who's that?" asked Yohaba.

"Nobody," said Rulon.

"Nobody?" said Magnus. "I'm your boss and your friend, but I'm nobody. Was that a woman's voice I heard? Who is she? Don't tell me. It's the chick from the luggage store. Ask me how I know. No, I'll tell you. Opposites attract. How was—?"

"Magnus, now is not the time," said Rulon.

"Oh, yes it is, my friend, because you aren't going to be alive much longer. I suggest you get married quickly so at least you'll know what you're missing.

"I don't know how you manage it, but in three days you've managed to reignite the Cold War. The Russians have half their teams in Europe on call, *and* they've dispatched a team from Serbia—three brothers—to finish you off. If you see these guys, you better run.

"You know I love you and your little hammer, but you are not in these guys' league. They play for blood. These guys will hunt you down, and if they can't find you, they'll go after your family to draw you out. And when they finally get you, they've got a suitcase full of power tools. And don't even get me started on your little friend, Isabella. Man, can you pick them. Are you following all this?"

"Magnus, take a breath, for crying out loud!" Rulon yelled into the phone. "I already know about Isabella, and there are only two brothers."

"No, there are three. I know these guys. They've got a reputation the size of the Cairo phone book."

"There are only two brothers now," Rulon enunciated slowly. "Well, I don't know where one of them is, but one's dead, and the other is in the hospital. Got it?" There was silence on the other end of the phone. A rare thing for Magnus.

"What are you trying to tell me?" he asked finally.

"I killed one of them less than an hour ago, and when I left the other one, he was in pretty bad shape. That's what I'm telling you."

"There seems to be a connection problem. Can you repeat that?" said Magnus. Rulon gave him the short version of what happened.

"You just scored a goal in the World Cup, my friend," said Magnus. "Congratulations. But listen to me very carefully. You should have run up the score and killed the other guy when you had the chance. Run, buddy. Ditch the girl and get your butt to Stockholm where I can protect you here. Or bring the bird, I don't care. Pretend you caught her in a raid like a real Viking. I'll set you up in a farmhouse in Tyresta, and you can grow a beard and become a Viking and raise lots of little Viking ski jumpers."

"I can't, Magnus. There's something I still have to do. And in case you've forgotten, I've been laid off."

"I didn't forget. I would have called you, but I was working on something. It's too late now, my friend. You are off the reservation, for sure. You are so hot, you're scalding. The Russians want you real bad, and they've complained to the Americans. Now Toby wants to you to come in so he can talk to you. Have you even bothered to check your cell phone lately?"

Rulon mumbled something evasive, but the fact was he had deliberately kept the cell phone off since the fight in the Desperado for just that reason. Cell phones can be tracked and even the microphone turned on remotely if the people doing the tracking have the right technology. He wasn't taking any chances. While Rulon talked, he put the battery back in his regular cell phone and turned it on. There were twenty-seven missed calls. He quickly took the battery out again and hoped whoever was monitoring him at the NSA was on a coffee break.

"Toby's got a few of his boys looking for you. Don't go back to your apartment. He thinks you went postal after you were laid off.

And that was *before* you killed someone."

Great. Even my own people are after me. Rulon filled Magnus in on Isabella and the Elsa thing.

"I'm real sorry the world is going to end someday," said Magnus, "but if I were you, I'd worry more about my world ending over the next two days. Are you with me?"

"Yes, of course," said Rulon. "But listen, you have to run interference for me for awhile. Can you do that? Explain to Toby what happened. Keep them off my back for just a few more days."

"I'll do what I can. Is there anything else you need while I'm feeling generous?"

"Sure, if you're offering. Try to track down a scientist with ties to Einstein named Steenberg, in his mid seventies. His last known whereabouts were in Geneva."

"I'll see what I can do. But now let me tell you how this works. Now that you've killed someone, the game is different, especially with these Serbians. Up till now you've been lucky. But from here on out there are no rules. Even in the boondocks of Idaho, your family is no longer out of bounds. Tell them to lay low and go stay with friends for a while. Are you with me?"

"Yes," he muttered.

"And what did I tell you about Isabella? Can I call them or what?"

Another mumbled "yes."

"And don't let your girlfriend hear this, but are you going to ditch her? You should, you know. She'll only slow you down."

"Drop it," Rulon said.

"Expected that," Magnus replied with a trace of a smile in his voice. "Okay, one last thing. I've been following these guys' careers for ten years. If things go wrong, don't, I mean *don't*, let them take you alive under any circumstances. These guys are certified psychopaths."

After he hung up, Rulon felt like throwing the phone out the window. He closed his eyes and let out a big sigh and then pinched the bridge of his nose. Yohaba reached over and stroked the back of his head.

"You should leave me," she said with conviction. "I'll only get in your way. You've got to save yourself now."

Rulon opened one eye and looked at her. "Where I go, you go. End of story." He pulled out the Colt and checked that a round was chambered. *Cocked and locked.* "Okay," he said, "let's go visit the sick and afflicted."

* * *

By happy coincidence, they arrived at the hospital during visiting hours. Dmitry had registered under the same name he used with Rulon, so finding his room was not a problem. When they reached his floor, Rulon had Yohaba hang back while he checked that the room wasn't guarded.

Rulon strolled past Dmitry's room and then doubled back to stick his head through the partially open door. It was empty except for Dmitry dozing on the bed. He waved an all-clear to Yohaba and she walked down the hall to his side.

"Let me do the talking," he whispered.

The room was sparse, clean, functional, orderly—in a word, Swiss. Dmitry, on the other hand, was a mess. Traction cables suspended one leg, and he wore an oxygen tube up his nose, fresh white arm casts, an asymmetrically rolled head bandage that totally covered one eye, and finally, the obligatory IV bag hanging from a pole. Looking at him, Rulon felt guilty; he thought he'd left him in better shape than this. He nudged the bed and Dmitry woke with a start.

"Mind if we sit down?" asked Rulon amiably.

At first, Dmitry stiffened, looking downright scared, but he quickly recovered.

"I'm hardly in a position to stop you," he said. "You'll understand if I don't get up and shake your hand."

"No offense taken," Rulon said. "I'm glad you haven't lost your sense of humor."

"It's all I have left," he said simply and without animosity. Rulon took a chair next to the bed. Yohaba took one in the corner. Dmitry looked at Yohaba and back to Rulon and nodded.

"You two have become quite the couple. A few hard core romantics at the Russian embassy are cheering for you two to make it. But my bet is that Rulon here, or whatever your name is, will be my roommate by tomorrow. Friday night I ordered a little surprise for you. They arrived last night. You should be meeting them soon."

"That's what I'm here to talk about," said Rulon, sounding calm and reasonable. "Things have gotten out of control. I've already met your psychopathic friends, and let's just say that when you fly them home they'll have an empty middle seat." Rulon could see his attempt at black humor went right over Dmitry's head, so he added, "I had to kill one of them. They kidnapped Yohaba to get to me. They were going to torture her."

Though not much of his face was visible, Rulon saw enough to know Dmitry didn't like what he heard. Dmitry frowned and said, "You killed one of them? Oh, my friend, that was the worst thing you could have done. Which one did you kill?"

Rulon never got a good look at the guy before he shot him, and after he shot him his only memorable feature was the hole in his head. "He was hard to describe," said Rulon.

"Never mind," said Dmitry, and in the way he said it, Rulon knew there was no love lost between him and those hired psychos. "With people like that you should never kill just one. They are from Serbia. They still hold grudges from five hundred years ago. With these people, you slip the leash, get out of the way, and don't ask anymore questions. I am sorry. I overreacted. I should never have called them, but you worked me over twice in one day."

"Yeah, after you attacked me twice that same day."

"Yeah, after you sent three of my team to the hospital."

"Yeah, after your team slapped Yohaba around and threatened to kill her." Rulon rose out of his chair. How convenient that Dmitry was already in a hospital bed.

"Boys, boys," Yohaba intervened. "Can we have a little focus, please?"

At Yohaba's rebuke, the two men looked at each other and declared an unspoken truce. Rulon sat back down. "Look. We can stop this, right now. You can't tell me these guys aren't controllable. Let's just make up our minds to walk away. We're professionals." Rulon played his last card. He pulled the Serbians' wadded note out of his pocket. "This is what your wild dogs left in my car after they snatched Yohaba." Rulon smoothed out the note and held it up for Dmitry to read. When he was done, Dmitry shook his head in obvious distaste. Rulon waited a full thirty seconds for him to say something.

"I'll see what I can do," Dmitry said finally in a tired, defeated tone. "These people I've been using, most of them don't work directly for my government. They are Russian mafia. Thugs. Or sometimes the Serbians. We contract them. I'll say it again—I regret what I've done. Those idiots who threatened the girl and started this whole thing, they are the ones who should be shot. Let me have your cell phone number. I'll let you know." When Rulon just looked at him and didn't answer, Dmitry smiled and gave Rulon his number instead.

"Call me tomorrow," said Dmitry.

"Thank you," said Rulon.

"But our little arrangement only covers the vendetta against you. We still want the trunk. We still want to talk to the girl." He shifted his attention to Yohaba. "If you would care to answer my questions now, we could end this. Right here. Between us."

"Not gonna happen," said Rulon firmly.

"Then I'm afraid we will be meeting again." Dmitry said those last words with a hard edge, but one that quickly changed into an amused smile. "Well, perhaps the meeting won't be with me." He held up his casts again to emphasize the point.

"I'm really sorry," was all Rulon could say.

"Yes, my friend, but I am in the hospital, having had the misfortune of a table falling on me while I was hoisting it up some stairs. And you? You have a beautiful woman who loves you. Hardly seems fair, doesn't it?" He went serious again. "Give me some time to see if an arrangement can be made."

Before they left, Yohaba went over to the bed. Bending over Dmitry's bruised and bandaged head, she kissed him lightly on the cheek. "I'm sorry I slapped you," she said. And then as she turned to leave, she asked, as an afterthought, "Do you have a wife?"

"Yes," he said, "and a sixteen-year-old daughter. They are flying into Zurich tonight to be with me. Even spies have loving families. Is that surprising?"

"Yes, a little, but I'm glad for you," she said with a warm smile.

18

"It should be possible to explain the laws of physics to a barmaid." —Einstein

Once Rulon did another bug sweep on the BMW and switched out his license plate again for good measure, he realized he was starving. As the car idled in the hospital parking garage, he considered his options. Going back to the apartment to cook was out of the question. Likewise, the Desperado was best avoided. There was, however, another excellent Mexican restaurant called Tres Kilos on the northeast side of town just a few blocks from the consulate.

As they drove, Rulon realized that strangely, he was still hyped over rescuing Yohaba, and even more strangely, the post-combat blues and guilt that normally trampled in like an elephant hadn't hit either. What had the Company psychiatrist said? *The time to quit was when you stopped feeling guilty.* Maybe that time had come. He searched his feelings. Nope. Not a shred of guilt.

Over dinner, Rulon and Yohaba planned their next move. Rulon hoped Steenberg's association with CERN meant that he still lived and worked somewhere in the Geneva area. They would find out soon enough from Magnus. Their plan was to track down Steenberg and ask him point-blank about the trunk. The man had no honest reason to hide anything as long as they could prove that Yohaba was related to both him and Einstein.

An hour later, as they got up to leave, Rulon saw that it was 6:00 p.m. Time for Dad's Sunday phone call and to tell him the good news about Serbian assassins maybe coming to Idaho. On their way out, Rulon stopped at the restaurant's pay phone.

"Yee-ello," said Dad in his typical phone greeting. "Is this my world-traveler son?"

"Yeah, Dad. How's it going?"

"How do you think it's going? I'm sitting on six hundred acres watching the wind blow. It's going pretty much like it did yesterday and the day before." Dad was eighty-one, tough as a boot, and as grizzled and weather beaten as the wind-swept Idaho flatlands. "What's the news from Yodel-ville?" he asked.

Without saying too much, Rulon told his father that he'd crossed some bad people and maybe it'd be a good idea if he stayed with a neighbor for a week or two.

As expected, his father didn't listen. His only concession was to say he would check that all the guns in the house were loaded and that he'd cut back on feeding the dogs.

"Dad," said Rulon, "I can understand why you would want to keep the guns loaded, but what on earth does feeding Gus and Molly have to do with anything?"

"It's how the Romans whipped up the lions," he said.

Rulon handed the phone to Yohaba and told her to keep him talking while he regrouped. Rulon listened while she nattered on pleasantly for a minute, having a perfectly normal conversation. *Why doesn't he talk like that with me?* When Rulon felt up for round two, he motioned for the phone.

"She sounds like a nice girl, son," said his dad, "but she has kind of a funny accent. I hope you didn't buy her off a Russian website or any such nonsense." After a few more minutes of that, they said good-bye. Rulon was worried. His dad had no intention of hiding out.

"He sounds nice," said Yohaba.

"Yeah. You just have to know what subjects to avoid."

"Like what?

"The Great Depression for one. But also Harry Truman, social security, the Federal Reserve, the Martin and Willie handcart companies, the twenty-first amendment, the—" When he saw the puzzled look on Yohaba's face, he stopped. "Trust me. It's a long list."

They drove to an all-night car wash in Zurich's Unterstrasse district and vacuumed out the broken glass. While Yohaba kept watch, Rulon took his time cleaning up the car. The sleeping arrangements had him stumped. They couldn't go to his apartment, and he had to assume Yohaba's apartment was also being watched. Even then, he didn't intend to never let her out of his sight. There was no way around it. He had to stay with her. A single hotel room was their only choice. *Dang it.*

He texted Magnus: *Any news on Steenberg*?

Getting close, was the quick reply.

After cleaning up the Beemer, Rulon and Yohaba sat there for a while, under the white lights of the car wash, talking about the day. Yohaba had a lot to work through. Her talking gave him a chance to rest. Mainly he just listened. But then she said something about them making a good couple after all.

"You've been reading too many romance novels," he gently chided out of the side of his mouth. He leaned back against the headrest and closed his eyes.

"You love me, don't you?" she asked. "You don't have to answer. Just stomp your foot twice for 'yes.' " That got a chuckle out of him. She continued. "You've caused me to revise my theory about men and love."

"Go on," he said. "This I've got to hear."

"I think with men, actions speak louder than words."

"You're just now figuring that out?"

"So, anyway," she said, ignoring his reply. "That's why I think you love me."

"Whatever," he mumbled, feeling sleepy now, fidgeting in the seat to find a more comfortable position. He wasn't going to argue the point about whether he loved her or not. He did. To him, love was more a decision than a feeling. Somewhere along the line he had decided to love her, and he was going to do his best to live up to that. Someday he might even tell her.

As they sat there, a coded text message came in from Magnus. It had two addresses, one labeled 'home' and the other 'work,' plus some rudimentary directions and the complementary closing, 'Watch your back.' The chase was on, and the destination was the small Swiss town of Meyrin, next to Geneva, where there was an entrance into the huge CERN complex.

They headed north to Schaffhausen—the opposite direction from CERN—which was forty-five minutes away on the German border. While there, he used a cash machine and took out another five hundred euros. He had no choice; he needed the money. They'd be pegged in seconds, but he figured if he used a cash machine in Schaffhausen and took out euros, they'd think they were heading for Germany. He also stole a car using tools from the spy kit in the Beemer's trunk.

Their new set of wheels was a red 2008 Clio Renaultsport. It didn't blend in as well as the BMW, but it was enough for a fast getaway if the need arose. He also switched the license plates with a nearby car and transferred all their gear, including Freya. Rulon noticed the back seat was small. One less temptation.

Once on the road, Rulon backtracked and headed southwest to Geneva, figuring he'd done enough to throw off their pursuers for a while. He could easily get there by midnight, but for security reasons, he didn't want to sleep in the city itself. To really confuse anyone trying to intercept them or looking for a stolen car, he decided to drive right past Geneva and head into France for the night.

Just over the border, about an hour past Geneva, was a touristy little town called Annecy. It sat on an alpine lake and had lots of hotels. Perfect. Just like any American traveling in Europe, Rulon always had his passport with him. Yohaba had her Swiss ID card, which was enough for her to get into France. Rulon figured that with any luck, they had until morning before the Clio was reported missing. With the license plates changed, and with them going back into Switzerland from France with the morning traffic, he thought it unlikely they'd be spotted. They settled down for a five-hour drive. It was 8:00 p.m.

"Are we there yet?" asked Yohaba fifteen minutes into the trip.

"Tell me about CERN," he said, figuring that would keep her occupied.

"Okay," she said, sitting up straight and suddenly all perky. "I'm going to assume you don't know anything."

"Good assumption."

"Okay then, let's start with the name. It's a French acronym for *Conseil Européen pour la Recherche Nucléaire*, in other words, the European Council for Nuclear Research.

"It was started in 1954, a year before my great-great-grandfather died. It's an amazing complex of buildings, all centered around a seventeen-mile tunnel a hundred meters underground. It houses six particle accelerators, including the Large Hadron Collider, or LHC for short. Basically, CERN is the largest particle physics laboratory in the world. At any one time, there are over ten thousand scientists on the various sites doing pure research into particle behavior. In other words, CERN is Disneyland for physicists."

"By particles, do you mean protons and electrons, stuff like that?" asked Rulon.

"Oh, that's kid's stuff for the CERN boys. These days, they're into things like W and Z bosons, neutrinos, antimatter, and anti-hydrogen atoms. It's mind blowing."

They chatted on, strangely happy despite all that had happened. As they talked, Rulon developed a theory: Love is a protection from the hardships and internal wounds of life, like a force field around the spirit. Eventually Yohaba drifted off to sleep. It was late Sunday night, and traffic was light. He let her sleep for a couple of hours. They stopped once to stretch their legs and hit the rest-rooms. Just before 1:00 a.m. they drove into Annecy and quickly found a hotel with an underground garage.

Now came the hard part. Rulon realized that James Bond wouldn't think twice about checking into a hotel room with a woman he wasn't married to. But he wasn't James Bond, and he was having a lot of trouble with it. At the front desk, he squared his jaw and bit the bullet, even though he turned beet red in the process. The only available room had a single queen-sized bed. It was late, and he took it. He flashed his passport and Yohaba's ID and filled out the registration form.

Yohaba, on the other hand, wasn't fazed in the least. She stood there, holding her gym bag, breezily chatting to the clerk in French while clutching Rulon's left arm possessively. Rulon couldn't follow what they were saying. His French wasn't up to snuff, and the French spoke too fast anyway. When they were all checked in, the clerk handed Rulon the key and winked. As they walked up the stairs with their bags, Rulon's curiosity got the better of him.

"What did you say to the clerk?" he asked.

She got a wicked gleam in her eye, and Rulon held his breath, but soon Yohaba couldn't hold it in, and she burst out laughing.

"Oh, don't worry, darling. I didn't make any allusions to us not being married. We joked about French politics. Everyone finds French politics funny, especially the French."

"Why did he wink at me then?" he asked, still not satisfied.

"He gave us the honeymoon suite," she said. "It was the only one available. He's a Frenchman. I'm sure everyone who gets the honeymoon suite gets a wink."

"I'm sleeping on the floor. Just so you know."

"I would have been shocked if you didn't," said Yohaba. "Don't worry. I'll make it as easy for you as I can."

The room had a single queen bed pushed up against the wall, a glass coffee table, a desk with a phone, two chairs, and a wall-mounted TV. It was cramped, but by moving the coffee table, Rulon managed to stake out a place for himself next to the bed. It must have been the chocolates on the pillows that made it the honeymoon suite.

They took turns changing in the bathroom. Rulon was in a wrestle with his conscience. He went first and came out in a pair of baggy gray sweats and a gray, cotton Boise State T-shirt. Yohaba was sitting cross-legged on the bed, with a big smile on her face, and his passport in her hand. *Uh-oh*, he thought.

"Gonville," she said. "Your real first name is *Gonville*?"

Rulon had his clothes in his hand and nonchalantly began hanging them in the closet. "Yes," he said casually, as he straightened his shirt on a hanger. "It's a perfectly fine name."

"Don't worry," she said. "Your secret is safe with me."

He sighed and sat down on the bed. "Look. I prefer Rulon—it's my middle name. Before I was born, my mom and dad had a deal. He could pick the first name, and she could pick the middle name. Gonville and Rulon are both old family names."

"Wow. They didn't give you much of a choice, did they?" she said mischievously. "But *Gonville*?"

"Remember when I told you about Hook, my relative at Rorke's Drift? Well, one of the officers there was named Gonville Bromhead. We think he must have saved Hook's life or something. All we know for sure is that after the battle, Hook named his next kid Gonville, and the name's been in the family ever since."

"Hey," she said. "My name is Yohaba. I'm cool with Gonville. A Gonville by any other name is still a great kisser." With that she tossed him his passport and jumped off the bed, heading for the bathroom to take her turn changing. He watched her disappear through the door and started to turn away. Just as he did, she stuck her head back out and said with a giggle, "But Rulon suits you better, Cowboy," and then she was gone.

Rulon finished hanging up his clothes and then sat in the room's one chair, waiting for Yohaba. Her progress in the bathroom was easy to follow through the thin walls; he could clearly hear the medley of pop songs she sang in the shower, followed by her brushing her teeth. Before she came out she yelled, "Close your eyes!" which he did. Then came the scampering of bare feet and the rustling of sheets and covers. "All clear," she said.

When he opened his eyes she was lying on her back with the blankets pulled up to her chin. His imagination took off. What was she wearing? *Get a grip*, he told himself.

He got up and found some extra bedding in the closet. A couple of pillows and a triple layer of blankets made a reasonably comfortable arrangement next to the bed. When finished, he flipped the switch by the door then made his way in the dark back to his improvised sleeping bag. He lay there on his back with his hands folded behind his head. The curtain was open and lights from the street lamps threw shadows on the walls. Within a minute, his eyes had adjusted to the dark.

"Good night," he said.

"Good night," came the reply, and the room was quiet again. Then he heard the rustle of sheets and squeaking of mattress springs. Suddenly Yohaba was looking down at him, her face no more than a foot above his. "What are you doing down there?" she asked. Her long hair hung down around his face, and they talked to each other from within a cozy little tunnel.

"Trying to get some sleep," he replied. She pulled away slightly and he could see her smooth, bare shoulders.

"Well, I'm not sleepy. Let's talk about something. What kind of music do you like?"

"I like both kinds. Country and Western. Now go to sleep."

"Sing me a song," she demanded. "Please? I'll bet you used to sing in the church choir."

"Still do."

"Sing me a lullaby then." She rolled away, and he couldn't see her anymore.

"I'm ready," she said.

He lay there thinking he should just roll over and blow her off. But then he decided, *Why not?* "All right. One song." With a loud sigh for a prelude, and without any particular thought behind it, he sang one of his favorite songs.

> Two weeks in a Virginia jail,
> For my lover, for my lover.
> Twenty thousand dollars bail,
> For my lover, for my lover . . .

"Tracy Chapman. 'For My Lover,' " she said when he was done. "Well done, cowboy. Why'd you pick that song?" Then she added flirtatiously. "Was there a message in there for me?" He couldn't see her, but assumed she was lying on her back, like him, looking up at the ceiling.

"Yeah," he said. "Being with you is like being in jail."

"No. You know exactly what I'm referring to." Then she leaned clear over the bed, her hair making that tunnel again around his face. "We're not lovers, remember?"

"You have a very narrow definition of the word 'lover.' "

For a few moments she looked stumped, and then she said, "Give me your hand."

He complied guardedly, and she took his hand in both of hers. "You might be right," she said. With trepidation, he wondered what was coming next, but all she did was tenderly kiss each one of his scarred knuckles. Then she rolled over so he couldn't see her anymore. "Good night, cowboy."

"Ditto," he said in the darkness.

They lay there in the dark. After a minute she started quietly singing Billy Idol's "Rebel Yell" until he finally had to tell her to shut up.

19

"PEOPLE LOVE CHOPPING WOOD. IN THIS ACTIVITY, ONE IMMEDIATELY SEES RESULTS." —EINSTEIN

A FEW HOURS AFTER RULON AND YOHABA HAD GONE TO SLEEP and several time zones to the east, the offered report disappointed its recipients. Such reports were not received well in this room of the Kremlin—a mere one hundred yards from Lenin's tomb. Seven men rendered out of commission. Nine, if counting the two Serbian brothers. One bullet. One dead. Eight in the hospital. One man was responsible for all this? Was this man Rambo?

Deep growls of mirth rose from the throats of five of the six old men sitting along the length of the briefing room table. A few further expressed their approval of the jest by rapping their knuckles on the sturdy wooden surface. The only persons who did not laugh were the old thin man with the hawk-like face, thin lips, and dark intense eyes who had made the joke, and the young captain in the SVR—the Russian Foreign Intelligence Service—who stood before the table in civilian clothes rigidly at attention.

"Who is he?" asked the thin man.

"A former cowboy and college hammer thrower and wrestler. An accomplished marksman. Eight years with OCD," answered the captain. "Mainly an investigator, we thought, until an incident in Marseilles last year. It did not involve our people. It was a smuggling operation. *Fashisty*—Nazis. A very rough crowd. Apparently he is easy to underestimate."

"*Fashisty?*" someone growled. "Maybe we give him the Order of Lenin."

The thin man said, "Go on."

"He graduated from Boise State University in Idaho, and—"

"Boise, Idaho," said a voice. "The entertainment capital of the world." And this time everyone roared.

When the laughter subsided, the thin man said, "No. Just Marseilles. I wish to hear what happened."

The captain paused for a second, not sure how much detail to supply. "It was in a bar. He'd blown his cover somehow. They arranged for a final meeting. It was a trap. He was alone. They were experienced. Armed. It should have been the end for him. We're still not sure what happened. We just know it was—it was quite the fight, sir. He tore the place apart. Our man in Marseilles checked it out later and said he never saw anything like it."

The room went silent for a few seconds.

"I see. But we are not a mere smuggling operation, are we?" said the thin man.

"No, we are not," replied the captain.

"This information strains credulity. But it happens," said an ancient voice on the far right. "There are always losses. Even setbacks. Order must be restored, and then we complete the mission with the same people, if possible. Teach a lesson, but no barbarisms. Nothing that would invite retaliation. Kill the cowboy in the usual way, a hollow-point bullet in the face, so they know who sent the message."

The young officer clicked his heels and saluted. Five minutes later, he crossed Red Square on his way to the shopping mall that bordered the eastern edge of the square. The fresh air was a relief. As he walked, he congratulated himself on his handling of this difficult meeting.

To have delivered such news and not be demoted was a coup. But there would be no third chances. He had eight five-man teams to choose from. Team two would do nicely.

* * *

Right up until the time she'd been tossed out of the car, Rulon had been pathetically easy to handle. He'd been a chubby seal off the waters of Capetown, and she a white shark rising from the depths. Everything had been under control. This made it doubly hard for Isabella to accept the magnitude of her defeat. When she heard that the Serbians had been hired for clean-up duty, she nearly whooped for joy.

Signing on with the Russians had been a good career move.

Petro-dollars gushed fountains of money on the various Russian intelligence services, oiling the palms of many contractors, such as herself. Surprisingly, the Russians were good bosses. They tolerated mistakes, just not the same mistake twice, which she could understand. Also, they paid well and took care of their own. This meant more than having a competitive medical plan.

It meant they didn't take any guff from rival services. Payback was part of the code. She hoped this little incident with Rulon didn't hurt her chances for advancement. Why should it? The males on the team had done a lot worse. At least she wasn't in the hospital racking up medical bills.

When the phone call came in, Isabella was in her apartment, licking her wounded pride and wondering how long before she got the good news. She leapt at the phone and, at first, couldn't believe her ears. Something had gone terribly wrong. Isabella had so counted on hearing the details of Rulon's brutal beating that she had already picked out the flowers she'd send to the hospital. It never occurred to her he would walk away from a meeting with the Serbians.

The Serbians were famous for always getting their man. When she heard, instead, that Rulon had killed one of them and that another one was in the hospital until he was well enough to go to jail, she rampaged around her apartment for ten minutes, stopping only to throw the occasional couch pillow. When that proved unsatisfying, she hurled a partially filled coffee cup at the refrigerator. She knew Rulon. He was an idiot. He was a hick. He was a romantic fool. He was from *Idaho*, of all places.

Finding the third surviving brother was difficult. He was doing his best to avoid the Swiss police, not to mention Rulon, who he assumed was hunting him down too. He was on the move constantly and communicating intermittently only on a secure message board. He hadn't even visited his injured brother in the hospital or claimed his other brother's body from the morgue.

She had no money to pay him, but she hoped they could forge a partnership rather than an employer-employee relationship. When she was just about to give up hope and accept another assignment in Germany, she received a text message: *Dietlikon, IKEA, front entrance, 10 a.m. today.* It was now Monday, 8:30 a.m.—plenty of time to get there.

20

"SCIENCE IS A WONDERFUL THING IF ONE DOES NOT HAVE TO EARN ONE'S LIVING AT IT." —EINSTEIN

BY 8:00 THE NEXT MORNING, RULON AND YOHABA WERE ON the road back to Geneva. They drove through the border without any problems and headed for the B entrance of the huge, spread-out facility that was CERN's Meyrin site.

As they pulled into line behind the other cars at the main gate, Rulon noticed a sign on the guard shack that said "All Firearms Must Be Declared." He was prepared for that and had hidden the Colt in the trunk. As it didn't look like they were doing any searches, he wasn't worried.

When it was their turn, the guard held firm and wouldn't let them in without a pass. She directed them to the security desk in an adjacent building, where Yohaba convinced an initially skeptical security officer that she was related to Dr. Steenberg and had a present for him—the scrapbook. It helped that the clerk was male.

Once through the gate, they headed for building 133 at the intersection of Einstein and Rutherford roads. Yohaba mentioned that Rutherford was the New Zealand physicist who discovered that atoms had a charged nucleus. Apparently, this was a scientific leap so earthshaking that it needed no further embellishment. As a former rancher, Rulon would have traded the discovery for an easier method of milking cows.

Twenty minutes later, they had successfully navigated the maze of streets and buildings and were sitting in the parking lot in front of Steenberg's office. It was 9:45 a.m. The pale gray building was as long as a short city block and three stories high.

He asked, "Do you know what you are going to say?" She nodded. Then he asked, "Got the scrapbook?" She smiled weakly and indicated her cavernous handbag. She was acting so strangely that he knew something was wrong. "What's up, kiddo?" he asked.

"He's my *grandfather*, and I've never met him," she said, looking down and forlorn. "He's a genius. I have to convince him that an asteroid is going to hit the Earth. Maybe he knows. Maybe he'll think I'm crazy. Maybe I won't be able to convince him I'm his granddaughter. Maybe he won't be there. Maybe we should have called him first. Take your pick."

"Come on," said Rulon, trying to sound confident despite her barrage of realistic objections. "This will be a slam-dunk. You two will probably look so much alike, he won't even question your pedigree. He probably has a nose ring and a spider web tattoo, just like you." That got a laugh out of her. "Seriously," he said, picking up steam. "Even if he doesn't think you're his granddaughter, he'll be pleased to spend time talking with you. You'll be without a doubt the most beautiful, sexiest physicist he's ever met. He'll probably want to adopt you." She gave him a smile and a determined nod. He squeezed her hand, and they got out of the car.

At the reception desk, they were greeted by a matronly-looking woman in her mid-sixties. She started out speaking French but in a German accent, so Rulon took a chance and responded in German. He told her whom they wanted to see, and she asked, in fluent German, if they had an appointment.

He said no, and immediately the room went cold enough to freeze a grizzly. She dialed a number, presumably Steenberg's. Rulon took this as a sign Steenberg was in the building. But when she hung up, she told them in a tone that brooked no debate that Steenberg was busy and wouldn't be seeing anyone this morning. When they protested, she gave them a look that would have turned lesser people into stone and repeated her previous edict.

While Rulon made one last-ditch attempt to change her mind, Yohaba paged through her scrapbook. Just as the curmudgeon's hand was drifting under her desk for what Rulon assumed was a hidden security alarm, Yohaba found what she was looking for. She leaned over and showed the receptionist the old photograph that had been taken in front of the Little Garden restaurant in Brooklyn over fifty years ago.

"See? Here is Einstein. And this young man is Doctor Steenberg. This woman here was my grandmother, and this is Einstein's long-lost daughter." Rulon was relieved when she had the good sense not to mention her connection to Dr. Steenberg. It might be a sensitive subject. "If you show him this, he'll want to see us, don't you think? I'm sorry we didn't make an appointment. We will next time, I promise."

The receptionist still said no. And rudely at that.

"Listen," Rulon said firmly. "Somehow, within the next two days, we will see Doctor Steenberg, with or without your cooperation. We have his home address. This young lady is related to him. When we show him this picture and explain what happened at this front desk today, do you think he will be happy with you?"

They watched her ponder the ramifications, and then to their relief, she slowly picked up the phone again with a sigh that could have been heard in Zurich. Before she could dial, Rulon jumped in and asked her to mention the picture but not to mention that Yohaba was a relation. She sighed again and made the call.

Five minutes later, they were standing in a long third-floor corridor in front of a door labeled "Doctor Leonard Steenberg, Managing Director, Area LS." Their security guard escort did the knocking. A second later they heard the click of an electronic lock. The guard stepped aside, and they went in.

Aware of Steenberg's Jesuit training, Rulon expected something a little more on the monastic side. Instead, what greeted their eyes was a kaleidoscope of colored pictures on every wall and a desk buried under stacks of paper. There were also a dozen medium-sized boxes stacked three high along one wall, and a large side table covered with unrolled architectural drawings prevented from re-rolling by a heavy book at each corner.

Standing over the drawings was a man in a black suit and charcoal-gray turtleneck, still looking every inch the Jesuit. He was tall with a thin ascetic face, and a broad, intelligent forehead under a shock of white hair. He looked up as they entered, his piercing, somewhat recessed eyes, alight with interest.

"It's not every day that an attractive young woman brings me pictures, especially of my old mentor," he said with a wry smile. He walked around the table and extended his hand. "Hello. I'm Doctor Steenberg. And you are . . . ?"

They shook hands and introduced themselves. With a slight gesture, he invited them to sit down in the two chairs beside his desk. "These pictures that you see around you," he said, gesturing towards the walls, "are of the various components of the Large Hadron Collider. Colorful, aren't they? Excuse the mess. There is always so much to do, so much to read. Are either of you mathematicians, by chance?

"I'm an honors physics student at the ETH," said Yohaba. "I contributed to the CMS experiment."

"Ah, yes, the Compact Muon Solenoid. Our expensive little project in that cavern in Cessy. Tell me what you did."

"I worked on the test for the heavy ion collisions," she replied. "The interaction point calculations. I was on the team that worked that out."

"That was good science, young lady. A good team that got results. You may call me Leonard. As you can see around you, I'm not particularly given to formality or titles." He directed his attention to Rulon. "And your friend here?" He looked Rulon up and down, or rather, observed him, but not in an unfriendly or patronizing way. "I would say," he offered, " that you are not a mathematician. Perhaps you are given to more practical pursuits? Tell me, Mr. Hurt, what do you do for a living?"

"I'm an unemployed spy, sir," Rulon answered truthfully. It was nothing to be ashamed of. Steenberg paused, considered that for a second, and then accepted it.

"So, we have a sorceress and her knight . . . and a photograph. May I see it, please?" He held out his hand. Yohaba opened the scrapbook on the desk and flipped it around so he could see.

"This is it," she said with her finger on the picture. "Do you remember that day?"

"Oh, yes, that was a most memorable of days. One of those life-changing kinds of days for me, I can assure you."

You can say that again, thought Rulon, his mind immediately leaping to Granny's story of the night-time tryst.

"Do you remember all the people in the picture?" asked Yohaba.

"Yes, I believe I do," said Steenberg. "I have quite a good memory."

"Do you remember anything special about this woman, Leonard?" asked Yohaba.

"Yes. She was utterly charming. I was but a boy at the time, and she completely swept me off my feet."

Rulon looked down at his feet and bit his tongue, trying not to chuckle at the image.

"I remember being quite taken with her," Steenberg continued. "Would you by any chance be related? Is that where this is going?"

"Yes, Leonard, that woman is my grandmother. And I believe you are my grandfather." The words hung in the air, completely filling the space around them.

Yohaba sat back and studied his reaction. Leonard got up slowly and stood behind the chair with his hands on the backrest. Then he pushed the chair into the desk and paced around the room with his hands behind his back. A few times he stopped to say something but then resumed his pacing, the words not quite there. When he was ready, he came back and sat down.

"And so that makes you also Albert's great-great-granddaughter."

"Yes, it does," said Yohaba. "My grandmother never told me that she told you about their relationship. You can call my grandmother for corroboration."

"Oh, then she *is* still alive. But there is no need for further confirmation, child. You even look like your grandmother. Tell me, did she marry eventually? How is she?"

For the next fifteen minutes, Rulon sat back and listened while Yohaba and her grandfather talked. Steenberg never asked about visiting the grandmother or even of speaking with her. At first that struck Rulon as odd, but then he remembered that there wasn't a rule book for situations like this. It's hard to know what to do sometimes, and maybe Steenberg's reticence was the wiser course. Himself, he was anxious to talk about asteroids, so he eventually pushed his way in.

"I was wondering," Rulon said at a break in the conversation. "Do the words 182 Elsa have any significance for you?"

Dr. Steenberg turned his attention from Yohaba and looked at Rulon with a slightly amused expression. Rulon could immediately tell that Steenberg knew exactly what he was driving at. "A main-belt asteroid," he answered. "Discovered February 7, 1878 by Johann Palisa. Named after a character in the Legend of Lohengrin. Oh yes, I'm quite familiar with it. At one time it held a great deal of significance for me, but not anymore. Tell me though, how did you come to know about that mysterious, insignificant little asteroid, and why do you care?"

The story came out fitfully as Rulon and Yohaba stumbled over each other trying to put the pieces together for Steenberg without him thinking they were crazy. He listened patiently, rubbing his chin in thought, and without giving away his feelings except when Rulon told him that Yohaba was physically threatened by the Russians. Then he looked uneasy and restive in his chair, but that was all the emotion he showed. Rulon never mentioned the Serbians.

"Albert was obsessed with that discovery," he said when they were finished, his head shaking slightly at frustration remembered. "I loved him as my own father, but I will say that he drove us all crazy for years with that asteroid business. We felt like monks in a holy order asked to keep the secret of the Holy Grail. No, more than that. Asked to not just keep a secret, but to build a dream, an impossibly complex dream made up of building blocks, all carefully calculated by that great man. But I don't regret it for a second.

"Just as the landing on the moon wasn't as significant as was the spin-off technology, the science that it funded, so too did this fools' errand over Elsa, this Don Quixote jousting at windmills, turned out to be a waste of time. But this, all this that you see around you,"—he spread his hands wide as he said it—"has spun out of it."

"Are you saying his calculations were wrong?" Rulon asked. "That Elsa isn't going to hit the Earth, here at Geneva?"

"That's exactly what I'm saying. At first we didn't believe he could be wrong. You realize, he really put this whole theory together just a few weeks before that picture was taken, less than a year before he died. He kept feeding it to us in dribs and drabs. We were quite staggered. At the same time, he was grooming us for other things. Suddenly, this was all he could talk about. We felt his passion and were animated by it. And then he died rather suddenly.

His heart, of all things. How ironic. I would have said it was his heart that most defined him.

"It wasn't until 1972 that we finally had the technology to once and for all put these theories to rest. For all that he got right, for all the miracles he performed, this one he missed. It was like the chess grandmaster not seeing the fool's mate. The asteroid will miss the Earth by thirty-seven million miles. We checked and rechecked. There is no possibility of a mistake. It's been independently confirmed by a dozen of the top astronomers in the world.

"And besides, how preposterous! To predict an asteroid will hit the Earth is one thing, but to predict the exact spot where it will hit? Well, we should have known. That is utterly impossible, even today."

He stopped talking, and his shoulders sagged. It was obviously an emotional subject. Rulon thought he sensed a lingering doubt and that, despite all the proof, Steenberg wasn't absolutely certain his beloved mentor had been wrong.

Yohaba and Rulon looked at each other, and frankly, Rulon wasn't feeling much, and he didn't think she was either. The idea of life on Earth being snuffed out by a meteor had seemed very far-fetched, even from the beginning, and it certainly didn't jibe with how Rulon pictured the world ending. In fact, he wasn't sure he ever really believed it. About the only thing he was convinced of was that Einstein thought it was real. He still needed more answers, though, and, it turned out, so did Yohaba.

They sat there for another hour while Steenberg patiently endured their questions. When it was time for lunch, he took them downstairs to the cafeteria where they continued their discussion. Most of all, Rulon and Yohaba wanted to know what was in the trunk.

"Everything you see around you, and many things you can't see, came from the depths of that trunk, that old seaman's steamer," said Steenberg with a wave of his hand. "Both things above the ground and below. Albert was forever saying that the Gutenberg press was the most important invention in the last two thousand years because it enabled mankind to better preserve and, most important, share information.

"Well, he left us ideas that eventually led to packet switching and then eventually to the Internet, and even to what lies a hundred and six meters below this building, the Hadron Collider. He thought we would need all this if we were ever going to stop Elsa. Intercepting an asteroid is quite a challenge. Much more than most people imagine. He really was a genius. Not just a mathematical genius."

"The Russians are looking for information that will increase the yield of nuclear weapons," said Yohaba. "Was that information in the trunk?"

"Yes. But I burned those papers one night. Or rather, the three of us did together. This was right after we discovered that Albert was wrong about Elsa. We decided that's what he would have wanted."

Rulon was curious. "Would it have worked? Would it have increased the yields?"

"We all three studied the formulas before we burned them. We concluded that Albert's formulas would have indeed increased the yields by a factor of sixty. Imagine that knowledge in the wrong hands! It wasn't simple, though. He kept saying it was obvious. Believe me. It wasn't."

Dr. Steenberg sighed, and his voice trailed off in a tinge of sadness, Rulon supposed, at all those missed conversations. "But I guess to him it was." Then Steenberg perked up again. "All these years, and I still miss him. Being with him was like being with . . . with . . . Adam in the garden. It was like seeing the world for the first time. Every day it was something new. He had a way of looking at the world that was so ingeniously odd.

"One time we were walking across the Princeton campus eating, ice cream cones. He suddenly stopped and looked at the cone in his hand. Right there, standing on a sidewalk between two buildings, he came up with a theory that black holes were shaped like ice cream cones. Then he promptly forgot about it. Years later his theory was confirmed. You are the first people I ever told this to." He looked directly at Yohaba. "If it ever comes up in a trivia contest, you can have the satisfaction of knowing your great-great-grandfather thought of it first."

After lunch, on their way back upstairs, Yohaba had another question. "Do you still have the trunk? It's not really that important. I'm just wondering."

Steenberg laughed. "We certainly do. We may not look it, but we scientists are soggy sentimentalists at heart. Come, I'll show you." They reversed direction and went back down, deep into the bowels of the building. His security card opened all the doors.

They entered an elevator and went down five floors, as far as they could go. They continued their descent down two more flights of stairs and then navigated a labyrinth of hallways. Finally, they came to a small, nondescript door midway down a corridor. Stenciled neatly on the door was the room's alpha-numeric identifier: G-14b.

Steenberg unlocked the door with a key from his key chain and flipped on the overhead light. The room was the size of a small office, with light green walls and a single piece of furniture sitting in its center: a plain, wooden table on four sturdy legs.

Sitting on the table was Einstein's trunk—an old wooden steamer, just as Steenberg had described it—two feet wide, three feet long, and almost as tall, with a slightly domed lid. The trunk still looked sturdy, but the wood was dry and rubbed bare in places. It had seen better days. Its corners were edged with black metal slats, and the lid was reinforced with five similar bands. On the front were engraved the words,

> Home is the Sailor,
> Home from the Sea.
> And the Hunter,
> Home from the Hill.

Everyone stared at the trunk for a few moments, all lost in their own thoughts. Rulon supposed that to each of them, the trunk represented something different. To Steenberg, it symbolized a lifetime of work; to Yohaba, a memory of a great-great-grandfather she had never known; to Rulon, four days of trouble—all for nothing. He caught himself. Yohaba stood next to him. No, not for nothing.

"I wanted to enshrine it permanently in a place of honor in the Center's museum, but I was overruled," said Steenberg, after a respectful pause. "A few of my brethren on the board are resentful of all the attention your great-great-grandfather has received over the years. They certainly weren't willing to share CERN with him after his death. I do have a certain empathy for their position. To most of the huddled masses, Einstein was the only scientist who did anything of note in the entire twentieth century. To people who spend their whole lives in anonymity performing miracles in laboratories, it really was too much to bear. But it doesn't matter. He never cared about such things."

Spotlighted by the single light directly overhead, the trunk lay there like a religious artifact, and Rulon said as much. Steenberg smiled. "Yes, a little like being in the Holy of Holies viewing the Lost Ark. Come, I'll show you what's inside. Don't be afraid, you won't be impaled by celestial lasers."

He lifted the single, unlocked clasp and raised the lid, sending wisps of dust rising in the slipstream. *Like incense*, thought Rulon. He peered inside and saw the trunk was half filled with papers and a few cigar boxes.

"Do you know what was in the original Ark of the Covenant?" asked Steenberg, not letting loose of the religious theme. "I'll tell you. Aaron's staff for one thing." Steenberg reached into the trunk almost up to his shoulder and pulled a slide rule out of its depths. He held it up for them to see then placed it on the table.

"And a portion of manna." Next out came a small fishbowl. He made a show of looking inside. "Sorry, no manna. Or loaves and fishes, either, for that matter." He set the fishbowl next to the slide rule.

"And finally, the stone tablets of the Ten Commandments." He used two hands to lift out a large, illustrated, coffee table book. He turned it around so they could see the title: *The Illustrated Pool and Billiards Book: From Breaking to Bank Shots*. "Well, not quite," he said with a frown and dropped the book on the table with the other things.

"Ironically, he told my colleagues where to find the trunk just a week before he died. He really cut it close. A woman had been there before them posing as his illegitimate daughter. It seems he told her about the trunk. We never got the entire story.

"I couldn't be there. Ferris and Whitehouse, rest their souls, had to do the honors. When we first opened the trunk, it was filled with papers and projects, right up to here." He touched the side of the trunk just a few inches from the top. "Some unfinished, some an utter waste of time. He allowed himself sometimes to be diverted into the fruitless search for a unified field theory, but I digress. Some of the papers, though, were utterly brilliant. World changing. Just the Internet alone I would say has changed the world, wouldn't you? At one time, all the papers were removed and studied. We're in the process of returning them now. That's why the trunk is only half full. We're getting ready to put it on temporary exhibit. A small concession on the board's part."

Yohaba slowly and contemplatively ran her fingers along the slide rule. Steenberg and Rulon stood there patiently watching her, respectful of her feelings. After a brief silence, she asked, "If he thought the Earth was going to be hit by an asteroid, why do you think he just told you three? Why not tell the US government?"

"Good question," replied Leonard. "At first, that's exactly what we wanted him to do. But he would have none of it. He also insisted that we keep his involvement secret from the world. He seemed to think that he had enemies who would refute his asteroid theory out of professional jealousy.

"But as to your point about the government, he wrote a letter in 1939 advising the US government to begin what eventually became the Manhattan project. It was a confusing time for the world. In any case, he felt betrayed by the way things turned out.

"After that, he didn't dare trust any government with the secrets of a higher yield. He had a dream that someday the world's scientists would band together across national boundaries to do the right thing for mankind. That is what CERN has become. We've tried to live up to his dream. We started with twelve member nations in 1954 and now we are up to twenty. Your great-great-grandfather would have been quite proud." Steenberg had been sitting halfway on the edge of the table. Now he stood up. "Are you ready to go?"

They nodded.

He reached over to put the slide rule back in the trunk but stopped and said to Yohaba, "If what you tell me is true, then all of this, the trunk and what's inside, really belongs to you. How do you feel about that?"

"I can't believe he meant it just for me," said Yohaba, touching

Steenberg's hand as she said it. "I think it was meant for his three stars *and* his daughter. I think he would be pleased for other people to see the trunk and maybe to remember him just a little. But if you don't mind, I'd like to have the slide rule and the fish bowl. I think my grandmother would appreciate both and find a place for them on her mantelpiece."

"By all means," he said. "But, please, take the book too. Someday, the trunk will end up in a museum; you have my word. But what would we do with the book? If word leaks out that Einstein was interested in billiards, the workers' union here will demand pool tables in every break room, and our budgets are already overtaxed. Please, take it. You'll be doing us a favor. Really, the trunk and the papers are enough."

Once back in his office, they continued to ply Dr. Steenberg with questions, and with the patience of Job, he continued to answer as if they were the most important people in the world. Rulon noticed his ringless left hand. It occurred to him that despite his one moral lapse decades before, Steenberg had most likely lived a celibate life since then and had to be acutely aware that Yohaba was his sole descendent. As Rulon listened to Yohaba and him converse, he could sense that Steenberg was leading up to something. And sure enough, he was.

"Now that you know all about the trunk," said Steenberg, "I have one other issue to discuss with you, my child. But first I must ask you a personal question about your young knight here. Would I be wrong in assuming that your relationship with him is more than platonic? I don't wish to imply anything indiscreet, but depending on your answer, I will either ask him to remain for our succeeding conversation or to leave."

As an answer, Yohaba leaned closer to Rulon and hugged his right arm with both of hers. "I love Rulon, and I trust him completely."

"Then, Rulon, what I have to say goes for you too: please, no questions until I'm done. Do I have your word?" They both nodded and sat up straight, perfectly alert.

"Albert's work was of immense scientific value; in many respects it was pure science, pure research. But the projects themselves required huge capital investment and were meant to lead eventually to practical applications. Your great-great-grandfather, Yohaba, in his wisdom and foresight, allowed for this.

"Not all of his ideas have borne fruit, but some have. Many of Albert's discoveries have become patentable over the years. Albert anticipated this, and he worked out a rather complex algorithm for distributing the funds. It was very much like him, I assure you. For as long as we three stars were alive, we followed Albert's instructions to the letter. Even after the deaths of my dear colleagues, I continued to perform my fiduciary responsibilities.

"I last checked the account in question only five days ago, the one that has been reserved for his daughter—or any of her female descendents if they tracked down the trunk. It held just over one and a quarter million dollars. I regret to say that before the world's current economic difficulties, it held a considerably larger sum.

"Now, I believe you, that you are his descendent. What makes this particularly joyous for me is that I also believe that you are my granddaughter. Nevertheless, before I can turn the money over to you, according to the terms of Albert's will, I must first enlist the services of a company that specializes in such things and verify your claim. He insisted on this. Once verified, the money will be wired to a bank account of your choosing.

Pausing for a moment to observe their reactions, Steenberg then asked, "Do either of you have any questions?" Yohaba suggested that the money was half Alex's too, but Steenberg corrected her and said the terms of the will were quite clear—that the money would go to the female descendent who managed to track down the trunk.

Steenberg fell silent, but Rulon's mind raced on. Yohaba was crying; her eyes were brimming, and a few small tears ran soundlessly down her cheeks. To most people, a million dollars was a lot of money. Not enough for someone to quit working for the rest of their lives, but enough to take some of the pressure off.

But Rulon didn't think it was the money itself that made Yohaba cry. As for him, he was struck by the poignancy of this loving gesture extended by Einstein over the decades to a descendent he knew he'd never meet and also by the honesty of Dr. Steenberg, who remained true to his charge after all these years. He suspected Yohaba felt the same way, only more so.

Money never held much attraction for Rulon. The most he ever wanted was enough to be free and to take care of the people who depended on him. So it wasn't so much the money that preoccupied his thoughts at that moment, but the way Yohaba had clutched his arm a few minutes ago and said she loved him. The fierceness of it went through him like a shiver but still managed to warm his cowboy heart.

21

"Few are those who see with their own eyes and feel with their own hearts." —Einstein

As they walked outside, having said their good-byes to Steenberg back in the lobby, part of Rulon was worried that now every time he reached for Yohaba, she'd think he was doing it for the money. Yohaba must have been feeling the same way because once they were back in the Clio, they turned to each other at the same time.

"The money doesn't mean a thing," she said, cutting him off, her words gushing out. "I'm the least materialistic person you'll ever meet."

"Me too," he said, glad to get it off his chest. They both fell silent, their initial points having been made. "I really like you, Yohaba," he began again, "and it has nothing to do with the money. I like being around you an awful lot. In a strange way, we work well together. Like two draft horses hitched to the same plow."

"Darling," she said, without the slightest hint of having taken offense, "please shut up. You're no good at this. Let's forget about the money for now. Long-term, a lot of it will go to taking care of Alex. That was always Grandma's greatest worry—what would happen to Alex after she died. This takes a big burden off both of us. But as far as the money is concerned, if I agree not to rush off and buy a tattoo parlor, will you promise never to try professing your love to me again?"

"Deal," he said. He pulled her to him, and they kissed, the tight quarters of the Clio making it tough to get too passionate. After a suitably romantic interlude, they drove off, back to Bergün to see Granny.

* * *

For the next five hours they chattered on like magpies, reviewing everything that had been discussed back in Steenberg's office as well as solving most of the world's political and social problems. Now that the asteroid wasn't going to hit, Rulon felt like mankind was worth talking about again.

"I'm right about this," he insisted as they drove through Andermatt after one particularly stimulating exchange. "Improvement is a generational thing. You don't go from mud huts to college in one generation. The first generation learns to read and write. Then the next generation graduates from high school, and then the *next* one goes to college. It takes three generations, minimum. It's the same reason why you can't ram democracy down people's throats. First they need to be educated, and then you get a free press, and then you stop the civil-service corruption. It's a process."

"You're wrong," said Yohaba. "There are lots of women who have gone from mud huts to Louis Vuitton in one generation. It doesn't take that long."

"But that's not the same thing," he almost yelled.

"Look at you," was her reply, "you've gone from riding bulls to driving BMW's all in one lifetime. There's another example for you. Give it up."

He spluttered a few responses, but Yohaba just laughed at his feeble comebacks.

They were a surprisingly jolly couple considering the circumstances.

I wonder what the Serbians are up to. The thought struck Rulon out of the blue. *And what about Jezebella?* He hoped Dmitry, or whomever she worked for, had moved her right into another assignment and out of his hair. Then he laughed out loud. "A picture just came into my head," he said, "of Isabella teaming up with the remaining Serbian. Wow! What a nasty outfit that would be." Yohaba smiled but didn't laugh.

About an hour outside of Bergün, Rulon took a call on the red phone from Magnus.

"All is well," Magnus said. "It's safe to show your face in Zurich. You'll have to turn yourself in to the police, but you'll be immediately released on your own recognizance. You can thank

Toby for that. Privately, the Swiss were angry that you didn't kill the second Serbian. They know those guys are a bunch of psychos. The guy you left alive is in the hospital under police guard, blind in one eye, with a serious concussion and months of plastic surgery to look forward to. Police are looking for the third brother and expect to have him on a plane back to Serbia within hours. And one other thing. The brother you never met is the family bull-goose loon bucket. Be careful."

After hanging up, Rulon quickly inserted the battery back into his other cell phone and gave Dmitry a call. Now that things were squared away with the consulate, he wasn't worried about the phone being used to track him, and he was extremely anxious to know if Dmitry had managed to pacify the natives.

Dmitry sounded tired, or maybe it was just painful for him to talk. "We can't find the third brother," he said. At those words, Rulon got a sick feeling in his stomach. But then Dmitry explained that they'd left the brother a message paying out the contract in full, and saying if he pursued Rulon and Yohaba, they would take corrective action. "But honestly," said Dmitry, "we wouldn't bother. He doesn't know that, of course. That's the most I can do for you."

Rulon said thanks, and then Dmitry added ominously, "This changes nothing between us. We still want the trunk. You can make it easier for everyone if you just let me talk to the girl." When Rulon said nothing, Dmitry eventually clicked off. Still, overall, Rulon was pleased with the response. Honor among thieves. A rare trait.

Right after he hung up, Rulon had second thoughts about how he handled the call. What was the harm now with Dmitry talking to Yohaba? The formula for the higher yield had been destroyed. The trunk was going on exhibit. There was no further need for secrecy. Rulon and Yohaba talked it over, and she made a good point about not wanting to risk making Steenberg a target. They decided they needed more time to think this through. Rulon dropped the idea. The exhibition was still four months away. They'd have it worked out by then, one way or the other.

It was nearly 10:00 p.m. when they turned into Granny's long, narrow driveway, and Rulon switched off the headlights. He parked two hundred yards away from the house and made Yohaba get out of the car and hide in the woods while he walked on ahead and did a careful surveillance.

Predictably for this time of night, the house was dark and peaceful. Rulon circled it warily from the woods. When he was satisfied, he walked around to the unlocked back door and let himself in. The home was quiet. He silently checked out the house with his Colt at the ready. All clear. He holstered his pistol, returned to Yohaba and the car, and drove the rest of the way to the house.

Yohaba was out of the car first and bounded for the front door. Rulon stayed behind to fetch the bags out of the trunk. The house lights came on. He heard a door open and glanced up to see Granny in a nightgown hugging Yohaba. He stopped to watch as they started inside, arm in arm. He was still watching when, just as they crossed the threshold, Yohaba leaned back and shouted, "Come on, slowpoke!"

A few moments later, Alex came out to help in his pajamas. Rulon asked him to clean out the car while he carried the bags inside.

When Rulon walked in the house, he found Yohaba sitting on the couch next to Granny. The old lady looked up with tired eyes. "Don't stand there like some kind of pack animal, Rulon. You know where the rooms are. Go make yourself useful."

Yohaba corrected her sternly. "He's not a pack animal, Gran. You'd better learn to get along; you're going to be seeing a lot of him." The look in her eyes when she jumped to Rulon's defense didn't go unnoticed by Granny, who now apprised both of them with a curious mixture of humor and wistfulness.

Rulon trundled off with a smile on his face, first dropping off Yohaba's bag, and then his own in Alex's room, along with a big sigh. He hoped this wasn't going to be another long night with Alex discussing the mutation patterns of swine flu DNA. Though he was tired, he went back to the living room and tried to be sociable.

Yohaba was telling Granny about the money. Granny was less than impressed. "Fortunately, it's not so much money that it will change your life," she said. "This old fool's advice is to forget about the money. Decide what your dream is as if the money didn't exist and then live that dream. Only live it with more money."

Granny felt the same way about the money as they did. What does it matter if you gain the whole world but lose your soul? Earlier, Yohaba had joked about buying a ranch, but now, in front of Granny, she and Rulon discussed the idea more seriously. When Yohaba was a teenager, she lived forty-five minutes from Zurich in the foothills of the Alps and learned to ride horses. She loved that lifestyle. Rulon loved it too, but he also knew the flip side—brutal hours and no security. How she was going to juggle that dream with a career in physics was anybody's guess. It didn't worry him, though. If they had a future together, they'd make it work.

While Yohaba and Granny talked, Alex walked in eating an apple from the car. He stood there in the doorway, chomping away. With a full mouth and without even waiting for a break in the conversation he nonchalantly asked, "What's so special about April 13, 2029?"

Yohaba let out an aggravated huff. "Not now, Alex. Can't you see we're talking? If you want to be part of the conversation, then come inside and sit down." Yohaba and Granny returned to their heart-to-heart. Not fazed in the slightest, Alex came over and sat on the plain wooden chair next to Rulon.

Rulon was ready for bed but thought it smart to check on the car one more time, especially if Alex had been out there fiddling around. When he got up, Alex trotted along behind him like a two-month-old calf.

Outside, Rulon was highly annoyed. Every car door, including the trunk, was flung open. Alex had gone through everything. The garbage bag lay tipped over next to the driver's side door, and the leftover grocery sack was disturbed, its contents partially strewn on the ground. Inside the car, Einstein's billiard book was spread open on the passenger seat, and some 4- by 6-inch photographs Rulon hadn't seen before were scattered on the floor. Truly annoyed, Rulon gathered up the scattered food and the photos, barely glancing at the pictures, noticing only that they were images of pool tables, and wanting to chuck them all away.

"What's so special about April 13, 2029?" asked Alex again.

"I don't know," replied Rulon angrily. "Is it Bastille Day, or something?"

"No. Bastille Day is July 14," Alex said simply, oblivious to Rulon's mood. It was freezing out, and Rulon noticed Alex was in his stockinged feet. *Good grief, boy.* Alex reached for the photographs, but Rulon snatched them away and handed him the repacked sack of food instead.

"Here you go, pardner," he said, hoping the food would keep him out of trouble for a while. "Maybe you should head inside. It's pretty cold out here."

"What's wrong?" asked Alex. Rulon looked at him standing there in his pajamas, in the cold, without any shoes, and felt a glimmer of compassion.

"Okay, Alex, you've got me. What's so special about April 13, 2029?"

Alex handed Rulon the sack but still held onto his apple, which he continued to munch slowly. With his free hand, he took the photographs back and laid them out on the floor of the trunk. He shifted a few of the pictures around into an order that made sense to his savant brain.

"There," he said, pointing to one of the pictures. "That one. What's so special about April 13, 2029?" Rulon strained to look at the pictures in the dimness of the trunk light.

"Alex, my friend," said Rulon, mustering every ounce of his patience, "this is a pool table and these are billiard balls. Where did you find them? I'll bet you got them out of that book on billiards, right? Which you shouldn't have been looking at in the first place. Right?"

"Oh, I'm sorry," said Alex with a start, followed by a look of genuine contrition. "I just saw the pictures and wondered why someone went to all the trouble."

"What trouble?" asked Rulon.

"To set up those balls to represent the night sky over Switzerland on all those days," he said matter-of-factly.

"You're crazy," said Rulon, and then instantly regretted it. Alex's eyes went terribly hurt and then angry. "I didn't mean that the way it came out," Rulon said quickly. "I didn't mean that you were crazy; I just meant that as an expression. I tell your sister she's crazy sometimes when she says something off the wall. Do you understand what I'm trying to say?"

Alex obviously didn't, because he wordlessly wandered off back to the house, dropping the half-eaten apple on the stone footpath. When he got to the door, he turned back to Rulon and said in a calm voice, "You shouldn't call my sister crazy. I don't want to be in Switzerland when that asteroid hits. Are we going to move?"

"What?" asked Rulon in complete befuddlement. "Yes. No. Of course not, everything is okay. What are you talking about?" Alex, his face expressionless, went into the house without answering.

Puzzled, Rulon gathered up the photos and got in the car behind the steering wheel to look at them. These were billiard balls. When had he told Alex about the asteroid? He honestly couldn't remember. Maybe he'd been eavesdropping. Maybe Granny had said something after they drove off yesterday.

Rulon studied the photos in the order Alex had placed them. Okay, there were subtle changes. All the balls changed position somewhat in each picture, but three of the balls moved further in each photo than the rest. Those three were circled in red with the numbers one, two, and three written next to them. He opened the Clio's sun roof. He wanted to see the sky. It was a brilliantly clear night, but the trees were blocking his view.

Something told him not to let this go. He studied the pictures again, and his focus was drawn to the last of the eleven photos. Two balls were touching. He backtracked through the pictures. One of those two balls also made a similar touch with another ball in picture eight. Suppose this *was* set up to be a sky chart; what was the purpose? Rulon knew he wouldn't be able to sleep until he talked to Alex.

Yohaba and Granny were still together, chatting away, when Rulon stuck his head in the living room. No Alex. The kitchen. Nothing. He moved to the back of the house, and before he even reached Alex's room, the tangy aroma of green apples reached his nose. He found Alex in bed.

"Hey, Alex," said Rulon in a friendly voice, as he sat down on the corner of Alex's bed. "I need your help. Tell me what you see in these pictures." Alex got out from under the covers and took the photos. He sat cross-legged on the bed, and Rulon watched while he laid out the pictures in front of him in two rows exactly as he had in the car.

"This one," he said, pointing to the first picture, "is November 22, 1954. And this one—" He pointed to the eighth picture "—is June 4, 2011. This one is April 13, 2029. What are we going to do about the asteroid?" Rulon looked at the pictures again and picked up the last one. He studied it and turned it over. On the back, in English cursive, was written, "A slow massé shot curves sooner, even though a harder shot spins faster."

"This is about billiards," he said, "not stars." He looked at Alex, who was now eating a sandwich he'd pulled from under the covers.

"If the asteroid or comet hits, it will be the end of the world, if it's big enough," Alex said casually between bites.

"Alex, how can you be so sure this is about asteroids? It could be about anything," said Rulon, gesturing in exasperation and disturbing the pictures.

"Like what?"

"Like, well, like . . . anything," Rulon blustered out, frustrated. "Anything. Maybe it's the table pattern of the 1931 billiard world championships. Anything."

Alex stopped chewing for a few moments and looked at him, puzzled. "But why would you say that when it shows star formations over Switzerland?" As if any other explanation was unthinkable.

"Have you got a computer?" asked Rulon, a sick feeling growing in his stomach, thinking they had missed something, then thinking, *Hey, I could miss something, but how could Steenberg miss something?* Then he looked at Alex, who was engrossed in one of the pictures. "Alex," he almost shouted, "do you have a computer?"

"In the other room," he mumbled while waving his sandwich in the general vicinity of the door. Rulon rushed down the hall, throwing open doors and flipping on lights until he found the right room. He sat down in front of the computer. What exactly he was hoping to find, he wasn't sure. The Google home page came up, and he typed in a search for 182 Elsa.

By this time, Alex had come in, his breath reeking of apple, mustard, and sausage. Rulon went through page after page, looking for something, anything, he didn't know what. He read paragraphs of data, biographies of Palisa, and numbers galore. He learned about Elsa's perihelion, aphelion, inclination, eccentricity, semi-major axis, orbit type, rotation period, and albedo. Very little of it made any sense to him. Alex read along over his shoulder.

"It's got a moon," said Alex at one point, as casually as if he'd just noticed a loose thread.

"How the heck do you know that?" Rulon asked, annoyed that their troubles might not be over. Oh yes, he knew Alex was onto something. Somewhere, deep in his gut, he knew it, just like he had known he was going to get busted up when he hopped on Spin Doctor the last time he rode a bull.

"The rotation period is too long," Alex said. "See here." He leaned over Rulon and pointed to a chart that listed the rotation period as eighty hours. "That doesn't make sense unless it's got a small moon."

Rulon sat there absorbing what Alex had just said. Another body nearby with a gravitational field sufficiently large to slow down Elsa's rotation? Okay, that made sense now that Alex pointed it out. But Rulon never would have thought of it in a million years on his own.

He looked up at Alex, amazed. And more amazed that he was about to count on him to give him the right answers.

"Alex, sit down please." Rulon pointed to a padded chair in the corner of the room and Alex obliged. "I need you to tell me what you think these eleven photos are trying to say."

"Two asteroids or comets are converging. Then on June 4, 2011, they either collide or pass close enough to disrupt each other's orbits. They then go off on a new trajectory, and one of them collides with the Earth on April 13, 2029."

Rulon asked, "Is that what you think is going to happen?"

"I don't know. But whoever made the pictures thought so."

"How do you know that?" he asked. "Show me." He offered Alex his chair and Alex pulled up Google Sky and searched through it until he found the right star pattern.

"See," he said. "This is April 13, 2029." Rulon held up the photo next to the computer screen. *Well, I'll be horn-swoggled.*

"Is it possible for people to know these things?" Rulon asked in wonder. "Could someone calculate the orbits of two asteroids millions of miles away and know they were going to collide?"

"Yes," Alex said. "It's not too hard if the asteroids are big enough. The hard part is knowing which of the tens of thousands of asteroids to perform the calculations on. The chances of following the right two asteroids are incredibly remote."

Alex's eyes lost their focus as he withdrew into his own world. After a minute, he blinked twice as if waking up. "They could possibly do it if they knew for certain at least one of the asteroids involved in the collision. But even knowing that would be next to impossible."

"Unless," Rulon said, "they had a reason for watching a particular asteroid." And now the name Elsa and its significance to Einstein took on a greater weight.

"Yes," said Alex.

"Could one man working by himself with the technology available in the 1950s have done this?"

Alex didn't hesitate. "No."

"We believe Einstein set up those pictures," Rulon said, and then asked, "Could Einstein have figured this out?"

This time, Alex was more thoughtful. He got up and paced around the room. After a minute, he announced his conclusion: "Apparently."

"Alex," Rulon said testily. "What's the answer? Could Einstein do this? Yes or no?"

"Well, apparently he thought he could."

Rulon started to protest that he hadn't really answered his question, but then stopped himself: *It was the only answer.*

As he listened to Alex, a thought came to him, a Sunday School memory, about the eye not saying to the hand that I have no need for thee—that everyone has a purpose. How ironic if Alex's strange neurosis ended up saving the world. How many people would have spotted this? Maybe Alex was the only one.

Alex was looking around, probably for something to eat. An odd young man. Rulon stood up and gave him a hug. As odd as he was, they were brothers.

Yohaba was still in the living room talking to her grandmother. When Rulon came in, both women looked up abruptly, and he suspected they'd been talking about him. With Alex at his side, he showed the pictures and explained this new situation. Once everyone was over the initial shock, they agreed they had to contact Steenberg immediately. Given the timeline they were dealing with, they decided it could wait until morning.

Later that evening, as Rulon lay in bed, with Alex snoring away on the other side of the room, he decided that for the first time he really did believe an asteroid was heading toward the Earth, or rather, would be after the June 4, 2011, combination shot.

22

"You cannot simultaneously prevent and prepare for war." —Einstein

Tuesday morning arrived way too soon for Rulon. It was 9:00 a.m. and still dark in the room, partially because the days were getting shorter, partially because of the thick forest around the house. He had no desire to stir. The memory of rescuing Yohaba in the Hönggerberg forest preyed instantly on his mind when he awoke. He lifted his head to check on Alex. He was in bed, sleeping peacefully. Rulon planned the day.

Once they got hold of Steenberg, they'd have to find a way to scan the pictures and email them. Then it occurred to him, it would be better if Alex explained the pictures to Steenberg face-to-face. The more he thought about it, the more that seemed like the right thing to do. He resigned himself to another long, cramped drive back to Geneva. He pulled the covers up to his chin to ward off the cold. Steenberg should see the photographs as soon as possible. They'd drive back to CERN right after breakfast.

The house was stirring now, and footsteps that sounded too sprightly to be Granny's were coming down the hallway. The bedroom door opened slightly, and along with a stream of light came a melodic voice whispering, "Cowboy, are you awake?" Not waiting for an answer, Yohaba came in and sat on the bed. "Wake up! You're burning daylight. Isn't that what you cowboys say?" He rolled over and pretended to ignore her.

"If you don't talk to me," she said, "I'm slipping under the covers with you. It's freezing in here. What did you do, open the window?" She got up to close the window, then came back. With a deep sigh, he rolled back over and sat up.

"I'm not talking to you until you put some clothes on," he said. Yohaba wore a bath towel around her and her hair was wet.

"Don't be a prude," she said while trying somewhat incompetently to hold the towel in place. "Listen. When I was showering, I got to thinking. We need to drive back to Geneva. Leonard will want to see the photographs as soon as possible."

"I already figured that out," he said. "I thought about scanning the photos, but I think you're right. We need to go back."

"Oh, yeah," she said. "I didn't think about scanning. So why can't we just do that?"

"This will turn his world upside down. There is no way he'll accept this just on the basis of some scanned photographs and a phone call." Rulon lowered his voice to a whisper and pointed to Alex's sleeping form. "Your grandfather needs to see him. None of this is logical, but it starts to make sense when you know where Alex is coming from."

Yohaba looked at her brother. "You're probably right. Well, come on then. I'll make you breakfast." She tried pulling the covers off but he manfully resisted.

"Geez, woman!" Rulon yelled.

She finally gave up, and he listened to her giggling retreat down the hallway and then got up and dressed. He pulled on his black Brax jeans and slipped a dark gray shirt over his head. He gripped the edges of the dresser and looked at himself in the mirror. *Gads, she's beautiful.*

Twenty minutes later, he sat at the large, round dining room table, showered and dressed, eating one of Yohaba's famous omelets. Granny was also there, sipping a cup of coffee. Alex was still in bed.

Granny blew on her coffee to cool it. "The boy sleeps a lot," she said. "It's because of his medication. It's also why he eats so much."

"Yohaba and I were thinking we should bring him with us," said Rulon between bites. "I'm sure Leonard will have questions for him about the photographs." Granny shook her head.

"Alex doesn't like to travel," said Yohaba. "He doesn't like anything that upsets his routine. I'm sure just having you in his room will take him a few days to get over." A floorboard creaked, and everyone turned around. There was Alex in the doorway.

"Where did you want to go?" he asked. "I don't eat as much as Rulon."

Rulon told Alex they were driving back to Geneva after breakfast and asked if he wanted to come along. Alex's eyes darted from side to side like he was looking for a way to escape. Rulon added. "We need to visit CERN and talk to one of the directors there."

From that point on, wild horses couldn't have kept Alex away, and eventually Granny gave in. With that settled, Yohaba tried to call Steenberg, but he wasn't picking up. They decided to get going anyway.

An hour later. they were on the road, this time in Granny's Toyota Camry. She said she hardly drove these days and had no plans to go anywhere. For Rulon, not driving a stolen car made things a lot simpler. Alex rode in the back with the picnic basket Granny had put together. Rulon did the driving. If they had to take evasive action it was better if he were behind the wheel.

Yohaba held Rulon's hand and massaged his neck from time to time. He tried engaging her in conversation, but she didn't feel like talking; she wouldn't even bite when he told her he didn't believe in time travel.

Around noon, Yohaba finally got through to Steenberg. She explained about the pictures, making the billiard theory sound a whole lot more plausible than if Rulon had described it. When she hung up, though, she was puzzled.

"He didn't sound that interested," she said. "Does that strike you as odd? He didn't even sound that happy to hear from me. What do you make of that?"

"You don't know him well enough to read him," said Rulon. "You've only met him once. Don't take it personally." But inside he did think it was odd.

"You don't suppose he's happy the way things are, and he doesn't want anything to upset his little world?" she asked.

"Could be," he replied. "But like it or not, his little world is about to be turned on its ear."

Eventually Yohaba and Alex fell asleep, and Rulon was left alone with his thoughts. He looked south. The sky was dark with billowing cumulus clouds, their centers black and edges tinged with gray. Now and again, there were lightning flashes and the sounds of distant thunder. They were heading into a storm. The hills around them were a thick rich green, as green as any Irish meadow, made greener by the contrast with the gathering blackness. A few drops of rain hit the windshield, and in a matter of minutes it was raining hard. Then it was pouring. He slowed. The rain continued for thirty minutes, and though it eventually stopped, the sky remained black and ominous.

An hour later, they drove through Meyrin, past small throngs of costumed children, reminding Rulon it was Halloween. Tomorrow was All Saints Day. He had to give it to the Swiss. While not a particularly religious people, they still managed to take off most religious holidays. Thanks to Steenberg calling ahead, they made it easily through CERN's security at the Meyrin entrance. Rulon looked at his watch. It was just after 4:00 p.m.—a little later than he had intended, but the storm had slowed them. Once through the gate, they headed straight for building 133.

Rulon figured that everyone makes mistakes, but if you correct them quickly, at least you haven't dug yourself a deeper hole. As he stepped out of the car in the parking lot, he remembered that he hadn't checked the car for bugs that morning. He hesitated. What were the chances? He half-expected the stolen Clio to get bugged, maybe, but not Granny's car.

But years of training left their mark, so dutifully he dragged his bug checker out of the glove compartment. To his great astonishment, he picked up a bug. Not taking any chances, his pursuers must have bugged both cars during the night.

Rulon examined the small device closely. Russian. He thought about the Serbian, but he would have attacked him at the house, regardless of witnesses. It had to be the Russians. They were after the trunk and would be more interested in knowing where Rulon and Yohaba were going. What should he do now? All this time Yohaba and Alex were standing on the other side of the car waiting for him.

"What's up?" asked Yohaba, seeing something was wrong. "Did you find something?"

"Yep," he said. "You go inside with Alex, and I'll be right

along. I'll fill you in later. Please, just go." He felt sick inside and blamed himself for putting everyone in jeopardy. This was bad. He might still be able to make things difficult for their pursuers, but the bad guys were homing in. He watched Yohaba and Alex disappear through the reception doors. At least they were safe for now.

As soon as they were out of sight, he jumped into the Camry and cruised the nearby parking lots looking for a license plate from the Graubünden canton where Granny lived. No luck. His other option was to find a car from a canton they'd driven through on the way to CERN that afternoon. For that he had to go back to the second parking lot where he remembered seeing a car from Valais, and there he planted the bug.

His hope was that once the bad guys caught up with the bug and saw it wasn't on the Camry, they would be confused, not knowing when during the journey he had made the switch, but it was a long shot. More than likely they'd figure out what he was up to, but it would take time. It all hinged on whether they'd been trailing the Camry closely enough to keep it in sight.

His conscience pricked him that he was potentially putting some stranger in a dangerous position, but he consoled himself that it was a small risk. And he didn't have any choice. Logically, once the bad guys saw the car wasn't the Camry, they'd realize they'd been duped and walk away. There was an unwritten rule that you left civilians alone.

He drove back to building 133, his heart pounding. He thought about the Serbian. It wasn't over. It was just the beginning. What had Magnus said? He'd find Rulon's family in Idaho. How could he have gotten so complacent?

As he drove, he used all his mirrors, constantly looking in every direction to see if anyone followed. When things had first gotten rough, he should have immediately run for the hills with Yohaba and come back in a year to solve the mystery of Einstein's trunk. His tires screeched as he took a turn too fast.

The 133 lot was emptier now, and he parked closer to the main entrance. He jumped out of the car, nervous from having Yohaba out of sight for so long. In his haste, he left the keys in the ignition and the car unlocked. He went through the first set of tinted glass doors into the vestibule and pulled on the second set. And pulled again. They were locked. Through the glass, he could see the reception area was dark and empty. For a second he was confused. Then he noticed a sign on the door. Despite his bad French, he was able to translate it well enough to figure out that the main reception area was closed for renovation. Visitors now had to use the secondary entrance on the opposite side of the building.

This was innocent, he told himself. He had seen Yohaba and Alex walk through these doors just a few minutes ago. Obviously, they'd gone around to the other entrance while he was replanting the bug. Surely they were with Steenberg now. Nevertheless, with a quick glance to make sure no one was watching, he drew the Colt chambered a round, and put it back in its shoulder holster. He wasn't wearing the Know-foam or his vest, and Freya was tucked away under the seat of the Camry. He had gotten sloppy. Well, that was going to stop. From the vantage point of the vestibule, he scrutinized the parking lot for any suspicious vehicles, most likely a van or an SUV. It looked clear.

He hastened around the building along the narrow path skirting the grass border and then through the doors of the temporary lobby. Inside, there was a front desk and a small waiting area. A young man, dressed in a clown suit, stood at the desk, trying to get past the receptionist, the same harridan from yesterday's visit. From the look on her face, her mood hadn't improved. In a corner, three people, also in costume, sat on cushioned chairs, chatting amiably around a small table. All looked peaceful. He breathed a sigh of relief and walked up to the front desk just as the downcast young man was leaving, obviously rebuffed.

"Remember me?" Rulon asked, keeping his tone easy and pleasant, despite his racing heart. "I'm here to see Leonard Steenberg again. Some friends of mine just came through a few minutes ago. It looks like they already went up to see him." As he talked, he scanned the guest sign-in book. His heart skipped a beat. He didn't see their names.

"Yes, I remember you," she answered sternly. "Mr. Steenberg left over an hour ago for an unexpected meeting. He said you would be coming by and asked that you wait. Please take a seat."

"Thank you," Rulon said, trying to keep the worry out of his voice. "Have you seen my associates? The young woman I was with yesterday came in less than twenty minutes ago with a young man. Do you know where they went?"

"Sorry, I haven't seen them. Please take a seat."

"Are you sure?" he asked coldly, his amiable aura now completely dissipated.

She must have caught something in his tone or expression because her voice went conciliatory. "I'm sorry, sir. I can see you were expecting your friends. But they are not here, and it's been a slow afternoon. I would have seen them. Do you see their names in the guest register?"

"No," he said. "And Leonard Steenberg?"

"He's not here. He said he would be back by five. I'm sorry, sir."

"Are you sure he couldn't have left with my friends?"

"I suppose it's possible, but they would have had to be here by three because that's when he left. Unless he came back early."

Rulon spun on his heels and ran for the door. Once outside, he sprinted for the car. His world was spinning. *Keep cool*, he told himself, fighting the sick feeling in his stomach. *Panicking accomplishes nothing. There's a simple explanation. Steenberg could have come back early and bumped into them.*

As soon as he turned the corner of the building, he could see the Camry—someone was inside. When he reached the car, Alex was in the front passenger seat alone. Rulon pulled at the door handle, but it was locked. He banged on the window. Inconceivably, Alex was looking to the side and not reacting. He yelled, "Alex!" and pounded loudly on the hood. Alex slowly turned his head. His mouth was moving and tears ran down his cheeks. Rulon raced around to the unlocked driver's side and threw open the door.

"Alex? Alex!" he screamed, leaning halfway into the car. "Where is she? Where is she?" He grabbed Alex by the front of his jacket and dragged him over the seat. "Tell me!" he demanded, inches from his face.

While he was shaking Alex, a familiar female voice behind him asked, "Anybody seen an easygoing cowboy around here?"

What the—? He let go of Alex and turned around. There was

Yohaba with her hands on her hips and Leonard Steenberg at her side. "Mine seems to have been taken over by aliens," she added.

Seriously embarrassed, Rulon backed out of the car and tried to regroup. "I can explain," he said quickly. Alex sat there looking perplexed and disheveled, but none the worse for wear. "Hello, Dr. Steenberg," Rulon said. He took a deep breath and cleared his throat. "Bet you didn't think you'd be seeing us again so soon." He held out his hand and Steenberg, after a moment's hesitation, reciprocated.

"Rulon," said Yohaba, "why were you beating up my brother in the car? I'll bet my grandfather would like to know as well." Steenberg folded his arms across his chest, bit down on his lip, and fixed him with a glare.

"I wasn't beating him up," said Rulon with as much dignity as he could salvage. "I was interrogating him while under duress." When Rulon saw his excuse wasn't working he confessed, "I thought you'd been kidnapped. I found a bug on the car. We're being tracked. Dr. Steenberg, this situation with Einstein's trunk is much more dangerous than we've led you to believe."

Before anyone could respond, a wave of paranoia came over Rulon, prompting him to suggest that a previously bugged car wasn't the place for a discussion. He told Yohaba to get Alex out of the car and that they all needed to get inside for their own safety. It took a few tries before Alex could be coaxed out. Once he emerged, Yohaba made a sisterly attempt to straighten his clothes. While she was fussing over him, Alex glared at Rulon with the heat of a thousand suns and ignored his apology.

They all headed back to the building. Rulon felt like a total idiot. Steenberg was kind and helped defuse the situation by walking ahead and chatting amiably with Alex. Yohaba drifted back to walk alongside Rulon.

He stopped in his tracks to face her and demanded, "Where were you?"

"Leonard spotted us as we were walking around to the temporary entrance. We waited by the garage entrance while he parked."

"Well," Rulon said, now feeling like an even bigger idiot, "it's an explanation. Not a great one. But it's an explanation." They resumed walking. "Why was Alex crying?" he asked. "And what was he doing alone in the car? That's what really threw me."

"Can you believe it?" she said, totally blown away. "While we were waiting for Leonard, he asked if he could drive part of the way home. I yelled at him for even bringing it up and told him to wait in front for you. Emotionally, he's still a child sometimes, and you have to treat him that way. You must have gone around one side of the building while he came around the other way and just spotted the car and got in."

"Oh," said Rulon.

"Are we happy now?" asked Yohaba. "Good. Now it's my turn. What the heck was going on back there? I thought you'd flipped."

"I almost did," said Rulon. "I thought they'd taken you again. You can figure out the rest." Rulon wanted to blurt out that his love for her was making him crazy, but the words got stuck in his throat.

"Oh, cowboy," said Yohaba, kindly. "You were beating up Alex for me? And it's not even my birthday."

"I wasn't beating him up. He was acting catatonic. I was trying to get an answer out of him."

"He gets like that when he's under stress. There is an autism streak with Asperger's." She grabbed Rulon's hand and swung it as they walked. "What would you have done, if they'd taken me?" she asked, almost lightheartedly.

"If they had killed you," he said in all seriousness, "I would have gone to the hospital, disabled any police guards, and killed the brother. Then I would have hunted the rest of them down, whoever they were, and killed them all."

Yohaba came to a dead stop. "You're joking," she said, her eyes boring into his, looking for some assurance that he hadn't meant what he said.

When he didn't say anything and looked down instead, she tenderly touched his cheek. "Oh, Rulon," she said, her voice carrying a note of sadness, or maybe it was pain. "Don't even go there, Cowboy. I know you love me. Your attempts at communication are primitive but effective."

"Then don't ever scare me like that," he said angrily. While they talked, he was continually scanning the area. Up ahead, Steenberg and Alex nattered away. From the previous day's visit, Steenberg already knew about Alex and the Asperger's.

Rulon escorted everyone back to the lobby and then rushed back to the car. With Steenberg's blessing and entry card, Rulon parked the Camry out of sight in the building's private underground garage. He still felt like a fool, but he also figured this was a wake-up call. It was time to sharpen up. Out of the trunk came the vest and Freya with her modified shoulder holster. He figured there was no need for the Know-foam anymore. Whoever was chasing them knew what they were up against. He was going tactical from here on out.

23

"Two things inspire me to awe—the starry heavens above and the moral universe within." —Einstein

"This is a perfect example of the intersection of scholarship and intuition," said Steenberg. "Quite brilliant, really, to recognize the star pattern in these photos. But it doesn't answer the question as to why Albert never pointed out their significance to us. It seems like an important detail to have omitted, don't you think?" No one knew what to say. Finally, Steenberg looked down, shook his head sadly, and answered his own question. "I guess for us mortals, death always comes too soon and never when we expect it."

Steenberg sat behind his desk with Rulon and Yohaba sitting on the other side and Alex standing by the wall on his left. The photographs lay spread out in front of him and Google Sky was on his computer screen. He looked like an Armani advertisement—sports jacket, turtleneck, and tapered trousers, all in black, his longish white hair providing a vivid contrast. "It's quite remarkable that Alex recognized the pattern. Well done, young man."

At those words, everyone turned to Alex, who was looking over his shoulder at the colorful pictures of the Hadron Collider on Steenberg's wall. When Alex didn't respond, Rulon and Yohaba turned their attention back to Steenberg, waiting for him to say more. His next question stunned them.

"Now then, what would you like me to do with this information?"

"Ah . . . no offense, sir," said Rulon, seeing for the first time the reticence Yohaba had earlier sensed on the phone, "but, is this a trick question? Because I thought the obvious thing to do would be to show this to your astronomer friends and get it verified." Rulon was still trying to burn off the aggression from the parking lot.

"And then what?" asked Steenberg.

"Well, I'm no scientist, but I'd say we build a big rocket and blow the thing up."

Steenberg smiled patiently then frowned. He got up and faced the window behind his desk. Without turning around he said, "You think it's that easy? For almost twenty years, all our efforts were focused on dealing with 182 Elsa. When we discovered the error and found out that Elsa wasn't going to hit after all, we redirected our mission.

"At this point, my young friend, it would take years to shut down the LHC and redeploy the engineers. I'm talking about shutting down projects that have been specifically funded by nations with specific expectations. This theory about colliding asteroids is totally unverifiable at this point." He threw his hands in the air. "A collision in space, millions of miles away and when only one of the asteroids is known . . . impossible. You have no idea what you're asking." At this he punched his left hand in frustration. "This discovery couldn't have come at a worse time. I'm being frank."

"Look," said Rulon, "maybe you're not expecting to be alive in 2029, but now you've got a granddaughter and a grandson here who just might be. How does that factor into your priorities?" Rulon sensed Yohaba looking over at him in horror.

Steenberg looked at Rulon for a long ten seconds before returning to his chair. "Strong words, Rulon, but not totally unjustified," he said humbly. "Just give me a minute." He closed his eyes and rubbed his temples while Rulon and Yohaba sat there quietly. After a minute, Yohaba asked if he wanted them to leave. Steenberg neither moved nor opened his eyes but simply replied that wouldn't be necessary.

In all this, Alex was forgotten. Now he turned from the photographs on the wall and said matter-of-factly, "It will be easy to verify after 2011, after the collision. Then you'll only have to track a single, known asteroid's trajectory. I don't think it will hit. The required calculations were too precise for the technology of the fifties. Einstein would have had to account for the rotation in both asteroids as well as for their orbits, angle of collision, and gravity from other passing objects to compute the correct path. There were too many factors."

Rulon was still trying to comprehend Alex's point when Steenberg, sounding suddenly energized, answered, "Yes, yes, that makes sense. We've got until June 5, 2011 before we can even verify. And eighteen years after that to prepare—if we have to. Plenty of time." Rulon looked in Steenberg's eyes and could see the wheels starting to turn.

"Yes," Steenberg said, his words coming quickly now. "We'll have enough time to satisfy most of our current contracts, and then when we have incontrovertible proof, we will change our charter. I'll talk to our benefactors, to the twenty member states. They'll get behind us. This will galvanize the entire staff. Money will come pouring in. It will have the same sense of mission as the US space program in the sixties. Only this time, no one will be able to question our purpose. We won't be inventing Velcro this time; we'll be truly saving the world."

"Can we do it without the increased bomb yield?" asked Rulon, not deliberately setting out to rain on the parade but feeling the question had to be asked. "You know, the formula or whatever it was that you burned up." Steenberg looked from Rulon to Yohaba and then back to Rulon again. Something was coming.

"Forgive me," he said, with a grimace that said he was about to make a painful admission, "but I still have it." He focused on Yohaba, needing her to understand, and continued. "Knowledge is knowledge, and inspiration comes from a higher source for a reason. Your great-great-grandfather was a conduit, I believe, from the Almighty, and there was a reason why we were given that information at that time. The thought of destroying it never entered my mind, though the others were adamant about it. Through some sleight of hand, I managed to burn only a copy that night; the original I smuggled and put back in my safe. After my colleagues passed away, I was the sole keeper of the secret. Ironic, isn't it? A serendipitous and decidedly uncharacteristic deceit on my part but perhaps a fortuitous one."

They conversation lasted for several more hours and eventually swung toward more personal topics, mainly driven by Steenberg's interest in the history of his newfound family. As they talked, they were occasionally interrupted by pirates, ballerinas, witches, and super-heroes sticking their heads in the door and wishing Steenberg a good night.

A little after 8:00 p.m., their conversation wrapped up, and Rulon's thoughts drifted towards other matters. It was too late to drive all the way back to Bergün. They still had to find a hotel room. Had the Russians been fooled? Was he in for a surprise when he got back to the car? By now the floor was quiet as a church.

Steenberg looked at his watch and with a kind smile asked when he would be seeing them again. It was decided they would all meet for breakfast the next morning before the drive back to Granny's. Because all the doors would be locked, Steenberg escorted them downstairs to the garage to let them out.

24

"REALITY IS MERELY AN ILLUSION, ALBEIT A VERY PERSISTENT ONE." —EINSTEIN

IT WAS TUESDAY NIGHT BEFORE A HOLIDAY, AND THE BUILDING was practically deserted. On the way to the elevator, they saw only one custodian, and after they got off there was no one in the hallway to the stairs. Rulon was on high alert, fearing the worst, but hoping that his little ploy with the bug had succeeded. With any luck, the driver of the car had left work early and was leading Rulon's pursuers on a merry chase. But because he didn't know for sure, it was with all his senses tuned that he took the lead through each door and then down the stairs to the garage, insisting that everyone wait behind him while he checked out each opportunity for an ambush.

Just outside the garage, Rulon paused with his hand on the door handle. He asked everyone to wait once more while he investigated their most vulnerable and obvious chokepoint. Up until then, Steenberg had quietly gone along with what he considered to be Rulon's excessive concern, but he now suggested, if the situation were really so dangerous, that perhaps they should involve the authorities. Rulon kicked himself for not thinking of that earlier. Steenberg offered to lead them to a police station only ten minutes away.

But first they had to get to their cars. The garage's gray metal door stared back at them. What was on the other side? He turned to Yohaba and Steenberg. "Just bear with me one more time. Everyone stay quiet. It'll take a few minutes to check out the garage, and then we'll head straight for the police."

He quietly opened the garage door and stuck his head out. For the count of three, he did a quick scan, and then pulled his head back in. This level had been nearly full, with at least fifty cars when he parked here four hours earlier. Now there were only three: Steenberg's Audi TT just to the right of the door, the Camry to the left at the far end of the garage, and forty feet away, between the Camry and the doorway, a black Nissan panel van that had ambush written all over it.

The van was so obvious that Rulon was tempted to dismiss it just for that reason. But then, maybe his adversaries anticipated his reaction and parked it there anyway. The garage ceiling was low, eight feet high, and supported by thick, evenly spaced concrete pillars every twenty feet in all directions. The pillars made for tight parking and a poor line of sight when backing out of a space, but they made for a good place to hide.

When Steenberg started to protest that surely they were safe here, Yohaba put her hand on his arm. "Leonard, let him do his job." Steenberg then suggested they go back to his office and call the police from there.

Rulon thought about it, and Steenberg was right. This was an unnecessary risk. "Okay," he said. "Let's go back."

Everyone, except oblivious Alex, was relieved. With a single phone call from Steenberg's office, the danger would be over. They walked back up the stairs to the first door. Steenberg's key card didn't work.

"Not to worry," he said, chuckling. "Of all the times for this to happen." He rubbed the card against his sleeve and slid it again and again through the card reader. Still nothing. There was an intercom next to the card reader and Steenberg pushed the speaker button. "Thomas, it's Leonard. The reader's not working again. Can you let us through, please?" Silence. Not even a click. Steenberg hit the button a few more times. "Hello? Thomas? Is anyone there?" He turned to Rulon with a worried look. "I think the intercom has been disabled."

By now all doubt was gone from Rulon's mind. He could feel it—they were here.

Steenberg caught Rulon staring at the door and misread his thoughts. "These doors are solid metal," he said. "You would need a blowtorch to get through." Rulon had already accepted that.

What he was worried about was being trapped.

Rulon grunted, pulled out the Colt, and thumbed off the safety. It occurred to him that these guys would be loaded for bear this time and that they'd be in an ugly mood. *Well,* Rulon said to himself, *I'm getting pretty good at ugly myself.* He reached inside his jacket and slipped off the thong that held Freya in her holster.

There was a fire alarm to the right of the door. Rulon flipped open the plastic guard and pulled the T-shaped lever. Yohaba and Leonard gasped, but nothing happened. Just as Rulon suspected.

He had one goal: to get them out unharmed. He explained to everyone their new reality. No talking unless absolutely necessary and even then only in a whisper. He asked everyone to pull out their cell phones and try to call the police. No luck. He wasn't surprised. They were at least thirty feet underneath a concrete building.

They walked down to the garage. As they did, Rulon assessed their state of mind. Yohaba was trembling. She knew how serious this was. Steenberg was worried but naïve. Alex was, well . . . Alex.

Rulon opened the garage door and stuck his head in again. Same three vehicles. He quietly closed the door and planned his next move. On the floor to Rulon's right was a large plastic bag filled with aluminum cans ready for removal to the recycling plant. He snapped the plastic tie-wrap that secured the top and pulled out a couple of cans. Signaling for everyone to stay quiet, he opened the door again and tossed the cans across the floor. As the cans rattled along, he scanned the entire garage but particularly watched the van. Nothing moved. He closed the door and asked Alex to turn off the lights in the hallway. Alex ignored him. Yohaba flipped the switch herself, and the hallway went dark.

Rulon opened the door once more and stood recessed in the opening, not showing himself, but having a clear view. He decided to watch and wait for ten minutes. His watch showed 8:24 p.m. The countdown began. All he heard was the background buzz from the fluorescent lighting. He waited.

The Camry was eighty feet away with the Nissan van in between him and the car. Was the van there when he first parked the car? He couldn't remember. After four minutes, the van dipped slightly in its shocks, suggesting someone had gotten out on the other side. Rulon pulled the dental mirror out of his jacket pocket. He dropped to his stomach, slipping the mirror beyond the edge of the door jamb, close to floor level. He was looking for feet under the van. And there they were. Two pairs in black combat boots. He eased the door closed and sat back against the wall. This wasn't good. He told Yohaba to turn on the lights.

"They're here," he said. "If we stay, there will be a fight, and they'll have us trapped between them." He looked at Steenberg. "What's downstairs?"

"The seventeen miles of the Hadron Collider tunnel and a lot of extremely expensive equipment."

"How far?"

"Sixteen flights."

"Is there a way out?"

"If we get out, we can use our cell phones," suggested Yohaba hopefully.

"There is a way out," said Steenberg, surprisingly calm for a man being trailed by assassins. "The service vehicles will be locked up by now, but if we go down to the bottom, we can walk along the service tunnel and exit at building 157."

"Okay, that's our new plan," said Rulon. "But just tell me one thing: Einstein's nuclear yield paper is in your safe, right?" When Steenberg didn't immediately answer, Rulon's stomach churned.

"Actually . . . no, I'm afraid not," said Leonard, with another one of his grimaces. "It's in the trunk. Like I said, we're in the process of collecting the original papers and putting them back in."

"Yes, but why put that one back in?" blurted Rulon in frustration, not quite able to believe someone so smart could do something so stupid. "Wasn't it better off in your safe?" Nothing was going right.

"Its safety was its anonymity, which, up until yesterday, I thought was airtight," Steenberg replied. With a deep note of regret, he added, "It originally came from the trunk. I wanted the exhibit to be a monument to his brilliant intellect. No one else would have appreciated if the paper were there, but I would have known. It was to be a personal tribute from me."

Rulon sighed wearily. "Look, we've got to go. I want Leonard to lead. Yohaba, I need you to stay between me and Leonard with Alex. I'll bring up the rear." Steenberg started off. As Alex followed after, Rulon grabbed his arm and whispered, "Sorry I yelled at you outside."

"You would never yell at my sister like that," he said, still bitter and hurt like a little kid.

"You're wrong," said Rulon. "Your sister and I have gotten into it a few times. It doesn't mean I don't love her. Same goes for you. Now buck up. We need to be a team in here. This is no time for holding grudges." Rulon didn't know how much of this got through, but he was going to treat him like a man, and he better darn well measure up.

"Can I hold your gun?" asked Alex.

"No," said Rulon forcefully.

"Can I hold your hammer, then?"

"Heck no," he said. "You'll get yourself killed. Now get down there and watch after your sister, or you'll be pulling my shoe out of your rear." At that, Alex's eyes went a little wide, but he did what he was told. "Hey," Rulon whispered after him. "Tell everyone to wait for me four floors down. I'll be a minute." Alex's face was losing its animation, and that had Rulon worried. The last thing Rulon needed was for Alex to freeze up.

While talking to Alex, Rulon had been keeping his eye on both the door to the garage and the door at the top of the stairs that led into the building proper. The one they couldn't get through. It was hard to know how to play this without knowing what their enemies were really after. If it was Rulon they wanted, he'd send the others off down the tunnel by themselves and sit here all night with the Colt in one hand and Freya in the other, daring them to come get him. But if they were still after Yohaba and the trunk, he didn't dare leave her alone.

What if they were already down there waiting? But Rulon knew they couldn't go up, and they couldn't stay here. To do either would guarantee a gun fight. While he was thinking this out, he opened the garage door a few feet and slammed it so the boys by the van would know someone was still around. He needed to catch up with his little flock. He pulled two more cans out of the recycling bag and then raced downstairs. Once he caught up with everyone, they continued down to the bottom.

"The collider tunnel is over a hundred meters below ground," whispered Leonard as they followed him down the stairs. "Normally we'd have people working around the clock, but because of All Saints Day, everyone's off."

The lights were dim and reflected poorly off the dull gray walls of the stairwell. The stairs were metal and clanged slightly with each step, despite their best efforts to walk quietly. Rulon looked over the railing. It was a long way to the bottom. When they'd gone down six more flights, he stopped and arranged the two soda cans on a step.

"What's that for?" whispered Leonard.

"I want to know if someone follows us," said Rulon. "If we're lucky they'll trip and break their necks," he added with a smile.

With the cans in place, Rulon told the others to step back. Covering his eyes with one hand, he busted the nearest wall light with the butt of his pistol. This made the stairs darker and the cans harder to see. They continued on, everyone walking as quietly as possible. Rulon's senses were on high alert, and he held his pistol at the ready. They'd only gone down three more flights when he heard the cans rolling and tinkling on the stairs above them.

"Keep going," he whispered. "Wait for me at the bottom."

"No," said Yohaba, "we're staying together."

"Listen," he said urgently, "do what I say. I can't have you around if bullets start flying." He crouched on one knee, trying to get a good look at the staircases above them. She came over and knelt beside him.

"Do you see anything?" she asked as she craned her neck to look up the stairwell.

"Just a pretty little filly," he said, kissing her quickly. "Now get," he said. "Wait for me at the bottom. I'll only be a minute."

"Okay," she said obediently and a little breathless. *Man*, Rulon thought, *I'm sure getting bold in my old age*. He watched and listened. Not a sound. He walked back up a flight of stairs, keeping close to the walls, listening and sniffing. You'd be surprised what your nose can pick up sometimes. He touched the floor, trying to feel for vibrations. Nothing. He waited another minute. Still nothing.

Slowly he backed down the stairs again, occasionally looking behind him but keeping most of his attention focused above. Every few steps he stopped and listened. Still quiet. When he got back to where he originally started, he turned and ran down the next three flights all the way to the bottom.

The others weren't waiting for him when he got there, which caused him a little consternation. He didn't want them to get too far ahead. After a short pause to take one last look up the stairwell, he pushed open the double swinging fire doors in front of him. He knew the main collider tunnel would be on the other side, but still, when he went through the doors his jaw dropped.

Despite Steenberg's description and the reality Rulon had envisioned from the pictures on Steenberg's office wall, he wasn't prepared for either the size or the brilliance of what he saw. Before him stood an exposed side of the Large Hadron Collider—a huge, fantastically lit collar, fifty feet in diameter, and bedecked with electronic components and wires, some glowing, some pulsating, and some dormant, as colorful as an artist's pallet. He did a slow scan, right to left, and in both directions stretched the tunnel so long and so far that it passed out of sight.

As he took in the scene, he caught a movement on his far left. He turned his head, expecting to see the others, and started to say something. But then he froze. There they were, each kneeling next to each other in a row, each with a burly forearm around their throats and a nasty pistol pressed up against their heads, each accompanied by a pair of evil-looking eyes peering through the slit of a black ski mask.

Steenberg's thug, the one in the middle, used his gun hand to remove his mask. He said slowly, in English, piling menace into every word, "Gun down now or the retard gets it first." To emphasize the point, the man holding Alex twisted his pistol harshly in Alex's ear.

In an instant, combat hormones exploded through Rulon's body like a flash flood through an arroyo. Everything slowed down. He noticed details that he normally would have missed. He saw the skin compress on the speaker's finger as he stuck his pistol back into Steenberg's ear and exerted just a little more pressure on the trigger. Rulon studied his face and eyes, in an instant seeing everything, and not liking what he saw. Maybe he could get him, maybe not, but in any case, the man was totally committed to pulling the trigger in Steenberg's ear no matter what.

Rulon looked at the men on either side of Steenberg and saw the same thing. If he shot it out with them, Yohaba, Alex, and Steenberg would die right there in front of him. While he was going through his calculations, there came the sound of running footsteps from behind. Without turning around, he judged that three more men had burst through the double doors behind him. He didn't have to look to know they were armed. He felt one of them move up close, then reach around and take the Colt from his hand.

"Are any of you Serbians?" Rulon asked as he put his hands in the air.

"Not us," said the man in front of him, who now stood up straight. "We're Russian." And despite the situation, Rulon was immediately relieved. The Russians had rules. They'd even the score with him, but he was pretty sure they'd leave the others alone.

"But I am," said a voice from behind—a voice like a serpent's hiss. Rulon started to turn but got clubbed with something heavy and sank to all fours. Blows rained down on him, and the lights went out.

25

"THE REAL PROBLEM IS IN THE HEARTS AND MINDS OF MEN. IT IS EASIER TO DENATURE PLUTONIUM THAN TO DENATURE THE EVIL SPIRIT OF MAN." —EINSTEIN

WHEN RULON CAME TO, HE WAS BEING PUSHED ALONG BY TWO men on one of those flat carts with no sides—the kind used for hauling material around. Two more men walked on either side. None of them was close enough to reach. They all carried Russian-made PP-19 Bizon sub-machine guns, a sidearm, and a combat knife. They wore military issue, cordura-nylon, black and gray urban camouflage clothing, including combat boots.

What worried him most of all, though, was that the ski masks were gone. Even in his addled state, he knew that was a bad sign. They obviously weren't worried about being identified by witnesses. His thoughts wandered. How did they get into CERN looking like commandoes? Of course. It was Halloween! Almost the entire CERN staff had been in costume. He lifted his head slightly but couldn't see Yohaba, Alex, or Steenberg. He heard lots of feet walking behind him, though, and hoped theirs were among them. He put his head down and lay there breathing hard and sweating.

"Cowboy, you okay?" called Yohaba. The pain and concern in her voice hit him like another blow. Then he heard a smack, and Yohaba broke—shattered, really—her no-swearing resolution. Given the circumstances, he cut her some slack.

He wondered where they were. He looked around and started to put things together despite his scrambled brain. With a start, he recognized the hallway they were in. To the left, doors flashed by: G-4b, G-5b, G-6b. They were headed toward the room with Einstein's trunk.

Rulon flexed the muscles in his limbs. His arms and legs were working. But he was still fuzzy, and his mouth tasted coppery. Every time the cart hit a bump, his head felt like a bell clacker was banging away inside. He was pretty sure he had a concussion.

They stopped in front of G-14b. *Sometimes I hate being right,* thought Rulon. When they realized they couldn't get the cart through the door, one of the thugs got Rulon to his feet while the others took a safe step back, their gun muzzles tracking his every move. Rulon could smell their murders and their hundred ugly fights. He could smell the years of drinking and drugs and thirsting for blood. This was a bad place to be. There would be no mercy here. With the barrel of his Bizon, one of them pointed into the room. Rulon walked through the door under his own power. He was slowly coming back mentally and physically. He rolled his neck to loosen up but had to stop because of the pain.

Three of the men were already in the room, spread out along the wall. Their machine guns were slung over their shoulders, but their pistols were out. The wooden table was in the center of the room. Rulon noticed for the first time that the legs were bolted to the floor. *That's odd,* he thought. The bolts meant he couldn't use it as a weapon and flip it like he did in the Desperado. Einstein's trunk lay next to it on the floor. Maybe that would come in handy. Overhead, the meager yellow light burned away.

Rulon turned his head and saw that Yohaba, Alex, and Steenberg were also there. Alex was in the far corner, rigid and catatonic, his arms held stiffly at his side, totally out of it, trembling and forgotten. Yohaba and Steenberg stood together in another corner, their hands behind their heads. There were now five bad guys in the room. Where was the sixth?

Rulon had trouble seeing and realized there was blood from a head wound running into his eyes. He wiped the blood away as best he could with the sleeve of his jacket. He noticed that off in one corner was a tripod with a camera. As he puzzled over this, someone stepped from the shadows. *Isabella.* Elegantly dressed as usual. He wanted to say something suitably devil-may-care, like, "I knew you'd be here. Always figured you for a party animal," but he couldn't get the words out fast enough, and she beat him to the punch.

"Well, stud, what a—" she began, her lips curled back in a snarl, but a curt word from the leader cut her off in mid-sentence. Fear pumped through the room. Rulon knew that this was going to get nastier than anything he'd ever been through. He braced himself. In 1879, a relative of his won a Victoria Cross at Rorke's Drift. Thirty years before that, another ancestor named Rulon had been tortured by Indians. He held up so bravely that they left his family alone forever after that. He reminded himself that he carried that name, and the blood of both ancestors ran through his veins.

Someone shoved him to the far side of the table, away from the door. The two guys there forced him to his knees. They straddled him with their guns out, shoving one pistol into his ear and the other into his neck. A knee in the back forced him up against the table. His arms were twisted and wrenched up tight behind him. He couldn't move, but he could still see what was going on.

Now the sixth man came into the room. He carried a small aluminum suitcase and laid it on the table. He spoke, casually, in a thick Eastern European accent as he worked.

"You killed my brother," he said. Rulon watched him pull a Black and Decker drill from the case and start unwinding the power cord. "My other brother can't see out of one eye, and his face is a mess." He turned to Isabella. "Are you getting all this?" For the first time Rulon noticed the camera record light was on. The guy worked the drill chuck and cinched it down a bit. "I owe you." He stared breathing harder and talking faster. "I owe you like I've never owed anyone before."

He plugged the drill into a wall socket and pulled the trigger. The drill whirred to life. "You will hate me for this," he said with a quiet laugh, more to himself than to Rulon. He put a knee on the table to brace himself. He kept talking as he drilled a hole through the hard wood. "My brother, the one you didn't kill, he gave me a list of instructions. You should have killed him too. That was a big mistake." He finished drilling two holes a few inches apart and looked at Rulon. Then a leather strap came out of the case followed by a couple of six-inch bolts. Rulon watched him secure one end of the strap through the hole. The other end was left dangling. "*Big* mistake," he whispered. He nodded to the men behind Rulon, and one of them clobbered Rulon again.

When Rulon came around—it couldn't have been more than a couple of minutes later—his left hand was strapped to the table. He couldn't move. One of the guys had his other arm wrenched up behind his back, almost breaking it.

"I was greatly involved in the troubles in my homeland," the Serbian said. "In fact, I approved of them. When they were over, thanks to your President Clinton, it left a void in my life."

He had dark skin and a neatly trimmed goatee. What hair he had was buzzed short. Narrow black eyes. He held Freya in his hand and softly tapped the table. Yohaba was crying. Steenberg tried to say something but got pistol whipped for his trouble. Rulon watched as the Serbian wove his hand through Freya's strap.

"You like using this? You put men in the hospital with this. This is a present from one of them. I always keep my word."

Rulon looked quickly at Yohaba. He couldn't tell what expression he wore, but her face was as readable as a book. He saw her pain, her love, her agony, and her disbelief. He knew at once that she was about to do something stupid.

The Serbian had his back to her and swung the hammer, feeling its heft. Without warning, Yohaba charged across the room with something shiny in her hand. It was the knife Rulon had given her. The one he lifted from Dmitry. At the yell of warning from one of the Russians, the Serb spun like a cat and raised the hammer. Rulon screamed, "No!" but Yohaba never broke her charge. *That's my girl.* He feared for her life and felt proud of her at the same time. She lunged for the Serbian's neck, but he deftly blocked the thrust and grabbed her wrist, twisting her to the floor, almost snapping her arm. The knife clattered to the ground.

"The little mosquito has a sting," he said with an amused look. He twisted her arm a different way and made her stand up. "See, doesn't she look nice." And at that, their captors laughed, the sound vibrating with cruelty, their faces pulled back like wolves closing on a kill. "Save your energy for later," he said to Yohaba. "You will be needing it." He shoved her toward the pair of Russians by the door.

Rulon went berserk at that point and almost broke free from his two handlers, but the strap held firm. They clubbed him and clubbed him until he couldn't move.

He wasn't completely knocked out this time. He lay slumped over the table, more groggy than unconscious. All the time he was aware of Yohaba, her arms pinned behind her, watching him from across the room. She struggled violently but had as much chance of breaking free as a bird did from a python.

Without warning, the Serbian swung Freya over his head and with a blood-curdling scream he brought the hammer down on Rulon's hand.

From somewhere far away, Rulon heard Yohaba scream before his world went white. Pain like he had never imagined tore through his body like a surge of molten lead. His hand collapsed, deflated, exploded. Blood spurted from under his fingernails. His eyes bulged until he thought they'd burst. The room stayed white. He screamed from deep within his soul, the pain made worse because of the certain knowledge that this was only the beginning. Before this was over, his body would be destroyed piece by piece.

He looked at Yohaba and collapsed again over the table. His Serbian tormentor lifted his head by his hair and spat in his face. "Now watch," he said, and he turned to Yohaba.

"No." Steenberg stood up between them. "This you will not do," he said. One of the Russians struck him again with the butt of his pistol. The old man lay there, his white hair smeared with blood and sweat, unmoving.

Yohaba backed away as five of the men went for her. She fought them. Rulon watched as they pushed her around between them. She cursed them. Somehow she broke free and made it to the table. Rulon's eyes had trouble focusing. She touched his face. Before she could say anything they had her again. They dragged her back screaming with her arms extended toward him, imploring him to help her, saying she was sorry, terrified out of her mind. He could have written an entire book from what he saw in her eyes and read in her face. But there was nothing he could do.

He tried to rouse himself, but he couldn't move. He jerked weakly at the strap. There was nothing he could do. Tears ran down his face, mixed with blood from his head wound. Someone beside Yohaba was screaming. With a start, he realized it was him. There were other sounds—laughter, deep and coarse. He tried to move again but couldn't. He could only watch. Isabella worked the camera. He was no longer the focus of attention.

He offered up a prayer like he had never prayed before. He ripped the roof off the building with his prayer. But he couldn't even move.

The scene barely made sense anymore. They were close to getting Yohaba under control. Rulon, collapsed over the table, tried again to rise and couldn't. The fingers of his right hand curled around the edge of the table, but he didn't have the strength to grip it. He was helpless, and all he could do was turn his head and watch without hope.

And that's when Alex came to life.

One moment he was as unmoving and stiff as the table leg; the next, he suddenly started up like a mechanical man. At first, Rulon wasn't even conscious of him moving. He seemed to float across the room toward him, eerily, with his arms still stiff at his sides. He brushed close to the pocket of men. They were frantic, laughing, all six of them, still trying to control Yohaba. She fought like a wildcat.

Alex kept coming. The invisible man. He walked right in front of Isabella and the camera, but even she didn't react, unable to take her eyes off the scene with Yohaba. Alex reached the table and stood there for a moment, looking at Rulon with a detached curiosity and something else Rulon didn't expect to see: compassion. Alex tenderly wiped Rulon's brow and eyes with his sleeve, helping Rulon to see a little better. Then he gently took Rulon's mangled hand between both of his and guided it tenderly and smoothly out of the strap. "See? All the bones are broken," he whispered.

Alex bent over, and Rulon lost sight of him for an instant. He quickly reappeared with Freya in his hand. Then he pulled Rulon's good hand through the hammer's leather strap and made it grip the handle. As he did, he smiled vacantly and stared past Rulon at the wall. "My sister would like you to help her now," he said, from far away.

Rulon's fingers curled around Freya's familiar handle. A shot of electricity jolted his system. A current ran up through his arm, slowly at first, and then surged powerfully through his stricken body. When the feeling reached his chest, its effects redoubled. Like a lightning bolt from Vulcan's forge, it pierced Rulon's heart and got it pumping like a bellows.

Suddenly, everything worked again except the one smashed and useless hand. All around him the action had slowed. He stood up. His furnace roared white hot. Like the Frankenstein monster, he was filled with precious life.

With his right hand around Freya, and with every muscle pumping an astonishing amount of something more formidable than adrenaline, Rulon roared. Every head in the room turned, all in slow motion. His eyes locked on Yohaba's and told her not to look. Later she swore he had said it out loud, but he knew without a doubt that he hadn't.

Then he was among them, Freya raised over his head, all his pain and all his anger surging through his uplifted arm. There too was all his love for Yohaba and his desire to protect her. Like a catapult tightening, his arm swung back as he charged. Then reality sped up to real time, and his arm, with all its force, hacked down its first victim, commencing the work of death among those sorry souls.

He swung again and again, instantly, rapidly, like a trip hammer, all his weight behind each blow. He heard cracking sounds. He sensed more than saw images of blurred faces frozen in terror, before they disappeared. They fought back like madmen, but they were doomed and fell like stones, quickly, one after another. He caught the leader and broke him over Einstein's trunk, three wicked swings as if battering through a wall. One man, the Serbian, escaped and ran limping through the door. Rulon caught him in the hallway four doors down. The man turned and faced Rulon with a knife.

Rulon never broke stride, but did a single, full-turn, hammer throw spin and brought Freya down with crushing force, catching the Serbian squarely where the shoulder meets the neck. When Rulon was finished, the Serbian lay there at his feet, unrecognizable, and Rulon looked down at him, breathing hard, in horrible pain from his butchered hand, the pain fueling his anger and his strength. He waited for the Serbian to move, *wanting* him to move again so he'd have a reason to strike. But he lay still, stoking Rulon's anger even more.

He heard sounds of racing footsteps receding down the hall behind him and knew without having to turn that it was Isabella. In the state he was in, he couldn't have caught her, but he still had enough left to take her down with a hammer throw. He played with the idea but let it go.

Standing there, he heard a sob and turned around, knowing it was Yohaba. He looked at her and it was as if they'd known each other a thousand years. She was crying, but she moved with confidence and strength. She was all right. She knelt in front of him and gingerly touched his dangling hand. She tenderly kissed it and looked up. "Both painful and grotesque," she said through her tears.

"Michael Caine, *Miss Congeniality*, 2000," he answered. Then he sank to his knees beside her. Despite their tears and the pain, they laughed in each other's arms. They would get through this. They would heal. After a minute, with Yohaba's help, he struggled to his feet.

"Let's check on the others," he said weakly. Back in the room, Alex was looking through the trunk as if nothing had happened, even though several mangled bodies lay just a few feet away. Rulon gave him a big hug with his good arm, and Alex looked puzzled. Leonard was sitting up with his back against a wall, shaken but lucid. They were all alive and safe. That was the only thing that mattered.

Rulon quickly got everyone out of the room. He couldn't stand to look at the bodies of the men he'd just killed. He knew he hadn't had a choice. There would never be any second thoughts about that. But he wished the sight could be forever cauterized from his brain.

Before he left, he holstered the Colt and Freya, pocketed the knife, and slung one of the Bizons over his shoulder. He searched two of the bodies for extra clips and stuck four in his belt loop. He wanted weapons, lots of weapons. He stood in the doorway with one hand on the doorknob and looked back one more time before he closed the door. Four of their tormentors were together in a heap, and their leader was by himself on the other side of the room by the trunk. How fragile and ephemeral life is, even for those who think they are invincible.

It was impossible to be angry with them anymore. There was nothing to feel but sorrow for their wasted lives. The trunk was a different story. Its open lid and rectangular wooden shape reminded Rulon of both a coffin and an open grave. Was it wrong to hate an inanimate object? He closed the door.

Leonard was unsteady, but he gamely led them back to the service tunnel. They had to walk around the dead Serbian in the hall. They reached the tunnel and then walked a few hundred meters, very painfully in Rulon's case, and emerged inside the neighboring building. They went directly to the security desk where the guards were dumbfounded but helpful.

By this time, pain and shock had reasserted themselves, and Rulon was on his way to losing it again. He lay down on a couch in the security office with Yohaba by his side. Within a few minutes the police and an ambulance arrived. Everything was going to be all right.

Steenberg took care of all the explanations. He was a celebrity in these parts, and his word carried weight. He even convinced the ambulance personnel to let Rulon keep his arsenal with him. Rulon couldn't explain it, and he knew it was irrational, but there was no way he was going to be disarmed until he was good and ready. Yohaba rode with him in the ambulance and watched as a paramedic injected him with pain killers. She held Rulon's good hand and made him laugh, claiming she had everything under control until he barged in.

"I kicked one of the guys right in the groin," she said. "I think it was the guy who hit Leonard. It was a perfect shot." She seemed quite proud of herself for that. She made a fist and brought it around in a big, slow-motion roundhouse and punched Rulon in the nose, the only part of his body that wasn't hurting.

"Ka-pow," she said.

"Ka-pow yourself," he replied. An outsider might have thought that nothing much had happened to her, but Rulon knew better. In between jokes, he watched her closely. Around her eyes was a sadness mixed with fear and shock. There would be scars. For her and for him. They would never forget that awful room. Not just for what happened but for what could have happened.

"Hey," he told her, "don't think I was so preoccupied that I didn't notice the swearing. That's called backsliding, and where I come from we know how to deal with backsliders."

"Does this have anything to do with irrigation pipes?" she asked.

"How did you guess?"

"You have an obsession," she said.

"It builds character."

"And calluses, no doubt."

"Same difference," he said.

"Well, you're out of luck. They don't do that in Switzerland."

"Yeah, well, that just means you'll have to come to Idaho." They looked at each other for a long second before Yohaba came back with a smart aleck response about what he could do with his pipes.

Rulon closed his eyes for a few seconds, and Yohaba asked him if he was all right.

"Just saying a prayer," he replied.

At the hospital, the nurse who undressed him stepped back and whistled when she got his vest and shirt off. His body was a mass of bruises, and he'd collected two more round ones just like the nasty one he'd gotten in the luggage store fight. She picked up the heavy vest, and there, plain as punch, were the remains of two bullets, flattened and turned inside out.

Rulon vaguely remembered hearing shots fired but didn't recall being hit. The power of adrenaline. Right now, every part of his body hurt, despite the drugs they'd pumped into him by the gallon. But even then, the external bruises were the least of his worries.

26

"A TABLE, A CHAIR, A BOWL OF FRUIT AND A VIOLIN; WHAT ELSE DOES A MAN NEED TO BE HAPPY?"
—EINSTEIN

SOMEWHERE BETWEEN JUPITER AND MARS, 182 ELSA WAS ON a trajectory toward a possible collision with another asteroid. Then possibly towards the Earth. This worried Rulon greatly. He was now one of only a handful of people in the world who knew about this. His money, though, was on Alex's intuition—that there was simply no way Einstein, even though he was Einstein, could have possibly been that precise back in the 1950s. Still, they would all be waiting with bated breath for June 4, 2011, to see if the collision took place.

Despite several surgeries and extensive rehab over the last six months, Rulon's hand still hadn't made it all the way back. He wore a SaeboFlex dynamic hand splint, which gave his hand a vaguely *Terminator*-esque look. The doctors said he'd eventually get back 90 percent of his hand's mobility if he stuck to the program. They wanted to know what happened, and he told them he dropped a grand piano on it. They all agreed that that's what it looked like.

But it wasn't so bad. He could still do everything he needed to around the ranch. He just wouldn't be playing the piano at church meetings or winning the hammer throw at the Olympics. The multiple concussions still gave him occasional headaches. That worried Yohaba. So did the nightmares. They both got them. For him, they came in spurts. He'd be fine for a few weeks and then wake up in the morning trembling and in a cold sweat. Most of the time, going outside and firing off fifty rounds settled him down.

With Yohaba it was different. He'd wake up sometimes in the middle of the night and see her there under a small reading lamp working on her physics. That's how he knew.

During the months after he got out of the hospital, he and Yohaba lived on his father's ranch, waiting there until his guys, mostly Magnus, could work out the situation with the Russians. In the end it was decided there would be no retaliation on either side. This struck him as a little too good to be true, and even Magnus couldn't believe it. But then Rulon got an email from Isabella, of all people, apologizing for what happened and expressing her hope that he and Yohaba were happy together. She said things had gotten way out of hand. She had expected him to be worked over good and proper that day in G-14b but nothing like what those maniacs had in mind.

It turned out she was the one who had made things right. She had kept the video from that day. When she heard they were assembling another team to go after Rulon, she turned it over to the Russian SVR. After that, she said, the word came down from the thin man: no reprisals. Rulon sent an email back, thanking her. It never hurt to be gracious.

Rulon also owed a debt of gratitude to Leonard Steenberg. He negotiated a deal with the Russians—they would pour some of their petro-dollars into CERN in return for—well, they never did get a straight story out of him on that. They figured it had something to do with access to Einstein's trunk—what the Russians were after from the beginning. Rulon just hoped he wasn't stupid enough to share with them the secret of the higher nuclear yield. All they knew was that the Russians dropped their hunt for Yohaba.

Rulon thought he was going to have trouble with the Swiss police, but it turned out he didn't need to worry. They made everything go away. The bodies. The bullet holes. The wrecked Volvo in the forest. The trouble at CERN. Even the surviving Serbian brother had been neatly tucked away without the formality of a public trial. By the time they were finished, it was as if none of it had ever happened.

The Swiss were a funny bunch. That's probably why he liked them so much. Who died? Bad guys. Let's go skiing and forget the whole thing. They even returned Freya, the Colt, and Dmitry's wicked little knife that Yohaba had used to try and save him.

After they got the good news, Rulon proposed to Yohaba officially while they were out riding one evening just around sunset. It was cold and quiet, and they were up in the hills by themselves. He poured out his heart to her and told her how she was the only person he wanted to ride the range with and that he thought she was more beautiful than a thousand sunsets. Later when they were walking the horses in to cool down, he asked her how he'd done with the proposing.

"You done good, Cowboy," she said in her best John Wayne accent. Then seriously and in her own voice: "It was the way I always dreamed it would be, my love."

They got to their wedding day in April with Rule Number One still intact. Sometimes, after they were married, they'd drop by the Rocking Rooster in Twin Falls for Wednesday night karaoke. He'd sing *For My Lover* and she'd sing *Rebel Yell*, driving themselves crazy just like that night in Annecy, only now they didn't have to say good night and part ways.

His dad had never met anyone quite like Yohaba. When Rulon first brought her home, Dad had circled her like a coyote checking out a trap. After a couple of days, he took Rulon aside and asked him if all the Swiss women were like her. Rulon lied and said yes. He said it was mainly the older woman in Switzerland who had the tattoos and nose rings but that Yohaba was a little old-fashioned. That seemed to satisfy him.

Eventually Yohaba and her father-in-law got along really well. She would listen to all of his stories and wouldn't complain even if she'd heard them before. Then she started getting up in the dark to rustle up breakfast for him before he went out to check on the herd. Little kindnesses. Usually it doesn't take much with people.

To reciprocate, he taught her to shoot, same as he did with Rulon. Said she showed real promise. By that time, Alex was also living with them. Granny wouldn't come. She said she was too stuck in her ways. But Alex really liked the ranch and didn't want to go back. They both had a feeling Granny would find her way there someday.

At sunset sometimes, they'd sit on the corral fence and watch the horses eat, daydreaming all sorts of things, like coming up with names for their kids. They decided to name them Albert and Elsa when the time came. They had thought about calling the girl Freya but decided they didn't want to be constantly stirring up painful memories. They tried their best to forget. They even buried Freya under the barn one day—they even made a little ceremony of it. Just the two of them.

But some things you just can't bury. For one thing now, at church, when people talked about the end of the world, it was a little more tangible. But also, even now as Rulon thought about all this, sitting on the fence again with Yohaba, his eyes never stopped scanning the landscape. Off to the east, toward the sage-covered hills that lined the property on that side, his eye caught the sun glinting off something shiny. He strained to see. It could be a reflection off some old barbed wire . . . or maybe off a telescopic sight.

He told Yohaba to get down off the fence, they were going inside. As they walked back to the house, he glanced back over his shoulder.

It wasn't over.

About the Author

Jim Haberkorn was born in Brooklyn, New York in 1951. When a teenager, he moved with his family to the west coast, settling in San Francisco for a time before moving south into Silicon Valley. After attending college, completing a church mission, and spending six years in the Marines, he joined a computer company in 1978 and is still employed there today. He has lived on three continents and done business in over forty countries but still counts Idaho—the home of Boise State University, his alma mater, and Rulon Hurt, his hammer-wielding cowboy—as one of his favorite places. Currently, Jim lives in Zurich, Switzerland with his wife Kim.